*The debut novel by B. A. Chepaitis presents the future of law enforcement in a society that has given up on justice . . .*

# the fear principle

In the aftermath of the Killing Times—when serial murder spread throughout the world like a plague—the Planetoid prison system was established. Jaguar Addams is one of an elite group of law enforcers working to cure killers of their murderous tendencies. Through empathic contact with her charges, Jaguar subjects them to their greatest fears.

But Jaguar's latest assignment—an assassin completely devoid of conscience—will show her the true meaning of fear . . .

*Ace Books by B. A. Chepaitis*

**THE FEAR PRINCIPLE**
**THE FEAR OF GOD**

# the fear of god

### B. A. CHEPAITIS

ACE BOOKS, NEW YORK

This book is an Ace original edition,
and has never been previously published.

Joy Harjo, excerpt of "Fury of Rain" from *In Mad Love and War* ©
1990 by Joy Harjo, Wesleyan University Press by permission of
University Press of New England.

THE FEAR OF GOD

An Ace Book / published by arrangement with
the author

PRINTING HISTORY
Ace edition / May 1999

The Penguin Putnam Inc. World Wide Web site address is
http://www.penguinputnam.com

Check out the ACE Science Fiction & Fantasy
newsletter, and much more at Club PPI!

ISBN: 0-441-00622-1

ACE®
Ace Books are published by The Berkley Publishing Group,
a division of Penguin Putnam Inc.,
375 Hudson Street, New York, New York 10014.
ACE and the "A" design are trademarks
belonging to Penguin Putnam Inc.

PRINTED IN THE UNITED STATES OF AMERICA

10  9  8  7  6  5  4  3  2  1

*To those who send the stories to me (you know who you are)*
*Long life, honey in the heart, no evil. 13 Thank Yous.*

# the fear of god

*"We are all in the belly of a laughing god, swimming the heavens, in this whirling circle. What we haven't imagined will someday spit us out, magnificent and simple."*

—Joy Harjo, *Fury of Rain*

# the fear of god

# prologue

THE FLY BUZZING IN THE ROOM WAS A DISTRAC-
tion. Sardis Malocco, Mother of the Revelation Sect, didn't
approve of its presence. It buzzed and then stopped, landed
and then flew and buzzed in circles around her head, then
stopped again. Intermittent, random, out of her control, it
drew her outward when she needed to think. Pray. Com-
mune with her destiny.

The fly ribboned around her head as she sat at her desk,
hands folded, large and luminous eyes focused on the portrait of mother and daughter that hung on the wall across
from her. Aside from the gray in her black hair, and the
few extra pounds on a frame that was always meant to be
ample, she didn't look that different now than she did
twenty-five years ago, when the photo was taken. She
pursed her lips in a kiss directed at the coal-eyed, curly-
haired little girl who smiled so serenely at her mother.
When the fly landed on her forehead, she didn't wave it
away. If it stayed there, at least it would be quiet.

"All will be washed clean," she murmured, "in the
blood of the lamb."

Sounds of singing, praying, weeping, reached her from
various parts of the house. Above her in the many bed-
rooms, people were preparing for the next phase of their
plans. She could hear a child crying. Jeremy, she thought,

from the high-pitched whine in his voice. Down the hall in
the communal room those who were ready were gathering
for their final stand. In the kitchen to the rear of this room
items necessary for their journey were being assembled.
She heard three voices rise in harmony to the tune of "On-
ward, Christian Soldiers."

She looked out the window and saw the Sassies, as the
press called the special artillery squadron. They stood at
attention, heavy and sexless in their gear, waiting for orders
to move. Half an hour before, their squad commander telecommed into her that they were prepared to make forcible
entry. She'd replied that she was sending the children out,
and needed time for the parents to say good-bye to them.
They were motionless now, giving her time.

Apparently, they'd believed her.

The fly left her forehead, circled the desk, and landed on
her right hand, exploring her knuckle with his tongue. The
small, tickling sensation was pleasant on her skin. She
smiled.

Slowly, very slowly, very carefully, without taking her
eyes off the portrait on the wall, she tilted her left hand
over the back of her right hand, and carefully brought it
down. The fly, unthreatened, continued feeding off her dead
cells as her hand closed over it like a dome. It took a moment for the signals of entrapment to go through its tiny
system, and then it buzzed and lurched wildly under her
palm. She waited until it grew quieter, then pulled it into
her left hand and held it up. It buzzed, and she shook it
hard. Quiet. It was quiet.

She shook it hard one more time, then slowly opened
her hand.

The fly wasn't dead, just momentarily quiescent. Perhaps
confused, if flies had enough neural capacity to allow for
something as subtle as confusion.

"I am confused," she said, examining the prisms of light
in the insect's wings. Flies, she thought, were undervalued
as a species. They could live off waste, sustain life out of
excrement. And they were as necessary as any creature in

the kingdom of heaven, she supposed. She pinched one of its wings between her thumb and forefinger and pulled it off. Immediately, the fly buzzed again, struggling to escape. She pulled off one leg, then another. It buzzed louder. If she released it now, it would try to fly away, just as if it could actually survive. In their insistence on survival regardless of horrific conditions, humans and flies were the same, she thought.

She sighed, and placed the fly on her desk, where it crawled in clumsy circles, attempting still to fly away. With a puff of breath, she blew it off the desk. She held the wing up to the light. It was beautiful. Like the wings of angels, she imagined.

" 'And I beheld an Angel in the midst of heaven crying with a loud voice, Woe, Woe, Woe, to the inhabiters of the earth,' " she said. She put out her tongue and touched the tip of it to the wing, then closed her eyes and leaned back in her chair.

The door to the room opened and closed softly. A man walked across the thick carpet and stood in front of Sardis's desk, regarding her with loving eyes. She opened her eyes, and her face brightened into happiness. He went around to stand in back of her and placed a hand on her shoulder. She rested her cheek against it briefly.

"Philo," she said, using his sect name, "Are you sure you want to do this with me?"

He stroked her heavy black-and-gray hair with his thin hand. " 'For the great day of wrath is come,' " he quoted, " 'and who shall be able to stand?' "

She leaned into him, and kissed his hand.

"We'll stand side by side in the new heaven," he said. "I'm sure of that. But we should begin."

Sardis released his hand, and he stepped back as she pushed herself out of her chair. "You're right," she said, standing and turning to face him. "Are the children prepared?"

"I saw to it myself."

"And those who remain know the hours and days to count? Where to go and—"

"All the plans are complete, Mother," he said rather sternly, using her title rather than her sect name. They would not be Philo and Sardis in the New Realm, but Mother and Father. "Why do you hesitate? Are you afraid?"

She shook her head. "No, Father. Not for myself. Only, it's so important that I've done my job correctly. That I don't forget anything before we go on ahead."

"I understand," he said. "But you've been perfect. The people are prepared, and the places all assigned. The accounts—you remembered to change account names, didn't you?"

"Yes. Of course."

"Then you've done everything. Now you have to trust to heaven."

She smiled at him, and held her arms wide, her white death robe spreading like wings around her ample shoulders and bust, her blue eyes alight with ecstasy.

Philo lifted a hand to caress her neck. "That's my girl," he crooned.

He pressed his hand hard into her neck. Her eyes widened and she gasped once when she felt the needle penetrate the skin. Adoration became confusion, and her lips formed the one-word question "What?" before she fell heavily onto the floor.

He stood over her and consulted his watch as the second hand swept around. "Good enough," he muttered, and grabbed her arm, dragged her across the carpet, out the door, and down the hall toward the great room where the others were gathered.

His intent was to put her in the middle of the huddled group of parents and children before he made his exit, but he was only halfway across the hall when he heard a voice behind him.

"There's a couple. Grab 'em."

Philo whirled around and saw four Sassies, weapons

pointed his way. He gulped air, and slowly lifted his hands high as they swarmed him, sensors beeping, the neural net wrapping around him. They lifted Sardis's limp form and levitated her down the hall as more Sassies rushed in.

"In there," the squad leader shouted, barreling toward the great room.

"I wouldn't if I were you," Philo said, his voice muffled and slowed by the neural web.

"What's he yakking about?" A Sassy asked.

"Says he'll never do it again, so could we please not take him to those nasty Planetoids."

Planetoids. No. He couldn't go there. That wasn't in his plans.

He tried to find a part of his arms that would move, a part of his legs that could kick the net that pulsed around him. Nothing worked. No part of his body would cooperate. Even the glass vial in his cheek was pointless now because he couldn't get his finger in his mouth to pull it out.

"Wait," he garbled at them, "don't send your men in. You don't understand. The children."

The Sassies laughed and dragged Sardis and Philo out of the house, tossed them into a vehicle, and slammed the door shut. Then they went back into the house and joined the rest of the Sassies at the door to the great room, where the sect members were gathered. The squad leader bent his ear to the door and listened.

"Singing," he muttered. He straightened up, nodded at his squad. Two of the Sassies kicked the door in. The others poured through and surrounded the circle of praying, weeping people.

"Face front, hands up, and nobody gets hurt," the squad leader barked.

The outer circle turned itself outward to reveal an inner circle of children. The Sassies moved toward them, weapons held ready. The squad leader spotted a little girl clutching a teddy bear to her white robe.

"Cute," he murmured.

Then he saw the blinking red light on the girl's chest, and the wire it was connected to.

*"No!"* he shouted. "Don't touch them. They're wired."

But it was already too late.

From the prisoner's van, Philo heard the explosion in the house, and he knew that at least part of their plan had gone off as expected.

### *Planetoid Three—Toronto Replica City Training Center*

The room was dark except for the row of small red lights that tracked the curve of the wall near the ceiling. They pulsed at one-third the rate of a strobe, casting the faces of the two women under them now in light, now in shadow.

"Boom," Jaguar Addams said, and she dove hard onto Rachel Shofet, laying her flat against the inside curve of the wall.

"Oof," Rachel said, pushing back at her. They struggled briefly, Rachel trying to unbalance Jaguar and throw her back on to the mats, but that went nowhere.

"Give?" Jaguar asked, poking a finger at her ribs.

"Okay. *Stop.* Don't tickle. I give. Now get off me. It's only training."

Jaguar rolled over and lay on her back, laughing up at the ceiling. "Don't worry, Rachel. You get to dive me next. It's a basic move."

The lights in training room seven came up and Jaguar could see the control booth, where site manager Stan Wokowski looked down and shook his head at them.

"You play rough for girls," he said over the intercom.

"Fuck you, Stan," Jaguar replied amiably, stretching out her long, lean body and tightening the piece of leather that held back her hair. She watched Rachel rub at her shoulder. "You want to call it quits?"

"No," Rachel said a little snappishly. "Why? You think I can't do this?"

"I know you can do it," she said. "I've seen what you can do. Did I say something wrong?"

Rachel grimaced at her.

Jaguar reclined against the wall, propped up on one elbow. When Rachel first came to Planetoid Three as a prisoner, Jaguar was her teacher. After her rehab she stayed on and became a team member, often working with Jaguar on other prisoner assignments. Now she wanted to start Teacher training, and had asked Jaguar to help her prepare. Rachel was pit-bull determined to do this, but the Planetoids demanded a great deal emotionally, mentally, and physically from Teachers. They had the most direct contact with prisoners, creating rehab programs to make them face their fears, based on the premise that all crime grew out of fear.

When Jaguar started work there, they'd required a higher degree along with Planetoid training. You couldn't test positive for certain psi capacities or post-trauma syndrome, or have a criminal record. Since Rachel had arrived, the Board of Governors had lifted the restrictions on psi capacities. Ex-prisoners could also apply for the position, if their Planetoid Teacher recommended them. Jaguar was glad to do so for Rachel.

"I didn't hurt you, did I?" she asked.

"No. Of course not."

"Am I being too hard on you?"

"I don't know. How hard are you on Teacher candidates, as a rule?"

Jaguar twisted her face around some and thought. "I think they start out tougher than you."

"Thanks," Rachel said. "A lot."

"I'm not being critical. But you're going into research, and I don't usually train researchers."

"If that's a different kind of job, why is it the same training?" Rachel grumbled.

"Because you still do fieldwork with prisoners. Interviews, assessments. You need to know how to be safe."

She pulled herself into sitting and put two hands on Ra-

chel's shoulders, rotated them, and felt the tension there.
Something not quite right. Something Rachel was working
out that Jaguar didn't understand, which was often the case,
because their friendship didn't make them any more alike.
It just taught them to tolerate each other's differences.

"You pissed off at me?" she asked.

"Of course not," Rachel said, shrugging Jaguar's hands
off her shoulders. Then she groaned and turned to face Jaguar. "Look, I'm nervous, okay?"

"About the training? I told you, you'll do fine. We just
need to put a little edge on you. You're not a naturally
edgy sort of person. But we don't have to do it all at once.
How about we skip the weapons work and go shopping? I
saw a great dress for you down at Wild Child's."

"I don't need an edge," Rachel said. "I don't need to
be like you, and I can't go shopping."

"Why not? Oh. It's Friday. The Sabbath. You still do
that, right?"

"No, Jaguar. Just listen, okay? I can't go shopping because I have a date."

Jaguar leaned back against the wall and whistled. "Well,
well. That's different."

Rachel rolled her eyes. "Don't start, okay?"

"Start what? Who is it? Miriam? I've seen her flirting
with you, but I—"

"Not Miriam," Rachel said firmly. "Pinkie. With
Pinkie."

Jaguar sat up hard. "Pinkie? Pinkie Horton? Don't tell
me you and Pinkie—" She rubbed the heels of her palm
together and raised her eyebrows questioningly.

"No. We have a date. Don't be lewd about it. Pinkie's
a great woman."

"Of course," Jaguar said quickly. "I love her dearly.
She's a great drummer, too. But she's—well, not your
usual type."

She looked Rachel up and down. Even the streamlined,
black-and-silver training suits didn't make her look like
anything but a nice Jewish girl. Her dark eyes, tight dark

curls, and small frame were a portrait from the shtetls of
long ago. And her demeanor matched, since no amount of
Planetoid rehab had tempered the demure ways she'd
learned growing up in a closed and very patriarchal ortho-
dox community.

"Jaguar," Rachel said, turning serious eyes to her, "I
don't have a usual type. It's been so long since I've been
involved with anyone, I think I've forgotten what to do."

"No, no," Jaguar reassured her. "It's like falling off a
bike. It'll all come rolling back to you. When did this
start?"

"About a month ago, but I didn't want to say anything
because I knew you'd get all helpful, and I've seen what
happens when you're helpful."

"Hey," Jaguar protested, "you know I have a policy of
noninterference."

"You? Dr. Jaguar If-You-Can't-Make-It-Better-Make-It-
Worse Addams?"

Jaguar was ready to protest further, with examples, when
a belt sensor began its insistent whine. The two women
simultaneously reached for their belt packs.

"Mine," Rachel said.

"Mine," Jaguar said. They looked at each other and
shrugged.

"Who wants you?" Jaguar asked.

"Looks like—Alex. Special duty. Report immediately."

"Thought you were on rest leave?"

"Called in."

"Big bad. Mine's easier. Gerry wants me at Silver Bay
to cover for a gig. Look, I'll call Alex and tell him I left
you incapacitated in training. He'll believe it."

"Don't play games with him, Jaguar. He's your boss."

Jaguar laughed.

"Okay," Rachel said. "That was stupid." She knew that
Jaguar had no boss except her own decision to do something, or not. "Then what about your noninterference policy?" she tried.

"That's not interfering. It's expediting. What's the code he's sending?"

"Brushfire."

"New prisoners? From where?"

"Doesn't say."

"Maybe Gerry'll know." Jaguar stood up, and extended a hand to Rachel. "If you won't let me get you off work, how about if I get Pinkie on to work with you?"

"Jaguar," Rachel said, "let it go."

"Can't," Jaguar said, "I never learned how."

And on the home planet, the sons and daughters of Revelation looked skyward.

Sardis was gone, and Philo with her. Some of them had disguised themselves and gathered to witness the shuttle flight that took them up and away, as prophesied. They knew that from now on they had to disperse, stay hidden, ready themselves. There would be three days of death, and ten days of imprisonment for their leader. Thirteen days to prepare, just as it said in Revelation. Those who saw her leave would tell the others how to count the days.

They would hide in the appointed places. Wait for the appointed time.

Time whirled around them, and they looked skyward, waiting.

# 1

JAGUAR STEPPED OFF THE ELEVATOR ON THE fifth floor of the Supervisors' Building and directly into two team members who were struggling with a man on the industrial-gray rug. She lifted her foot and placed it delicately on the exposed thorax of the man, and with a small twist forced him onto his back before she addressed the team members.

"What gives, Gail? This guy want to learn *capoiera*?"

Gail lifted her head and laughed breathlessly. "No, Dr. Addams. He just dropped a contact lens and we're helping him look for it."

"I see. Well, maybe he can do without it, and you can just lead him blind." She turned her sea-green eyes down to the wide dark eyes in the pale face under her foot. "You'll let these nice people help you down the hall, won't you?" she asked, moving the heel of her sandal to press against his carotid.

He made a choking sound, which she took for an affirmative, and she released him. "Have a nice day," she said, and walked on down the hall, toward the office of Alex Dzarny, who was her supervisor on Prison Planetoid Three.

She was surprised at the level and the kind of activity in the building. Though prisoners often went through these halls on their way from the holding tanks to their program sites, usually by the time they arrived here they'd been tested, a program determined, a Teacher assigned, and implants tucked into them to keep them in line. Most prisoners never even saw this building, but were sent directly to one of the regular houses or one of the special sites Planetoid Three boasted.

Jaguar had been a Teacher in the Toronto replica for more than five years, and she knew most faces and many of the names of Planetoid workers in this zone. But today she'd run into a glut of unfamiliar people in the lobby, a few she would've sworn were Federal Agents arguing about interview techniques in the elevator. And now this. She was glad she'd decided to come in.

After Rachel had left, Jaguar had gone to the Silver Bay Bar, where Gerry was setting up his band. He'd wanted Jaguar to take over for the weekend. He'd been called in for brushfire duty, he'd said. Big rush of incoming prisoners from a cult disaster.

"Cult disaster? Which cult?" Jaguar had asked him. Gerry had pondered the ceiling, waiting for the information to come down the pike between his brain and his mouth.

"Elevation?" he'd asked at last. "Relegation? Evolution? Degradation?"

"Would that be Revelation?" she'd suggested.

He'd scratched his ear. "Very likely. Will you take the gig?"

"For tonight," she'd said. "If they're calling us back, you can't count on me for the weekend."

But she hadn't been called in, and by the next morning, curiosity took over. She'd wanted to know what was going on. If it was interesting, she'd get involved. If not, she'd disappear for a while. Even within the limits of this replica city of Toronto, she knew many ways to do that.

"Hey. It's the big cat." Pinkie's voice came up behind her.

"Hey. It's the big hair," Jaguar said as they drew parralel.

Pinkie grinned and twirled the blue portion of her hair with her silver finger. "They call you in?"

"Not yet. I'm beginning to feel left out. You seen Rachel?"

"Yeah," Pinkie said, grinning. "Not as much as I'd like, though. Why?"

"I heard she had to cancel a date for work. Too bad, huh?"

Pinkie slapped Jaguar hard on the back and ambled down the hall, chuckling.

Jaguar briefly considered the prospect of Pinkie as Rachel's partner. She shook her head. There was no accounting for sexual chemistry. Many scientists had tried, and none of them got anywhere further than the obvious. "Opposites attract," she muttered, and kept walking.

When she got to Alex's door she put her hand on the knob, and then stopped. From inside, she could hear the low rumble of his voice, followed by a high, light, silver stream of laughter. Not his. She pulled the door open.

The first thing she saw was Alex sitting behind his desk, leaning back in his chair and smiling broadly. Then she saw a woman with sleek strawberry-blond hair and an even sleeker gray suit, sitting across from him, one elbow propped on his desk and her chin propped in her hand. She was showing pearly teeth and full red lips in an abundant smile.

Jaguar pushed the door closed hard. The woman twisted toward the sound and reined in her face. A slow pink spread across her fair skin.

Alex leaned forward too hard and righted himself quickly. "Jaguar—Dr. Addams—what are you doing here?"

"So sorry," she said. "Didn't mean to disturb you."

She pulled her gold-rimmed sunglasses off her head and looked from Alex to the woman and back to Alex. "Gerry said you're calling in all rest leave. I came to protest." She addressed the woman, holding out her hand. "Agitation is one of my particular domains. I'm Dr. Addams."

The woman took Jaguar's hand, shook it firmly, let it go. "Carolan Shannon. Special Federal Agent." She looked to Alex. "Who's Gerry?" she asked him.

Jaguar lifted her shoulders and let them fall, took two steps forward, and placed herself deliberately between them on Alex's desk, making herself comfortable on the edge of his blotter. Carolan leaned left in order to look around her.

"Special team member," Jaguar replied, leaning as Carolan did. "Very special. He's got a band, Moon Illusion, and I sing with them now and then. Your basic technopoet visionary with a criminal record, soft heart, and strange mind. Or is it the other way around?"

She twirled her sunglasses by the earpiece and swung a leg back and forth. It tapped against the side of Carolan's chair.

Apparently, Alex noted, she was in a mood. He wheeled his chair so that he wasn't trying to speak around her, and addressed Carolan. "Dr. Addams is one of my teachers," he said, ignoring her cluck of disapproval in response to the possessive pronoun. " I was about to call you in, Jaguar. In fact, you were just on my mind."

As he spoke he felt the stab of subvocal communication from her.

*Is that so, Alex? It seems to me you had something entirely different on your mind.*

He stabbed back.

*Not so different, Dr. Addams.*

A small cluster of cognitive dissonance, then her cool, clear thoughts.

*That's what you think.*

Jaguar turned a careful smile to Carolan and spoke aloud. "Watch it, Alex. Agent Shannon will think we're empaths."

Carolan frowned, then nodded to herself, as if concluding a conversation she was carrying on inside her head.

"The ruling against psi capacities was changed some time ago. With this Planetoid." Carolan beamed at Alex.

"You were active in getting the prohibition lifted, weren't you?"

"I was," Alex said. "Good Teachers were locked out whether they used psi capacities or not. Besides, in our system the empathic arts make sense, even if they're not officially approved."

"But they're not punished either, are they?"

Alex was about to make a judicious response when Jaguar cut in.

"What would you suggest," she asked, her leg swinging harder, "flagellation with pine boughs?"

Alex allowed himself a moment of silent, heartfelt profanity. Jaguar didn't like Feds. She didn't, in general, like people from the home planet intruding in Planetoid work. And she probably didn't like strawberry blonds.

He held her with his eyes.

*Please, Dr. Addams. Observe the common courtesies.*

*Common,* she replied, *is right.*

But he felt her bristle into stillness, and he moved forward. "We're calling everyone back," he said. "There's been a cult incident on the home planet. The Revelation Sect. The leader staged a siege that ended—badly."

Jaguar stopped twirling her shades, stopped swinging her leg. Checking her mental files, Alex thought. Seeing what she knew about Revelation. He waited for it.

She pressed a finger against her forehead and held it there. After a while she ran the finger down her nose and let it rest on her lips. She twisted around to Alex and said, "Revelation's an End of Days cult. They adhere to the Christian book of Revelation as superseding all other Scripture. Expect the second coming any day now, in noisy glory. It's a pretty big group."

"Almost a million, if you count the second-order members who don't live in the sect houses. About ten percent of them under sixteen. You know anything about the leader?"

"Sardis Malocco? She's fifty-seven years old, born and raised, married and widowed in L.A. One girl child. Deceased. She formed a rescue team in the Killing Times and built her following from that. Received a Congressional Award for bravery, and a Mother Teresa Humanitarian Award from the UN—in spite of the rumors that she started the Safety Squad responsible for burning most of Hollywood. Her theology's a mix of gender mysticism and economic conservativism. God as Capitalist Mama, with an emphasis on the mother-daughter relationship, much like the father-son relationship in Christianity.''

Jaguar turned a grin to Carolan. ''If I'm thinking of the right person, that is.''

Showing off, he thought. And she had the ability to do so, with her background in ritual practice, her doctorate in world religions, and her understanding of the spirit world. She'd read all the sacred texts and had the memory to quote chapter and verse. She also knew who was who in the world of leadership for both the sacred and the profane.

''That's right,'' he said. ''She started out okay. Revelation took in a lot of abandoned kids and homeless pregnant women after the Serials. She got legislative funding, and she recruited heavily, got a few businesses running. About five years ago she started preaching the End of Days.''

''How come? Were her ratings falling?''

''Still going strong. She said Revelations indicated the time was right. The Serials were just the first sign of the Apocalypse.''

''Funny,'' Jaguar said. ''I thought they *were* the Apocalypse.''

And her leg started again, back and forth, hitting against the side of Carolan's chair.

Alex watched Jaguar's face, guarded and closed. She had survived the chaos known as the Serials when she was a child living in Manhattan, and he was probably one of the few people who knew her specific experience in the violence of those years.

She'd been living with her grandparents, who were murdered while she watched. He knew that sometimes she still felt it, as would millions of people caught in the ubiquitous bloodletting. The cities in North America were decimated by murder and homemade biobombs and incendiary weapons. And while Jaguar was keeping a precarious hold on her life in Manhattan, Sardis was providing services to survivors in L.A., grieving the death of her daughter, and according to some people, running one of the most virulent vigilante squads of the Serials.

But if that rumor had any basis in truth, nobody was willing to talk about it then or now. Sardis was one of a group of religious leaders who were courageous enough to provide the little help available to those who sought shelter or escape from the cities. She'd saved thousands of lives and risked her own probably thousands of times. She was a true hero at that time, and up until recently her sect had been a moderate one, known for social welfare works and a strict adherence to biblical code. Nobody had expected the siege in Vermont.

"How badly did the siege end?" Jaguar asked, her leg going still.

"Very," Alex said. "The Feds found out they were stockpiling weapons and showed up with a warrant, but were locked out by laser fire. When the Sassies went in, the kids were wired with explosives and the adults were holding them."

Jaguar closed her eyes. Opened them again. "Ugly," she said.

"Two hundred and fifty people gathered in the great room of their main house," Alex said. "About eighty children in the center of the huddle. Sassies only got a few dozen adults out."

"And lost six of their own." Carolan said. "You'll have maybe twenty sect members by the end of the week, if we can keep them alive. They have a taste for cyanide."

"Great Hecate's cloak," Jaguar said. "Shouldn't they just be rehabbed on the home planet? Harvesting from cults isn't that difficult."

"We want them tested and interviewed first, and we haven't got the facilities you have."

Jaguar cast a glance at Alex, and he shook his head almost imperceptibly. There had been more than a little bit of turf battle over use of the Planetoid's advanced testing facilities from the Federal Bureau, as well as resentment of the Planetoid's freedom to act outside of home planet jurisdiction. It wasn't a battle he wanted to see fought in his office.

"We're heading a long-term research project," Carolan continued. "We want to establish a better predictor profile for cult meltdowns."

Jaguar's leg swung back and forth, its arc widening. She propped her shades back on the top of her head. Alex braced himself.

"How interesting," she purred, "and what're you hoping to learn here?"

"Well, we know there's a significant correlation between cult involvement and psi capacities," Carolan said, enthusiasm for her topic blinding her to danger, "which indicates a link between empathic talents and the manipulative behaviors associated with cults. Hypnopaths, telepaths, mind control—that's the triangle, but picking it up isn't easy with our equipment. We'll get a lot of data here with your instruments."

Alex watched the narrow line of Jaguar's jaw tighten, saw the flash of fire in her green eyes and the rush of color into the amber-smooth skin of her face.

"Marvelous," she said. "And while you're here, you can research the Lilith Effect."

"The—Lilith?"

"You know," she repeated. "Lilith. She goes to men in the night, and sucks their penises dry. You can collect data on that, too. Participant observer is the preferred methodological approach."

Carolan opened her mouth, then closed it tight.

Alex sighed. Not too bad, he thought. It could have been much worse. And personally, he found Carolan's face very attractive when it was that particular shade of pink. "I believe Dr. Addams takes exception to the implication that empaths are inherently manipulative,'' he said, by way of explanation.

"I see," Carolan said. She placed both hands firmly on the arms of her chair and pulled it well back, out of range of Jaguar's leg. "Well, I'm not here to argue proven facts. I'm here to collect new data. The sect's dispersed and their bank accounts are emptied, but we can work with the ones we have to learn about cult behavior, maybe avoid another fiasco like this one."

"Bad for your image," Jaguar agreed, then looked to Alex. "What's she mean, they dispersed?"

"Disappeared," Alex corrected. "Sect houses emptied. Accounts emptied of money."

Jaguar tilted her head inquisitively. Good, he thought. She's getting the implications, too.

"Any sign of weapon stocking elsewhere?" she asked.

"None," Alex replied. "And all the standard tests were applied. Radiography and telemetrics are still coming in, but so far they've been negative."

"Who'd she leave in charge?" Jaguar asked.

"We don't know. Her right-hand man is here. Name of Philo. That's his sect name. They all had sect names, with no surnames because they ackowledge no parentage except the Divine."

"Gag me," Jaguar commented. "They got rich from a line of snake oil they sell, didn't they? Silicon REM stimulators, red algae. What did they do with all that money?"

"Maybe they figured out how to take it with them, Jaguar," Alex said.

"But where would they spend it?"

"We've implemented the usual procedures to track the funds," Carolan said firmly. "It's slow because we're spread pretty thin and we want to keep a tight three-day surveillance just in case they follow the usual Resurrection model of trouble. But we expect them mostly to sit around weeping in their sackcloth."

"From the news clips I've seen, Sardis seems to prefer silk," Jaguar said. She leaned over and caught the material of Carolan's suit between thumb and finger, and rubbed it thoughtfully. "Nice suit. What's it made of?"

Carolan's hand twitched as if she'd slap Jaguar's away, but she restrained herself. Although Jaguar's back was to Alex, he knew her well enough to read the laughter in her spine. She was having too much fun with this, he thought. When she twisted around to face him and he saw the smile trying to hide in the corner of her mouth, his opinion was confirmed.

"Did Sardis precede her flock to glory?" she asked, then twisted back to Carolan. "Did she bite it? Buy the farm—"

"She's being tested," Carolan answered curtly. "Preliminary reports say her fear is God."

"Which one?" Jaguar asked, and Carolan looked at her blankly.

"Her own, of course," Alex answered, and Jaguar turned to him.

"Big guy?"

"Yes."

Jaguar wrinkled her nose. "I never liked Him. He talks too much."

She pushed herself off of Alex's desk and sauntered to the window, where she stood, looking out onto the busy street below and saying nothing.

Carolan mouthed a question at Alex—what's she doing?—and he shook his head. She was thinking something through and he didn't want her disturbed. Soon enough she stretched, walked back to her spot, and stood between him and Carolan.

"I saw some team members bringing a guy in," she said. "One of hers?"

"That's Philo. Gail and Mark had him. Rachel's probably interviewing him now."

Jaguar's eyebrows creased down. "Rachel's not trained for interviews."

"I chose her from a list of religious types," Carolan said. "I've been requesting religious types."

Jaguar scowled at her, then turned to Alex. "Which room is she in?"

"She's a big girl, and you're not her teacher anymore. Let her grow up and do her job."

"I'm helping her get ready for Teacher training. I want to observe."

"Jaguar, she'll be fine."

"I want to observe, Alex," she repeated.

He narrowed his eyes, but when he saw the real fear in her face, he relented. "Forty-two," he said.

She exited the room, walked swiftly down the hall. Carolan rolled her eyes at Alex, who shrugged, and stood to follow.

By the time they caught up with her, she was standing at the one-way mirror, her eyes glued to Rachel, who sat in a chair facing a man with skin as pale as an albino lizard, and eyes that seemed equally bleached of thought and emotion. Hair plastered away from his face, thin, venous, and badly shod, he had a number of nervous tics and twitches that contrasted with Rachel's very still demeanor. He coughed into his hand, a dry sound emerging from a hollow chest.

Alex took his place next to her. Jaguar chewed on her lip, then shook her head. "Rachel shouldn't be in there alone. The guy's way off."

"They're all way off," Carolan noted. "They blow up children. Don't worry. We checked them. When we arrested them, after testing, and when they got here. There's no danger."

"There's always danger," Jaguar said. Carolan couldn't possibly understand the thousand and one things that could go wrong, get overlooked, just happen, in this kind of situation. Jaguar knew because she was trained to hyperattentiveness. Rachel was not.

Rachel bent over a laptop, taking notes. Her voice stayed calm and smooth as she asked questions, her face stayed quiet as she listened to replies. Philo, eyes twitching, laughed, rubbed at his face. Coughed into his hand again.

Stuck his finger in his mouth and picked at his teeth.

"Be picking his nose, next," Carolan commented.

Jaguar ignored her. Rachel bent over her laptop. In the background, the voices of men and women moved down the hall. Philo picked at his teeth, coughed again, covered his mouth, and then brought his hand down.

"Alex," Jaguar said, and then more urgently, "*Alex*, there's—*no*, *Rachel!*" she shouted, slamming her palm against the glass. Rachel, startled, looked to the mirror, and Philo dove at her, pressed a hand into her neck.

"Something in his hand," Jaguar shouted over her shoulder as she dashed toward the side door. Already on the move, Alex saw Philo release Rachel, saw her body start the chaos of convulsions, saw Jaguar throw open the door, and beeline to Rachel as Philo inched his way along the wall.

Alex pointed Carolan toward the hall, shouting "Cover it" as he rounded the corner and joined Jaguar, kneeling next to Rachel.

She raised fearful eyes to Alex.

"Heart stopped." She started pressing rhythmically against her chest. "Do the breathing. Masks in the table kit."

Alex opened the drawer under the interview table, found the medikit and rescucitation mask. He bent over Rachel, masked her, and tilted her neck back as he breathed into the mask opening. Out of the corner of his eye he could see Rachel's laptop, lying on its side, her notes still on-screen. Then Jaguar spoke subvocally, urgently.

*Kiss of Life, Alex.*

Kiss of Life. An energy exchange between one empath and another, used either in lovemaking or in times of great need. Jaguar wasn't thinking straight. The Kiss of Life needed direct contact, and two empaths. Rachel wasn't an empath.

*Won't work, Jaguar.*

Wordlessly, Jaguar's mind moved from insistence to frustration to focus on her task. He kept breathing, working

in sync with Jaguar's pressing hands, hearing her mumble
encouragement to Rachel, saying with her, come on, Rachel. Breathe. You can breathe. He was reconsidering the
Kiss of Life, ready to try anything, when he felt a shiver
in her muscles that built quickly into a trembling and the
sharp intake of breath.

"She's alive, Jaguar. Hold off—get her legs. Don't let
her hurt herself."

They struggled with her spasmodic thrashing until it qui-
eted into twitches and jerks. Then Alex looked up from her
to see Carolan standing in the doorway.

"Philo's not in here?" she asked.

Alex's attention snapped around to the corners at his rear.
No Philo. He heard Jaguar 's breath catch in her throat. He
saw her face blanch, her gaze directed to the screen of
Rachel's laptop.

"What?" he asked

"Rachel's notes," she said. Alex looked down, and read.
*And her children I will kill with deadly plague.*

Jaguar licked her dry lips and stared at Alex.

"Stay here," he said. "I'll get the medics."

# 2

*day two—evening*

CAROLAN SAT IN HER HOTEL ROOM AT THE DESK, facing the telecom. On the viewscreen her supervisor Karl Madden regarded her with a scowl.

As she'd tried to anticipate the questions he'd ask and how she could respond without self-incrimination, she thought wistfully of Alex. When he'd found out Philo had escaped he'd cursed the situation and asked if she'd been hurt. He was angry, but his main concern was how to solve the problem, not how to find someone to blame for it. He was a nice man, she'd decided then. Someone who cared for the well-being of those he worked with. On the other hand, the Federal Research and Criminal Investigation Agency, child of the defunct FBI, was always willing to sacrifice its people on the altar of political expediency.

And the female sacrifice was so much easier, especially if the female happened to be a junior agent working the edges of research on psi capacities. Seeing Madden's scowl, she wondered how soon she'd start cross-filing records in the archives.

"One of the cult members slipped a concealed poison or infectious agent past you, stabbed a woman—a team member—with it, and then got away from you," Madden reiterated.

"Yes, sir," she said.

He made a temple of his hands and worshiped there briefly. "Is she dead?"

"Not yet, sir."

"Prognosis?"

"Uncertain. The medics still haven't ID'd the substance he used. The other sect members are secure, though, now that we know what to look for. He had a glass vial in a cutout in his gum."

He lowered his hands. "An isolated incident, then."

"It looks that way, sir."

"It *is* that way, Shannon."

That sounded final and official. She allowed herself to relax. They'd cover her to cover themselves. Or, perhaps the body politic had another agenda to pursue. She waited.

"What about Dzarny? Is he cooperating?" Madden asked.

"Very much so. He's crowded, though. Too many prisoners, not enough people here."

"That's right." He nodded. "So he won't object to our people helping out."

Of course. Good strategy. She'd wondered why he was sending them all to one zone, and now she understood. In an atmosphere of chaos, agents would be freer to move around and appear helpful at the same time. She was once again impressed with the agency's ability to take a potentially bad situation and turn it to their advantage.

"I don't think he'll object. Not now. He's got enough on his mind."

"Maybe before this is over, he'll be thinking about career opportunities. Someone with his talents could go far in strategic development or liaison work."

She felt her feathers ruffling, and smoothed them down before Madden could see. That was a clear order to do some recruiting, and it explained why he had put her on the job. Not for her intelligence or experience in working with empaths, but because she might prove attractive to Alex, and Madden wouldn't mind having Alex on board. In fact, Alex fit the profile perfectly.

He was ex-army, so he understood a chain of command, he had connections on the Planetoids, and he was an empath. Their investigation into the empathic arts wasn't as heavy-handed as NICA's or the Pentagon's, but they didn't mind having an empath quietly on their team. Only, they wanted the best, and they wanted discretion.

She'd read Alex's files and seen the testing reports on his psi capacities. Strong theta activity indicated empathic and telepathic ability used on a regular basis, but he didn't use it openly enough to call attention to himself. And his holographic wave imaging showed the strange attractor formation of neural pulse motion associated with precognition.

In the parlance of the empathic arts, he was almost certainly an Adept.

Adepts saw in metaphoric visions and dreams the various possible futures of a situation, and either found ways to direct those possibilities toward a desired future, or followed the express direction of their vision, with no knowledge of what the results would be. This, along with telekinesis, was considered the most valuable of the psi capacities for intelligence work. Skilled Adepts could negotiate the highly complex scenarios of intelligence work. They could be excellent leaders, experts at the invisible manipulation of people and events, using exquisitely subtle maneuvers based on their visions. Though the downside of the Adept was a certain poeticism that didn't match the pragmatic nature of Federal Agency work, at its best the personality of the Adept was subtle and complex, balancing authority and flexibility, creativity and structure.

While she resented the implications of the assignment, she was excited by the prospect of getting to know an Adept that closely, and she thought she'd probably enjoy the results.

She nodded. "I think I'd like to work with him, sir," she said.

"Good. We've got no reports of further activities by the sect here, so we're treating this as a cleanup job, as far as the press is concerned. We'll track the house leaders, but there's no point wasting energy on the other members. Who'd they assign to Malocco?''

"Nobody yet."

Madden ducked his head down, a sign that he was pursuing a line of thought he wasn't sure he wanted to reveal fully. When he brought his face up to the viewscreen, his expression was decidedly neutral.

"Get Addams," he said. "Dr. Addams. First name of Jaguar."

"Addams?" Carolan said, then quickly smoothed the surprise out of her face.

"Any objections?" Madden asked, indicating that he wanted none.

"No, sir," she said swiftly. "You know about her?"

"I know her history," he said, "I've been through her files. Have you?"

Carolan nodded. She'd read up on her Jaguar before arriving, on the advice of a coworker who used to work for DIE and moved to the more staid and stately Federal offices when that group disbanded. "Watch out for Addams," the coworker said. "She's the one who closed us down."

Carolan had been surprised that Jaguar's testing records indicated no psi capacities, until she learned that the technology broke down when they tried to use it on her. Three times. A fourth attempt made less than a year ago had the same result. Equipment failure. Consequently, her psi capacities remained officially nonexistent. But she was booted off Planetoid One for insubordination and breaking code, both charges euphemisms for using the empathic arts. And stories about her abounded: that she killed a coworker; that the glass knife she carried was the ritual sacrificial tool of her Mertec ancestors; that she carried mint to cover the smell of death; that she practiced forms of the empathic arts still unnamed by researchers.

Other than that, she was a bundle of contradictions. She used the arts openly, but was masterfully elusive in talking about them. She was openly against governmental experimentation in the empathic arts, but openly for their use on the Planetoids. She avoided having any record of her capacities, but never avoided using them. She wouldn't cooperate, and she wouldn't hide.

People who were unwilling to compromise were trouble, Carolan thought, and Jaguar proved her right. After being booted from Planetoid One, she'd been retained in the system only because Alex intervened. Since then, she'd managed to create a major political incident out of a straightforward execution judgment, blow up a corporate Lear shuttle, close down DIE, and get a Board Governor impeached. The record of her controversies was as long as the list of her psi capacities was brief.

And she had a 98 percent success rate with her prisoners—the highest on all three Planetoids. The other 2 percent weren't necessarily failures. They were merely dead.

"She's difficult," Carolan said.

"I know," Madden agreed.

Carolan waited. There was more, she could sense it. Madden was just trying to figure out how to say it without saying it.

"How much do you know about Virtual Reality systems?" he asked, unexpectedly.

"A little. They've got a site here, don't they?"

"That's right. It's pretty new, but they've run a few successful programs with it. The testers say Sardis's program is best suited for the VR, and we figure there's a lot to learn there. I've already discussed it with the Governors' Board, and they're amenable to your presence."

He paused, considered his fingernails. "Given Dr. Addams's history, and the difficult political nature of the case, the Board is concerned. They'd like someone to keep an eye on the assignment, but the Planetoid people will be too busy. I've offered your services, since they've been so good about allowing our presence."

"I see," she said.

And she did. Jaguar's history as an empath was anecdotal. Madden wanted solid data. Readouts of her neurosyncratics and empath points. In a heavily charged system such as VR, they'd get some interesting stuff, Carolan thought. She'd need the z-monitor, and she'd utilize the induction wave to feedback corollaries if the designers could bring it up to prolateral level.

Carolan felt a shiver of excitement run through her. "I'll be glad to help out, sir," she said.

"Okay, Shannon," Karl said. "Do your job. But if anything goes wrong—if Dr. Addams can't do her job, we have people here who can. Remember that. You just stay on top of your job."

"I understand," she said. They didn't care if Jaguar succeeded. Not that they'd deliberately sabotage her, but if she screwed up, they wouldn't go into mourning. And she was to concentrate on the testing, not worry if it interfered with the assignment. That made her life easier. "I'll stay with it."

He nodded once quickly, and was gone. Carolan continued to sit at her desk, making mental lists of what she needed to do in the morning. A good place to start would be Alex. That, potentially, offered the greatest personal reward.


Alex Dzarny sat in his rocking chair, facing the windows that overlooked the replica of Lake Ontario. He touched the inside of his elbow lightly with two fingers, felt the slight sting where medics had drawn blood to make sure he hadn't breathed in any infectious agents, even though that was exactly what the mask was supposed to prevent. Merely a precaution, they assured him. For insurance purposes. Alex supposed he'd know humans had really evolved when they no longer acted for insurance purposes.

He released the vein from under his finger and turned his attention back to the lake.

This was, for him, the heart of the Toronto replica city. The gleaming towers of glass, sparkling-clean streets, silent subway and air-shuttle system, even the Kensington Market replica successfully mimicked the home planet city they were modeled on, but the lake felt like home.

He rocked, and watched the play of moonlight over silver, ruffled by the spring winds. The Planetoid was turning toward summer, its orbit and revolution steadied through the mass generator that created an atmosphere, making bubble domes unnecessary; its climate regulated by ratifier panels that captured and transmitted ionic energy from the solar winds. Planetoid Three, a smaller version of the home planet, was the last one developed and the one with the greatest variety of options for prisoner programs. Along with replica cities and their secure houses, they had ecosites that allowed them to reintroduce endangered species, grow food, allow a natural environment to balance itself around them. They had a few unique sites that Jaguar had lobbied for, such as the house of mirrors and the hermitage, and they had the first Virtual Reality site. Which Jaguar disapproved of, and said she wouldn't work.

She objected, and he thought rightly so, to the decision to let creative designers plan and implement the programs that testers recommended for VR sites. Teachers had to either play along or play elsewhere. Why, she asked Alex, would she work a program that she had no say in?

She also said that because she was an empath, she was sensitive to the induction waves on VR sites. They gave her raging headaches. So, he noticed, did Carolan. He supposed that would only get worse.

Carolan had let Philo escape, and with him went all evidence of what he'd done to Rachel. The hunt started immediately, but by the end of the day, there was no word of him. Alex left a smoldering Jaguar at the hospital with Rachel, and suggested to Carolan that she might want to steer clear. She left, looking dejected at the prospect of dealing with her superiors.

It was late, already past midnight. He'd been at the hospital for longer than he'd thought while the medics went over him and Jaguar. They'd be poking at Rachel all night, trying to name the toxin that had stopped her heart and lungs. She was out of immediate danger, but she wasn't well, and nobody knew what would happen next. It wasn't

unusual for terrorists to hide viral splices in toxins, so that
what looked like recovery from poison became inexplicable
and sometimes infectious illness. Alternatively, Philo could
have been armed with a paralytic that would allow him time
to escape. That was the simplest scenario and, Alex hoped,
the correct one.

Jaguar would stay at the hospital, of course. Trying to
shift her from Rachel's side would be like trying to get the
white off rice.

Rachel had been one of Jaguar's prisoners a few years
before, and they often worked together now. They were
good for each other, Alex thought. Jaguar laughed more
when she was with Rachel. Rachel was more assertive
when she was with Jaguar. He remembered watching them
closely when they first started working together, because
some prisoners had a hard time transitioning to being a
team member, but they'd sailed through it easy as wind.
Though they were very different, or maybe because they
were very different, they made a balanced team.

Perhaps Jaguar had something to learn from Rachel's
capacity to connect with people. And perhaps, after almost
losing herself within a rigidly organized community, Rachel
had something to learn from Jaguar's fiercely guarded in-
dependence, which resisted grouping in all its forms, but
particulary where institutions were concerned. He didn't
blame her where religious institutions were concerned, especially when murder walked on stage flashing God's
name.

Alex wasn't sure at what point Revelation's agenda had
shifted away from social action toward the End of Days,
or if that had been written in from the start and simply
became visible over time. Perhaps as the horror of the Serials faded, Sardis needed new ways to keep her flock intact, and an expectation of the Rapture did the trick. If he
didn't know better, he'd say she was simply mad. But the
prelims cleared her for all the usual organic forms of psy-
chosis, rated her intelligence as moderate to low normal,
and her emotional stability as unreadable under the circum-

stances. They also said she was immersed in fantasy and her core fear was God, which got them no further than saying she was mad, because for Alex, the real question was what the sect would do next.

The Federal Bureau said that searching for members was unwieldy, and Alex knew they weren't particularly concerned with salvaging a large group of people they saw as crazy. Sect houses were under continuous thermoscan, and kinetic patterning scans would be utilized to detect any unusual urban activity, but only for four days, to account for the traditional time between death and resurrection. Alex wanted more. Or he wanted something different, and he knew only one way to get it, though what knowledge he gathered would be dressed in strange metaphoric gowns, never direct or easy to interpret. Harder to interpret than Scripture, and just as dangerous.

He brushed his hand across the book of Revelation that rested on his lap, and it tumbled to the floor. He let it stay.

He lifted his hands up toward a moon that was moving to the full. Light poured over the network of lines in his palm, and he opened himself to it, letting his skin drink it in.

This was where the visions poured in, through the play of time apprehended in the lines of his hands, the web, the space of the Adept. Ephemeral and laughing time, lines spinning out a multitude of possibilities.

It was the art of the Adept to read these lines, test these possibilities, negotiate reality around them. Jaguar regarded Alex with some suspicion because of his talent in it. Spider magus, she called him, when she was being kind.

But it was his art. Part of his being, his participation in a universe that heaved and yawned and tossed out strange magics that would not be denied.

Alex dropped his hands into his lap, and his body opened, as if molecules separated to allow the entrance of air. Solid dispersed to liquid and he became light and motionless within the crack of ephemeral and laughing time, spinning him, motionless, to a constantly moving center.

He knew that he continued breathing and that his heart continued beating only as an article of faith. Because he always came out of it alive.

Here, where vision danced, he saw—darkness. And inside it, a greater darkness, crouched low over an abyss, waiting to leap.

He could see nothing. See nothing. The abyss was filled with nothing and the crouched figure wanted to leap into it. He watched, waiting, knowing he had to be there stay there

*Wait don't go away.*

In the nothing, watching, he saw a death.

A death, moaning, a great wind sweeping a broad plain. Death, distant and sweeping and

There. Sorrow, unmovable, unless the earth should crumble beneath them all.

One sorrow. Profound and immutable and there.

There. Watching. Watching. *Hold on. Hold on.*

But something tugged at him, stroking his arm, pulling him away to

Here. This place. Light. Warm and inviting.

*Come away from there why stay there lonely when here is warm and sweet and*

He followed to the smell and feel of silk and sleep sleep sleep so he slept smiling and rolled through warmth in his sleep. Yes. Here. This possibility and

A roar, and the crouched figure leaped. *No No No You Can't* He stretched himself out to stop her, and the earth crumbled, and he reached for her to pluck her out felt fur brush his hand and

*Don't let go. She won't let go.*

Falling Falling all around him and he, helpless to stop the motion and

There a death, not so distant.

Flung out over the edge and falling, falling, his arms reaching helplessly and a sweeping wind screaming in his ears his hands over his ears and death screaming in his hands over his ears and his hand reaching because she was falling flying away from him and his hand

arm stretched to its limit his hand
trying to hold and muscles stretched to their limits and
trying to hang on and
The sound of his telecom buzzing.
The sound of his telecom buzzing.

He sucked in air. Blinked hard.

The Adept space was gone, sucked back into unlived
time, and he sat in his own rocking chair, listening to his
telecom buzz.

He didn't get up to answer because he couldn't move,
knew he couldn't respond coherently. It took a while to
retrieve himself from that swim through the play of time.
It would take him even longer to begin to understand the
information he'd gotten there. Right now he had to sit still
and let the knowledge integrate, articulate itself into what
might become action and words. At least he'd gotten no
initial sense of world disaster or even group disaster. If he
held on. If he remembered to hold on. Then, only a sense
of singular sorrow, profound and particular.

His message machine asked the caller to leave a name,
and then he heard a warm and calming female voice. Carolan. He wondered if she ever had a private practice as a
therapist, and thought she'd be very good at it. She had the
right voice, rich and warm and true.

"Just wanted to check in. We haven't turned up Philo
yet, but we will. And I think in the morning you can expect
some interesting news about Sardis. I—hope you're okay.
See you soon."

Nice of her to call. A nice woman.

Alex closed his eyes and rested.

The closet was dark, and infused with so much scented
herbal air purifier that he was feeling nauseated by it. But
he waited until he could hear a change in the pattern of
motion on the other side of the door before he opened it,
stepped out, and walked slowly down the hall.

This was the tricky part. He was still in prisoner's

clothes, and that could give him away. His eyes, trained to see fast, took in the length of the corridor, the nearest exit sign, the number of doors in between him and it, the street-light shining into the western window, and then—there. Stairs. What he wanted. He opened the door and went down.

Kept going down, not stopping, until he couldn't go any further. The door was marked COMPUTER BANKS: CODE AA ONLY.

He saw that it had no knob. Just a slit for Ident cards, a voice scan, and a weapons scanner. He peered at the ceiling. There'd be cameras, and they'd pick him up. The clothes would tag him as Philo, escaping prisoner. He was debating his next move, thinking of going up, when he heard footsteps on the stairs. Coming down. Coming down. He pressed himself into the wall, got small, waited.

Whoever was coming down was whistling, jogging lightly. He saw the feet descending. When they were about ten steps from the landing, he grabbed an ankle and yanked it hard. The whistling stopped, and the man went uncontrollably forward, smashing headfirst into the cement floor.

"Perfect," Philo said as he pressed a finger against the dead man's neck and listened to the pulse go away. He pulled the body into the corner and stripped his clothes off, replaced them with his own prisoner's outfit. In the man's pockets he found Ident card, cash card, keys to wheels. Everything he needed and more.

He wrapped a thumb and finger around the young man's chin, turned his face left, then right. "Don't I know you?" he asked the staring eyes, the gaping mouth.

It was the Planetoid worker who'd dragged him down the hall. Mark Halloran, his Ident card said. Nice looking, trying to be tough and not succeeding very well. Better off out of the genetic pool, the world being what it was. But he'd have to find a place to hide him. If he could hide him, he'd be able to hang around the building, gathering information from the computers until he was ready to leave. It was the last place anyone would think to look for him, and even if they did, they wouldn't recognize him.

He stood and took a look at his face in the dark glass of the door. He looked like a man crazed with God. A big God. He brought a hand to his hair and rubbed it rough. That was a little better. He pressed his thumbs against his eyes, his cheekbones, his mouth, observing the changes as they occurred, watching his face begin to unpinch itself from the aspect of nervous fanaticism.

It took time to achieve the kind of transformation that he wanted, because it was partly about a transformation of attitude, a shift in internal image that would be affected by the attitudes of those around you. He had to decide who he wanted to be.

Someone official, he thought, but nothing dramatic or showy. Just a worker bee, doing his job in an inobtrusive, efficient way. Nobody too noticeable. He continued to press at his face, watching in the mirrored glass as he ceased to be Father in the new heaven's nuclear family, which was how he appeared to Sardis. Then he ceased to be Philo, crazed cult member, which was how he appeared to everyone else. Soon he'd be an obscure worker on this Planetoid. A way of smiling could change a whole face. A way of brushing your hair could change your political affiliation, in some people's eyes.

He knew how to be anybody. Anybody at all. Anybody who was needed at the moment. And he was ready to be somebody else.

Then he could look for a place to hide this body, check the computers, find out where Sardis was. He'd have to deal with her before he left the Planetoid. But there was no hurry.

In spite of a few minor setbacks, everything was going his way.

# 3

## day three

''LOOK,'' ALEX SAID, ''IF YOU PUT PINKIE on it, she'll spill coffee all over the matrionic slides and then you'll be nowhere. I want someone I can trust. Get—'' He realized he was about to say Rachel, and clamped his mouth shut. The Teacher he was speaking to, Brad Deragon, shuffled his feet as he watched his supervisor's expression shift from one inexplicable mood to the next.

''You were saying?'' Brad asked at last.

Alex blinked up at him. His twenty new prisoners had become twenty-five, and each one required a different testing run, with each run correlated to extra tests the Federal Agents wanted to set. This, along with the regular run of criminals from the home planet. He didn't have the people to handle it, even with everyone called in and a number of team members acting outside their normal expertise.

He looked at Brad and pressed a hand against his forehead. He was getting a headache.

''Where's Mark?'' he asked. ''He's on today, right?''

''Um—he didn't come in yet.''

''Call him at home. Probably he just overslept.''

''I did. No answer.''

''Shit, piss, and corruption. All right, then. Try Gail,'' he said. ''She's new but—'' His telecom buzzed, and he grimaced. ''Gail. Let Pinkie do some gofer work.''

Brad exited, waving over his shoulder, as Alex flipped the receive switch and Board Governor Paul Dinardo's face appeared, his face puffy and his eyes swollen, as if he'd been without sleep for many days. Alex didn't waste energy on sympathy. Paul always looked that way, though he rarely did without sleep unless he was up too late watching football.

"Alex," he said. "I got one more for you."

"Jesus, Paul. We're stretched already. Try another zone."

"Can't, Alex. Not with this one. The Feds insist."

Alex wanted to ask since when did the Feds have anything to say about Planetoid operations, but they were the primary source of workers he had right now and he couldn't afford to lose them. He drummed his fingers on his desk.

"Who?" he asked.

"Sardis," Paul replied. "She's yours, so listen good."

Alex listened, a growing sense of unreality enveloping him while Paul explained. He kept waiting for the punch line, thinking it must be a joke. No punch line. No joke. Alex gaped at Paul, shook himself, and tried for a reasonable tone of voice.

"You want me to do *what* with her?" he asked.

"You heard me, Alex. Just set it up," Paul replied. "She's to start it by end of day."

"But I thought she was going to Two," Alex said.

"Not anymore. Word from on high, Alex."

Alex considered. "What about the VR people? They'll have to run a new program for this scenario. It's pretty complex, isn't it?"

"We talked to them. They got two hotshit programmers—sorry. Creative designers, they call themselves. Jesus Almighty, spare me. But they say they just gotta tweak the formula, whatever that means. I mean, they've been up and running for almost three months with no trouble, so I suppose they know what they're talking about even if nobody else understands a word they say."

Alex leaned back, rubbed a hand across his face. "Okay,

Paul. I'll do my part. I don't know who we'll get for the assignment, though. The only Teacher I know who can manage Sardis is—well, I suppose you wouldn't want *her*."

Paul pulled at his lower lip thoughtfully. "Funny you should say that. The Feds requested her."

"What?"

"You heard me. Special Agent Shannon went through the files and picked Addams. You meant Addams, right? Shannon's boss—guy named Madden—confirmed it. And if I knew why, I'd tell you, but I don't, so don't give me shit about it. Maybe for the same reasons you thought of her."

"Maybe," Alex mused.

"Anything new on the one you lost?" Paul asked.

"Nothing," Alex replied.

"Why didn't you guys put an implant in him when he got there?"

"Tested allergic to the coating. They were afraid he'd go into seizures, so they put an external nodule on him. Apparently he pulled it right outside the building."

Paul leaned away from the telecom a minute and looked around as if checking for spies before he leaned back in and spoke in a whisper. "Ever think it was an inside job, Alex? One of your people involved with Revelation?"

Alex shook his head. "We've been checking, and there's no sign of it yet. More likely," he added cynically, "it was one of the Feds."

"You aren't serious. Are you?"

"They're from the home planet, had more contact with the cult than any of my people."

"Yeah," Paul said. "You got a point. I'll see what I can see about that. But for God's sake don't mention it to Addams. We don't want another shuttle blowup, and since she's involved . . ."

He let the sentence trail, and Alex finished it for him. "I'll feel a lot safer," he said.

"What?"

"Whose ass did she save on that assignment, Paul?"

Paul's mouth twitched. "Just keep an eye on her."

"Always do," he said pointedly. "She's too valuable a commodity to risk losing."

He flipped the telecom off and made the calls necessary to set up a fake execution. They had a few execution rooms, since death was frequently the fear a criminal had to face. After he'd booked the injection room and signed off, he reached for the telecom again, but his hand stopped its motion as he realized he didn't know which woman he was about to call.

He tapped a finger against the slick surface of his desk, then punched Jaguar's home code.

No answer.

He tried her belt sensor.

Turned off.

He sat back and mused on her visage, checking for her empathic signals, which he knew well.

All he got was a sense of enclosure. She was blocking any empathic contact.

"Elusive," he mumbled to himself, "as the cat that goes with the grin. Dammit." He knew where she was. Still at the hospital. He could go and pull her out by the ankles, he supposed. There were two problems with that idea, though. He wasn't sure if he could take her, and he didn't want to find out.

So instead, he tried Carolan, who appeared much more receptive to his call.

Sardis tilted her head back and laughed, revealing a mouthful of perfect teeth and causing the skin of her face to stretch back from its own deep wrinkles.

" 'Let us be glad and rejoice, for the marriage of the lamb is come, and his wife hath made herself ready,' " she declaimed.

"Just," Alex said, "keep walking."

He held her elbow firmly, glancing over at Carolan, who had hold of her other arm, pulling her up when she stumbled. Sardis responded with a guttural noise, and continued dragging her feet as they made their way down the long gray hall toward the iron gate at the end. The two Federal Agents taking the role of guards in this small drama walked a silent attendance behind them. The glances they exchanged showed their opinion of the proceedings. A fake execution for a madwoman was a waste of time, a waste of money, and a waste of their most minimal efforts.

"Are you sure she knows what's happening?" Carolan hissed across her to Alex.

He shrugged. "We told her. Many times."

"Try again."

He took in a breath and stopped walking, took Sardis by the shoulders, and forced her to look at him. "Sardis, you're about to be executed for twenty-two counts of premeditated murder, for depraved endangerment, for— Sardis?"

She beamed at him ecstatically and nodded. " 'The devil shall cast some of you into prison, that ye may be tried; and ye shall have tribulation ten days. Three days and a half shall ye be dead. Be thou faithful unto death and I will give thee a crown of life.' "

"Right," Alex said. "Then let's proceed."

He turned her toward the iron gates and walked forward.

"I hope this works," Carolan muttered. "She seems a little too pleased about the whole thing."

One of the Federal Agents cleared his throat, Alex was sure to hide a laugh.

The guard at the gate responded to Alex's nod and the bars swung back to admit them. They helped Sardis onto a long low table, strapping down her arms and legs. A number of monitors buzzed over her head, reading blood pressure, heart rate, brain activity in all zones. They were rigged to indicate a cessation of body function. She offered no resistance until they adjusted the pillow under her head so that she could better observe her own purported demise. Then she struggled briefly, gasped.

"Wait," she said. Alex and Carolan, stopped, looked down at her.

"Is my hair all right?" she asked. "I don't want it to be messy."

Carolan gazed down at her, patted the streaks of gray at her temples. "Fine," she said. "Your hair is fine."

"Thank you," Sardis said, and lay back as they inserted the needle into her arm. A tranquilizer dripped from an IV into her vein, slowly, so that consciousness left her slowly. It contained a NeoSyn-inhibitor as well, which would lower the neural noise that surrounded her thoughts. Alex had ordered it without Carolan's knowledge, hoping this would clear her enough for him to make brief empathic contact. He'd tried contact when he met her that morning, but she was filled with a static he couldn't penetrate.

He wasn't sure if the NeoSyn would help him get through, but he'd used it in the past with some measure of success. And though he was keenly aware of Carolan watching him with interest, not sure he wanted her interest, he knew this was the last chance he'd have for contact.

Sardis sighed and leaned back into herself. " 'These are those who came out of great tribulation,' " she crooned dreamily, " 'and have made their robes white in the blood of the lamb.' "

He reached across the table and pressed two fingers to her forehead. She started, looked up at him, said nothing.

"Sardis Malocco, see who you are. Be what you see," he whispered, holding her eyes with his.

For the next few minutes he wasn't aware of Carolan frowning, at her frown smoothing into a speculative gaze, at her hand reaching to his and pulling back. He felt only the crack and hiss of Sardis's internal life.

He drew back more quickly than he'd expected to, and rubbed at his hand. Like trying to talk to a toaster, he thought. A toaster with a short. The NeoSyn didn't help at all. Jaguar would have to manage on her own. He leaned his face close to hers.

"Sardis, you're dying. Is there anything you want to say?"

The drugs were carrying her out to a sea of unconsciousness. Saliva dribbled out of the corner of her mouth, and she slurred as she said, " 'The spirit of life from God entered into them, and they stood upon their feet. And in the same hour, the city fell.' "

She smiled broadly, closed her eyes, and slept.

"Well," Carolan said, "that was fun."

"Fun," Alex repeated. "Pass the wine, please."

Carolan turned a wry smile to him and handed him the bottle of Merlot. She said they both needed good food and wine, and insisted they go to his favorite restaurant for lunch. Her treat.

About halfway through the soup, Alex decided *she* was a treat. Nice to be sitting with an attractive, courteous woman who wouldn't pull out verbal knives and fling them at you, wouldn't put your belly in knots over complex moral issues, wouldn't walk around inside your thoughts uninvited. Obviously, he'd been working too hard, and spending far too much time with Jaguar.

Nice to be eating a good meal on the Feds' tab, too. The Planetoid hardly ever sprang for expenses, and when they did, it was within very unfortunate limits.

They received ample operating funds from home planet legislation because the good men and women of the government wanted to keep the prison system out of sight and out of mind. But the Governors' Board controlled the flow of that funding, and more often than not they chose to put it into new technology rather than new people or perks. Sometimes that was the right move. For instance, the technology of the ecosites made for a more pleasant place to live than the bubble domes of Planetoid One. But when Alex was short on Teachers and remembered that he lived in a rather small apartment and ran a pretty old set of wings, he recognized that new technology wasn't always just the thing.

Carolan, on the other hand, wore a very nice new suit, and ordered a good wine that was just the thing. He poured himself a full glass, took a sip, and felt himself expanding in the warmth of the wine and the woman.

"I think it'll be a very interesting case, don't you?" Carolan said.

"I do," Alex agreed, "though my interest is less theoretical than yours."

"Mm. How's Rebecca?"

"Rachel. So far, no change for the worse, and that's good. They still can't name the toxin he used, and that bothers me. That, and what he was saying when he used it."

"You're worried about the End of Days scenario," she noted.

"Uneasy would be a better word. All the sect members are immersed in it."

Carolan reached across the table for the saltshaker, her hand stopping briefly to touch his reassuringly, a gesture he didn't mind at all. "We've got the houses tagged, and all the usual points of interest under three-day extra security. Shuttleports, government buildings. Cathedrals, too. And you know, we're experts at that kind of work."

"Among the best," Alex said. "Worrying just gives me something to do. I like to keep busy."

She smiled, brought her glass up to meet his, and then drank. "Then you can help me. I want more context for the data I have, and I'm going to request your assistance on it."

"Oh? In what way?" Alex asked, and found himself retreating slightly from her. He didn't feel quite up to discussion of the empathic arts, if that's what she was getting at.

Her laughter broke over him like cool water. He lifted his dark eyes to her clear blue ones.

"What?" he asked.

"You look so dark and portentous."

He smiled grimly. "It's my Lithuanian side. You should see me when my Irish is up."

"Irish? That's bad," Carolan said. "Worse than Lithuanian. I should know."

He shook his head. She was fair and filled with warm sun. "You don't look as if you ever had a dark day in your life. It's refreshing just to sit with you."

She clucked her tongue solicitously. "Tough work on the Planetoids, I know. And the home planet's glad enough to leave you alone to do it, unless something like this comes up. Then we just barge in and make your life tougher, right?"

"Well," Alex admitted, "that's about how it feels."

"I know. That's why Dr. Addams is so—" She paused, searching for a socially acceptable word.

"Rude?" Alex suggested. "Insulting and tactless?"

Carolan laughed. "Not really. Just defensive, I suppose. Only natural, given her proclivities."

Jaguar's proclivities. As if that word covered what the empathic arts could mean or do, especially as far as Jaguar was concerned. He was only beginning to understand her proclivities, very slowly drawing closer to the wildness that both encompassed and composed her being. What was she? A Mertec magic woman. Empath. A chantshaper, or so he suspected. A woman who could call fire out of stones and teach you the speech of the stars.

Since the Rilasco case, she'd become a part of his life in a way that was beyond coworkers, not at all like lovers, and different than just friends. Whatever it was, she had begun to share with him her knowledge of the arts. Her proclivities.

They spent a night at the animal sanctuary watching the jaguars, Hecate and Chaos, who ran free for certain hours to encourage them to breed and hunt. At the cusp of day, she'd acted as conduit for empathic contact between him and them, and he realized that she occupied a world few people knew existed. He became aware of the profundity of her power, so much like the raw and complex power of nature. And for her, this was just the simplest ritual teaching of her people. She knew more, and he found the prospect of learning from her as exciting as the dance of lightning in a storm-tumbled sky. Her world was as elemental as lightning, and potentially as dangerous.

"What do you know about Jaguar?" he asked.

"A good deal. Her grandfather's politics made the family of interest. He held one of the first UN seats for Native American Tribal Representation. You knew that, of course."

" Of course. What else?"

"Nothing more than we'd know about other important Planetoid workers," she said noncommittally. "Our files are fairly extensive."

"Your files," he suggested, "include me?"

She ducked her head down, and raised her eyes to his. What she said next confirmed what he saw there.

"Look," she answered. "I didn't mean to insult you by what I said about the empathic arts. I know they can be useful and humane. That's why I'm involved in this research. I'd like to see our progress directed humanely. I'd like to influence the research toward those ends, if I can."

"That's a good ideal to keep close to," Alex said, watching her face, her cool sky eyes. No empathic signals there. Just a sleek and shining surface, open and easy, unprofound and attractive as a summer sky.

"It's a difficult ideal," Carolan said, "when those who practice the arts most wisely are the least willing to share their wisdom."

He leaned back in his chair, picked up his wineglass, and swirled the red liquid at the bottom. "Go on," he said.

She laughed. "Don't encourage me. I'll go on all day. First, there's cloaked empaths, who hide what they are, and, if psi capacities show up in testing, deny using them. Then there's people like Dr. Addams, who don't hide, but who refuse to talk about the arts except to other empaths. She runs from any kind of scientific study, and then she's offended when people are ignorant."

Carolan had a point, but her worldview put the empathic arts in the realm of science. For Jaguar, they were spiritual acts, and the government didn't often respect her definition of sacred. In fact, they might not even recognize it, since it was so unlike the Christian God who still was intimately involved in running North American politics and morals. Prejudice on the home planet against empaths was widespread, and often violent. Between science, government, and popular opinion, Jaguar's self-protection was wise.

"Ignorance isn't always benign," he noted. "Empaths hide for good reason. Such as, they like to stay alive. Or they don't want their sacred space hooked to monitors and described in graphs."

"I know that," Carolan said. Enthusiasm for her topic brightened her face. She was on her own crusade, and for all Alex could tell, her intentions were good. "But if those who know better behave ignorantly, the ignorant will never learn a thing. Mostly we see the megalomaniacs and misfits. They skew the data to the negative end in a big way, which doesn't help change the general opinion that empathic arts are for weirdos and evil Satan worshipers."

"But can you guarantee you won't use the arts for Federal dirty work. There's no regard for what some of—" He paused. Some of us, he was about to say. "There's problems, Carolan. They don't all belong to the empath."

"Maybe," she suggested, "you could help me find some solutions."

"How could I do that?" he asked.

"Teach me," she said simply.

He was startled by the directness of her request, more startled when she stretched her hand across the table and slid it under his. She let it rest there, offering rather than demanding, the skin of her palm warm and smooth against his. When he asked himself how this felt, the one-word answer came back. Good. It felt good.

"I'm not an empath," she said, "so I only understand in a theoretical way. But I want to learn more. I don't even know what the—the empathic touch, it's called, isn't it? I don't even know what that feels like, and I should know if I'm to research it. I was hoping I could find someone here who would discreetly cure *my* ignorance."

"Ignorance," he agreed, "is a terrible blight."

She smiled, curled her fingers in on her palm, pulled her hand back. "It is," she said. "And I look forward to shedding mine."

Alex saw that there could be many positive facets to this work, but he was inclined to go slow, and she seemed inclined to let him take his time. He let the tingle in his hand pass, busied himself with a sip of wine. Then he brought the conversation back toward work.

"Carolan," he asked. "Why did you request Jaguar for Sardis?"

"She's the logical choice," Carolan said, "given her background. And I thought she'd be able to make an emotional connection, since Sardis lost a daughter in the Serials, and she lost her family."

"She's not that careless," Alex said.

"Pardon me?"

"She didn't lose them. She saw them killed."

Carolan picked up her napkin, twisting it at the end. "I'm sorry. I seem to keep stepping on your emotional toes."

Alex reached over and tugged at the end of the cloth in her hand. "No," he said. "My apology. It's just that euphemisms make no sense in the context of the Killing Times."

"You're right. I'm accustomed to official language. And I managed to miss all the violence of the times. Odd, isn't it? The single most important historical moment of my lifetime, and I'm out of town."

"Sounds like a good place to be. How did that happen?"

"My parents were professors." She shrugged. "They were taking a year to teach in Eastern Europe. Funny to think that Eastern Europe was in better shape than North America, given the twentieth-century history they had. Anyway, when the trouble started, they decided to stay on for a few more years. We didn't come back until the cleanup was well under way. Even then, we lived in the suburbs, so we didn't see much.''

''A blessing,'' Alex said.

''Of course. But I think there's a certain depth and compassion people develop when they've known suffering. I hope I didn't miss out on that.''

''Or a certain madness and intolerance,'' Alex added, thinking of Sardis.

''Did you see a lot of the violence?'' she asked tentatively, the question that people still asked each other, twenty-five years after the event. Where were you during the Serials? What did you see? How did you survive?

''I saw enough. I was in an army Domestic Patrol Unit in Manhattan in '62.''

He had also been isolated from the early part of the trouble because his family lived in rural Montana. The impact on rural areas was indirect, but what was happening in the rest of North America was engraved in his consciousness. He'd hear newscasts, and the horror of what he heard made him feel guilty at his own safety, and guilty at being so glad he was safe. Maybe in response to that, and certainly over his family's objections, he joined the army when he turned eighteen and requested domestic duty in a city zone.

He was sent to Manhattan as part of the rescue teams in the third year of the Killing Times, when the violence had slowed down enough to allow for organized intervention. He was there for a year and he saw—enough.

''Then you're a survivor, too.'' She looked sympathetic and mildly awed, a typical response to survivors and one that made him uncomfortable. It stroked his ego for something he couldn't really take any credit for. He'd done nothing beyond staying alive through a horrible time. ''So is Sardis, and Dr. Addams, which, like I said, I thought would be an advantage,'' Carolan continued. ''Did you give her Sardis's files yet?''

Alex shook his head. ''First, I had to decide if I'd let her take it on. I understand the Federal interest, but on Planetoid Three, in Zone 12, I'm the final authority in these matters."

"Understood," she said.

"Good. Because I won't let you put her under a microscope for your research. This is not an opportunity to study her—proclivities. It's an assignment with a prisoner. Is that clear?"

Carolan opened her mouth and gaped at him. "Well, why ever not?" she asked. "It's not as if we're doing anything except observing."

"Observing influences outcome," Alex said. "And I don't want her in any more trouble with the Board, or the Feds. She has a propensity for that sort of muddle."

Carolan spent some minutes carefully refolding the napkin she'd been twisting, placing it on the table next to her plate. "You take good care of your people, don't you?" she said softly. "That's admirable. I think you're probably a very good specimen of humanity, Alex."

"Maybe," he said, "but you haven't promised to take as good care as I do, and until you do—"

"I won't get her in any more trouble than she manages on her own. How's that?"

"Not good enough. I want your promise that you won't collect data on her, or use the situation to conduct research for your agency. No monitoring. Just let her do her job."

He watched her face, which indicated signs of a struggle. Like the Islamic saying, he supposed he'd have to trust, but tether his camel.

"I promise," she said at last. "But I promise reluctantly, under protest, and in the hopes that you'll change your mind once all is going well. Will that do?"

"It'll have to."

"Good. Is there anything else delaying the process?"

Alex shrugged. "I have to find her. She can be elusive."

"But aren't you, well, her boss?"

"Sort of. When she allows it. There's not such a strict hierarchy here as there is on the home planet. You follow the army model. We're more like guerrilla warfare, I sup-

pose. Jaguar has her own way, and if I don't let her pursue
it, I won't get good work from her.''

Carolan frowned as she absorbed this concept. "It's very
odd to me," she admittted, "but I suppose it's right, since
she has such a high success rate.''

"The one thing nobody can argue with," Alex said.
"She's very good.''

"She better be. There's still a whole bunch of Serial
survivors ready to jump at the suggestion of cult trouble.
And a lot of them are Senators.''

He smiled at her reassuringly. "It's all right, Carolan.
Keep an open mind, and you'll see how we work here.''

She didn't look convinced. She lifted her glass with one
hand, and sipped, but said nothing. He noted that her glass
was full, but her hand was empty.

And merely by way of reassurance, he took care to rem-
edy that situation immediately.

# 4

*day four*

THE MEDICS WORKED AROUND HER, THE MASKS ON
their faces making them inclined toward silence. Occasionally, Jaguar heard the muffled call and response of instructions on appropriate techniques for drawing blood,
removing skin, scanning breath contents, but that was all
done very efficiently, with a minimum of interaction. As
soon as they entered the sealed chamber between Rachel's
room and the hall, they'd strip out of their protective wear
and become human again, but for now they were just so
many automatons, doing a nasty job.

The medics were still treating the case as potentially contagious, though only at level-two precautions. At least they
didn't bubble her, Jaguar thought. As it was, she hated the
protective suits, the blur of Rachel's face in isolation behind
a plastic tent. Hated the loneliness of it, and the irretrievable
nature of the moment that put Rachel there.

As the medics finished up and left, Jaguar grabbed the
last one out. He or she—impossible to tell—turned and said
nothing, eyes peering over green mask.

"Anything yet?" she asked. "Any indication at all?"

The medic shook a neutral head. "We'll know more
when the blood work is back."

"But when the blood work's back—" Jaguar started to
say, and left the sentence unfinished, let the medic go.

When they were all out the door, she peeled off her face mask and walked over to Rachel's bed.

"You shouldn't do that," Rachel said, her voice muffled by the plastic tent, the hum of monitors and oxygen machines.

"You're not contagious, Rachel. They're just being anal-retentive, for insurance purposes."

Rachel shook her head. "If you lift the tent, I'm getting you kicked out of here."

"Rachel—"

"I mean it. You might be willing to take a chance, but I'm not. Get it?"

"Got it," Jaguar said reluctantly. "How do you feel?"

Rachel propped herself up on one elbow and grinned weakly. "Like I'm running out of blood," she said. Then her grin transformed into a grimace as she collapsed onto her back and clutched at her belly, gasping.

Jaguar turned on her heel and took a long quick step to the door to retrieve a medic.

"Wait," Rachel whispered. "Jaguar—wait just a minute. I don't want them coming back."

Jaguar stopped, took a second to smooth the fear from her face, and turned back, pulled a chair up, and sat by the bed. Rachel pressed her hand against the plastic, and Jaguar placed hers against it, on the other side.

Rachel's face went tight as she breathed in deeply, breathed out deeply. "Just the peritoneal work. Big needles."

Jaguar nodded. "Big fucking needles. I've seen them. Hurts."

"Hurts," Rachel agreed.

The spasm passed, and Rachel lay still, while Jaguar sat in silence beside her.

By pressing a hand against her forehead, feeling the movement of cells, the shout of her spirit in pain, she might be able to determine where Philo had hurt Rachel's body. She knew some of that art from her Mertec grandparents, and thought she'd remember how to find the elusive scent of a wound, feel any residual wound palpable in her hand. But she'd need direct contact. Healing required touch. If she stayed long enough, Rachel might fall asleep, and then she couldn't protest.

"Better?" she asked.

"Mm," Rachel said. "Better. Just tired. I'm really tired."

"Then rest," Jaguar said. "I'll sit and rest, too."

"Don't you have work to do?"

"Yes. And I'm doing it. Making sure you rest."

Rachel smiled, stirred, closed her eyes, laid a hand across them. "Do you think you'll ever stop seeing me as a little sister?" she asked.

"I don't see you that way," Jaguar protested.

Rachel chuckled. "Yes you do. It's okay, Jaguar. You're older than me. You could be my big sister."

"If I was, you would've gotten in even more trouble. You know that."

Rachel's smile dissipated. "Even more than this?" she asked pointedly.

Jaguar didn't answer. She sat and let Rachel's eyes accuse her and tried for no defense because she had none. In a moment of irrevocable fear she had made Rachel look away, and nothing would recapture or undo that moment except the capacity to reverse time and become someone not Jaguar at all. They both knew that. She felt heavy with culpability and rage, as if she'd swallowed stones, chewed on flint.

Rachel brought a hand to her mouth and pressed it against her lips as if to keep more words from escaping. "I didn't mean what that sounds like—"

"It sounds like the truth," Jaguar said. "I'd say I was sorry, if I thought it would help."

"Don't. I don't want you to feel responsible for me anymore."

"How about if I feel responsible for my own actions? For what I did."

"Look," Rachel said, "if you need to beat yourself up,

go ahead. But leave me out of it, okay? I'm the sick one here."

Jaguar tried a smile and found it almost worked. "You're right. It doesn't matter, anyway. You just get some rest. Get rested and well."

Rachel sighed, closed her eyes again, and was quiet.

Jaguar waited while she drifted into deeper sleep, into her dreams, wondering what her dreamscape would be like. Was it the same as her ancestors—Eretz Israel, desert and sea and mountain, the olive groves, fig trees, and lush river lands of those who wrestle with God? The portion of the wall where she wasn't allowed to pray? Rachel had described all of this in vivid detail during the long hours of her program as Jaguar's prisoner, sometimes sobbing at the loss of her self within that oppressive beauty, sometimes keening for her people, who had turned their backs on her, sometimes screaming in rage at the God of her fathers— the God who had betrayed her mothers. The God she confused with her father, and the father she confused with God.

Rachel said the trouble started when she realized she liked girls the way most of her girlfriends liked boys. She never told her parents, but the sharp-eyed looks they gave her around other girls told her they suspected something.

Her father claimed the trouble started when she sang so loudly at services the men could hear her female voice, which was a sin. He punished her with silence, not uttering a word in her presence for two weeks, and pretending to be deaf to her voice. It made her feel crazy, she said, and she'd started on a set of more public sins that eventually involved State and Federal laws. She went from shoplifting to car theft, stealing cars to drive them nowhere, and walking away from them when her anger was spent. She hoped the visible sins she committed would hide the one sin of being she couldn't accept in herself, or change. The sin of being who she was.

Her last car theft ended in a high-speed chase that killed two policemen. That landed her on Planetoid Three. For baggage she brought her Sabbath candles, a millennium of inherited guilt, and a profound fear that her very being kept her separated from her God. Jaguar thought that was a realistic fear in her community, where being a woman was enough to keep her away from God. Rachel sat behind the Mehitza and prayed silently. She couldn't read her holy book. Every day she listened to her father thank God that he wasn't made a woman.

Then, to be the lover of other women. To be a lesbian made her anathema. Dirty. A thing of pity and derision and shame.

"The walls that men build stand between you and the Divine," Jaguar told her. "You can't tolerate them, nor should you."

Just being away from the emotional complexities of that environment helped her heal. It also helped that Jaguar was willing to let her argue God forever, talking, listening, showing her own anger. Rachel needed to speak her truth after a liftetime of being silenced, to find a voice and use it with someone who believed differently, but respected her beliefs anyway. Jaguar encouraged her to take risks. Be openly and all of who she was. Don't hide your sexual preferences, she told Rachel. Nobody worries much about that on the Planetoids anyway. Stay here and be a team member. Try for the Teacher training. You can be who you are and that's very good. In fact, that *is* what's sacred.

And all of those good intentions got her exactly here. Maybe bad intentions would bring them somewhere better.

Jaguar watched Rachel breathing, the slower and easier breath of deep sleep, and saw Rachel's eyes scan the back of the lids for information on the status of the soul. She moved a hand toward the tent, and Rachel gasped. Jaguar pulled her hand back.

Rachel opened her eyes and stared dully for a minute before she found her focus. "Jaguar," she whispered, "did I die?"

"No," Jaguar replied firmly. "You didn't. He used a paralytic toxin and your heart stopped, but you were still alive."

"I think I was dead," Rachel said, ignoring Jaguar's response. "I saw Rachavia. Red anemones. Bloodred. I thought it was heaven, and then I realized it was just Rachavia, but that was good enough. The next time I die, I won't be as afraid."

"It'll be a long time before the next time, Rachel. Don't worry about it."

"No. That's just the way *you* want it. But you're not in charge." She returned to silence, closed her eyes, and her breathing grew softer.

Jaguar lifted the tent slightly, slid her hand under it, and pressed it to Rachel's forehead. Warm. It was warm, and she didn't wake. *Hush. Rest, Rachel. Sleep. I'm here.*

She prepared herself for this level of empathic contact, so visceral and so direct. She opened, her breath working with Rachel's to find the right rhythm, the right way of being within her body And as she opened she felt the movement of another mind within her own.

Shit, she thought. Now what?

Then Alex's voice, unmistakable, clipped and formal.

*Dr. Addams, I need you ASAP. You've got work to do.*

Caught within her own opening, she had no choice but to respond. She'd been staying closed to him, and had forgotten how persistent he could be in searching for her. Now he'd know where she was, what she was doing, why. She replied in equally clipped tones.

*I'm busy.*

His voice. His laughter. His knowing he had her in an inescapable bind.

*I'll wait right here for you.*

"Rat fuck," she said out loud, and tried not to scrape her chair too hard against the floor as she got up to leave.

He stared at the computer screen, folded his delicate hands, and held them to his mouth.

The VR site. The computer log said Sardis was on the VR site. That's where he'd find her. But where on this blasted Planetoid was the VR site?

Everything was going so well, he didn't want to give himself away by asking stupid questions like, excuse me, do you know where I can find the nearest VR site? Why? Well, there's this cult leader I was scamming, and I'd like to make sure she's good and dead before I go back to the home planet and access the funds she put in my name. My name? Well, she knew me as Philo, but actually that's not the name the funds are in. They're under the name Carl Barlin, but my professional name is Proteus.

That's right. *The* Proteus. The one you've heard so many stories about.

No. He wouldn't need to get stupid. So far, he was doing fine. He'd found a cart and put Mark on it, covered with his prisoner's clothes, then dragged his body up to the closet where he'd originally hidden. It seemed like nobody used that for much, and by the time they noticed the smell and figured out that the guy's Ident card was missing, he'd have found another one to use.

Mark's had already served its purpose, since it allowed him access to the computer banks, and from there he'd learned that Sardis was on the VR site. But where was the VR site, and what was the password to tell him?

A hand came down on his shoulder and he turned to see a young woman he recognized. He squinted at her. Yes. Mark's partner. The woman who had dragged him to the interview room by the ear. He couldn't remember her name, but a quick scan of her thoughts gave him that. He smiled.

"Hello, Gail," he said. "How's it going?"

"Pretty good. You look lost, though."

She didn't recognize him at all. He wasn't projecting the image of Philo's pinched, fanatical face anymore. He'd become someone else altogether. His transformation was complete.

His was such a handy talent. He figured it out when he was in college, trying to hide from a girlfriend he'd stood up. He was in a bar, and when she walked in he wished fervently that he could be someone else. Anyone. An insurance agent. A cop. Anyone. He braced himself for her tirade as she approached the bar, but she walked right by him as if she didn't know who he was.

He turned and caught a look at himself in the mirror behind the bar, and saw—someone who had much more the look of an insurance agent than a second-year college student.

Confused, disoriented, he dropped his beer. His girlfriend helped him clean it up without recognizing him, and just to see if he could do it, he ended up taking her home and bedding her. She never knew who he was.

He was not a religious young man, and he didn't go in for the spiritual searching popular at the time. He never had past-life regression therapy, never sought his Higher Guide, never talked to dead people, and didn't have a patron saint. He'd been raised to observe the proprieties of a Protestant ethos, and held basically to the theory that it was best to keep a low profile where God was concerned. But this was a strange miracle, he thought. God looking out for fools and drunks. He couldn't come up with any other explanation.

A few weeks later he signed up to be a paid subject in a psychology experiment. It was really some early work in detecting psi capacities, but in those days they had to call it psychology or lose any chance of funding. It was an easy twenty dollars. He answered a barrage of questions and was hooked up to an advanced ENG while he watched pictures flash by on a screen and listened to music and answered more questions. When he was done, the psych major looked at his chart and whistled long and low. She asked if he knew about Protean Changers. He didn't.

She didn't explain. "You should go into politics," she said. "Or religion. Either one'd work."

Protean Change, he found out later, was a psi capacity. The capacity to change aspect in response to environmental demands. Politicians, religious leaders, actors and actresses were probably using it without being aware of doing so. And he had the indications of it in spades.

Over time he learned how to control it. Mostly it was a

matter of finding out from those around him what kind of aspect would be most comfortable for them, and projecting that outward. Having telepathic talents allowed him to pick aspects directly from people's thoughts and simply assume them. He'd gotten so good that he could even give different aspects to two different people at the same time. One reason he had no rap sheet was because he was hell on witnesses. In the early days of the Serials, when he hired on as mercenary for a terrorist group, his science background wasn't half as helpful as the talent he had for blending into a crowd.

Proteus, they called him. The Greek sea god who changed shapes to slip the grasp of humans.

"I'm checking activity patterns for the areas surrounding the VR site," he said, asking Gail to see him as a research worker. Someone new to their system. "But I think I have the wrong codes."

"Easy," Gail said. She leaned over his shoulder, pressed three keys. "That's your site," she said. "Now you can access activity stats according to section numbers."

His smile broadened as the schematics for the site appeared, surrounded by normal houses, the breeding complex, and the Toronto Animal Sanctuary. Nice. The VR site was in the zoo.

"Great. Thanks. Just the thing."

"No problem. I guess you Feds have different systems on the home planet, right?"

"We're not allowed to talk about that, Gail," he said.

"Oh. Right. Sorry. Well, good luck."

When she left, he was able to retrieve details about the facility's layout and security system. Then he sat back and considered.

He wasn't in a rush to return to Earth. In fact, he was beginning to appreciate the good luck that had brought him here. He had a hiding place in the Caribbean, but this was really so much safer. He'd get back to the sun and the beach, but he'd take care of Sardis first. She was perhaps the only person alive who could give him away, if the rehab here was as good as rumor said.

Besides, if they rehabbed her, she'd probably call off the game, and he didn't want that to happen. A few million less stupid people on the planet sounded good to him. And the people left would be so hungry for the right leader. The right face. Maybe it was time to go into politics, like the psych major said so long ago. Surely he could cash in on disaster.

He'd find her, and see to it that she didn't talk. And according to all his calculations, he still had plenty of time to do so.

The door to Alex's apartment opened, and Jaguar stepped inside. He was stretched out on the couch, rereading Saint John the Divine, which he put down on the coffee table.

"Come in," he said, as if she needed invitation. She knew how to work the lock without a key, and she'd been entering his apartment uninvited since she started working for him. Sometimes she needed a place to hide, or had something to talk to him about. Other times he had no idea what impelled her to be there, or to go away. She'd wander his living space like a misplaced cat, then leave without a good-bye.

She seemed to be stalking the edge of something, but he didn't know what. Sometimes it felt as if she was testing him, as an empath, as a Supervisor or a friend. Other times it felt almost like sexual attraction, though he knew better than to travel there with her. She was volatile, unwilling to be attached and equally unwilling to let go. The combination made for a bad choice of bed partner, and he'd long since made an agreement with himself not to lick lightning. If this was her form of seduction, she'd have to remain disappointed.

Alex swung his legs to the floor and sat up, considering her. The amber skin of her face was smooth. Her sea-green eyes were sharp, taking in everything. Her hair was an un-ruffled fall of dark honeyed silk down her back, shining and smooth. She was containing herself, using a lot of control to maintain a smooth surface.

"Have you been at the hospital the whole time?" he asked.

She lifted her chin. "None of your business," she said. "I'm on rest leave."

"Not anymore," he said. "I have an assignment for you."

Her chin came down a notch, and she narrowed her eyes. "I'm busy," she said.

"Mm-hmm. How's Rachel?" he asked.

"Conscious, and stable."

"No residual damage? No fever or secondary infection?"

"Maybe a slight fever," Jaguar admitted reluctantly, "but that's to be expected. That doesn't mean anything."

"Good. Then you're free to work and I'm calling you in for assignment with Revelation."

She swiveled her head away from him and made a sound very like growling at the back of her throat. "I don't do cults," she snapped.

"You'll do this one."

"Why?"

"You're being assigned to Sardis."

He saw her pause, skip a beat in the conversation. Clench and unclench her hands. She walked across the living room and stood in front of him, hands on her hips, chin still high.

"Feds approve that?"

"Requested it."

"And you'll do anything they say, right?"

"Don't be ridiculous. Assigning you to Sardis is the best use of your talents."

"Sardis is living proof that it doesn't matter what genitals you have, everybody's got an asshole. Why don't you shoot her and get it over with?"

"If we do that," Alex noted, "we'll just be making another martyr for them to worship."

"We meaning you and Carolan?"

He drummed his fingers on the table. "Say what's on your mind, Jaguar. Don't hold back."

"C'mon, Alex. You lost your judgment the minute that cutesy Fed tossed a smile your way. Don't gawk at me like that. I know what I see. Who let Rachel interview Philo, and how'd he smuggle in a poison dart? How'd he get past the sensors?"

He reached over the small table between them and grasped her wrist. She stood looking down at his hand as if it were a mosquito she'd decided not to bother with just yet. He could feel, under his fingers, the holder for the retractable glass knife she wore at her wrist. He pressed the button that snapped the blade into the palm of her hand.

"You know how easy it is to slip glass past the sensors, Jaguar. You, of all people, know that. Whatever he gave her was encased in glass. Hidden in a cutout just below the gum. And I don't use my people to score points with a woman. I don't need to."

She pulled her hand away from him, glowering, saying nothing as she retracted her knife.

"Or," he commented, "is this about you not getting in there in time? As if you could have—"

"I got there," she said. "I hit the window, and she looked away from him. Remember?"

Alex closed his eyes and opened them, slowly. So that was it. Of course.

"Jaguar, it's not your fault," he said softly. "Not yours, and not mine, and not even Carolan's."

She returned his gaze and said nothing. He saw her face close against him, the narrow line of her jaw working hard. In spite of her reputation as a loose cannon, she had a remarkably overdeveloped sense of responsibility. She didn't see that at least she was there in time to get the medics. She saw only what happened, and that she hadn't prevented it. She'd take full responsibility, feel it all, and she'd do it alone, thank you very much. No point trying to storm that fortress.

She walked away from him, toward the windows that

looked out over the lake, staying out of his view. "Caro-lan's recruiting you, Alex. Personally and professionally. I see it, and if you don't you're either being deliberately blind, or you're thinking with the wrong part of your anatomy. In either case, I'm not sure I trust your supervisory instincts."

"Come back over here and sit down, Jaguar," he said.

He heard her stirring, but she didn't appear. He twisted around on the couch and saw that she was facing him, which was progress, he supposed.

He lifted a hand, moved a finger up and down. "A direct order from your boss, who likes his job on the Planetoids."

She walked over and sat on a chair across from him, at the edge of her seat, ready to bolt at a moment's notice.

He nodded. "That's better. Sort of."

"It's what you get," she said.

"Right. *I* want you on this assignment," he said patiently. "I would've recommended you no matter what, because you're the best Teacher for the case, and it'll be a tough one. I can't get anywhere with Sardis. I can't find a way in."

Jaguar raised her eyebrows.

"I tried," he confirmed. "Nothing except a brief flash of—of something sharp and twisted."

He held a hand out, leaned toward her, and felt her opening to his touch. He showed her what he felt with Sardis. No clear thought. No visual image. Just the feel of something piercing. Then total confusion, like driving into the glare of a sunset, road disappearing into elaborate light.

She puffed her cheeks out, ran a hand through her long hair.

"Her barriers are intricate and effective," he said. "You can get lost going around them and never find your way in, or back out. It's almost beautiful."

"Is she psychotic? Any of the biochems read wrong?"

"All normal, though she reads functionally psychotic, immersed in fantasy."

She thought some more. "Possessed?" she asked.

Alex lifted his shoulders and let them fall. This was not an official diagnostic category, but empaths didn't discount it. Possession, psychological or spiritual, was a condition they recognized as real and dangerous.

"It's a possibility," he said. "Now name me one other Teacher who's capable of finding out."

Jaguar ran a finger over her lips, smoothing them as she thought. She loved her work enough that it drew her beyond herself. The challenge of someone like Sardis would tempt her. But she had concerns, and he supposed some of them were serious, beyond her general snit over the Feds.

"Alex," she said thoughtfully, "you know that Christians don't like me much."

"What?"

"I mean, her sect is Christian. To her, I'm a savage Mertec. A pagan. And an empath. She hates me on principle. How can I find a way in? And if she's possessed, how can I deal with that? My ways aren't Christian, and I'm not sure if they'd work on her."

"In her program, she'll never know what you are. And if she's possessed, evil is evil. You know how to deal with it. Besides, what if her End of Days scenario is real?" He let that idea sink in.

She brought her gaze to a level with his, staring hard. "Have you been shaking your web, spider magus?" she asked.

"I have," he admitted, "but I'm still interpreting. The question is theoretical. If Sardis left her people with plans for self-destruction, what will you do?"

Jaguar shrugged. "You know. I'll stop it. Any way I can."

This, said as if there was no other possible answer. He nodded. "That's why I want you on it. Nobody much cares if a bunch of wacko cult members kill themselves. And maybe you don't care either, but you'll do the right thing regardless."

She settled back in the chair, her left hand drawing spirals on the arm of her chair. "What's her program?" she asked.

Good, he thought. She wasn't committing to it, but she was getting close. The next part would present the greatest difficulty, though. And there wasn't any way to pretty it up.

"She'll be on the Virtual Reality site," he said.

Jaguar's entire body rippled into attention as she sat up and glared at him.

"Beautiful, Alex. I hope Carolan remembers how manipulative empaths can be," she said sharply. "Especially Adepts. Or were you hoping I just wouldn't notice I was working VR?"

"Jaguar, don't get all—"

"All what? Pissed off? As if I don't have reason." She began counting them off on her fingers. "First, you're asking me to break leave. Second, you're asking me to break leave for an assignment with a woman you know I despise, who would despise me. Third, you're asking me to risk my ass with the Feds and the Board, who're circling like vultures to see the empath fall down and bleed. *And* you're asking me to work a VR site, which you know I don't do. Did I miss anything?"

"One thing," he said.

"What's that?"

"The asking-you part."

He heard the sound of fingernail tapping on wood.

"The Feds and the Board won't take a no from you, Jaguar. Not without consequences."

"Consequences such as?"

"I'm not sure. Something unpretty, I'd assume. The Board'll put you in research, maybe. Let you make coffee for Carolan and the Feds. Transfer you back to Planetoid One."

"Xipe Totec flay them all," she said, considering the prospect. "Goddammit, *let* them put me out to pasture for a while. At least I can be with Rachel."

"I can't," he said gently. "I need you on this. So does

Rachel. Sardis might know what toxin Philo used. She might know an antidote.''

She was midway to pointing an angry finger in his face when she heard what he said. She dropped her hand. Alex tasted something as sweet as victory in the gesture.

"Jaguar," he said, choosing his words carefully, "you ask me if I've been shaking my web, and I have. Maybe I don't understand all of what I saw yet, but I do know this is your assignment. If the Board wasn't putting your back to the wall on it, I would."

Her fingernail went *tap tap tap*. He waited.

"If my back's to the wall, who'll cover my front?" she growled.

"I will," he said, without a moment of hesitation.

She looked at him hard. "No matter what? And not just within reason. I mean, no matter what."

He didn't even have to think about it. "Of course. I pick you. I cover you. One hundred percent."

That did it. He saw her jaw unclench and knew she was done arguing. She'd take it on.

"Okay," she said, staring at her hands, "okay. But I'll have to see her before we go to VR."

Alex shook his head. "You can't. We've got her in suspended consciousness. We faked an execution. She's to think she's been killed and has woken up in the afterlife."

"What?"

"She'll think she's died and gone to heaven."

"Alex, that's appalling."

"Makes it clear why we have to use the VR, doesn't it?"

"But—heaven?"

"The testers say her fear is God."

"God," Jaguar said, then a wicked smile formed on her face. "Is that the part I get to play?"

"That would be typecasting," Alex said. "Listen up, Dr. Addams, and I'll explain the program. You've got tonight to go through the files, and you're on first thing in the morning."

• • •

Creative designers Andy Spodris and Dave Halpern sat and stared at the computer's panoramic screen, the wideness of their eyes an indication of the condition of their egos at this moment. The four quadrants of the VR site rolled across the three feet of screen in majestic and logistical order. The Moroccan bazaar, where vendors hawked their wares and women in chadors floated down cobbled streets, peacocks trailing them, was followed by a formal Italian garden on a grassy knoll that led gently to a quietly flowing stream where angels strolled under weeping willows. Green grass gave way to pavement, free of litter, where one could walk in peace to view the cars for sale at the Celestial Corners Lot, or easily stroll over to the entrance of the Heart of Heaven shopping mall, where happy holofamilies shopped happily.

"I love this, Dave. It's all so—real."

"That's why it's called Virtual *Reality,* you dirigible. I'm not so sure about those peacocks, though. Are there peacocks in Morocco?"

"What's it matter? It's my heaven."

"*Our* heaven, Andy. Hey—get that angel in the formal garden. Wing's crooked."

"Damn. Floppy wings. I hate that. Wait—just lemme—" Dave twirled a knob, said a magic word that sounded like an invitation to a sexual encounter, and the angel's wing righted itself.

"There. That should do it. How's tracking for the prisoner?"

"Fine. She should be in the mall to start. Get a close-up on Q4 Section 14."

"Huh?"

"SleepTight store. Main Hall."

"Oh. Right. I love this mall."

It was a leftover from a previous program, with more appropriate characters, softer lighting, and a new music track. The testers wanted Jerusalem, paved with gold and

jewels, but they'd requested it too late. The designers had
to come up with an equivalent fast, and Dave was proud
of his quick thinking. What better heaven than a mall where
everything was free? And it was so easy to tweak an existing program. He'd saved them a month of time and a
year's budget.

He flipped the grid to a close-up view, and they saw
Sardis in abundant white flowing robes, asleep on the florid
quilt of a queen-size bed.

"She's not supposed to come out of it for a while, I
guess," Dave said.

"I hope she doesn't screw up the works," Andy commented.

"The works wouldn't be here if she wasn't. This is not
art for art's sake, Andy," David noted.

"Yeah. I know. Seems a damn shame, though, to let
people in."

"There's gonna be people in and out like crazy until this
is done. Wait'll the Teacher gets here. Everyone says she's
a—you know." He wiggled two fingers in the air, snaking
them toward Andy's forehead in imitation of the gesture of
the empath. Andy brushed them away.

"Cut that shit out. Gives me the creeps."

David laughed. He didn't share Andy's horror of psi capacities, and didn't care if they put an orangutan on the
site, as long as his implementation schedule ran. "I won't
let her bite you. Besides, she's the least of our worries. We
got the Feds coming in tomorrow to look over our shoulders. You might want to wear something presentable for a
change."

"What's that mean?"

"It means change your shirt. And your pants. There's
pizza stains on 'em from last week."

"So?"

"So, I hear the Fed's a looker."

"So again," Andy said. He tapped on the screen, the tip
of his finger landing on a holowoman blanketed head to

toe in white robes. "I'm telling you, Dave, from what I
know of women, I'd rather have one of these any day."

"Your favorite women are all fictional, aren't they?"

"Damn straight," Andy said. "And I'm the writer."

# 5

*day five*

RACHEL STIRRED, OPENED HER EYES, AND SMILED
at Jaguar. "I was dreaming about your sisters," she said,
raising a hand to the plastic tent around her. "Yael and
Devorah."

Jaguar lifted her hand to meet Rachel's and smiled in
return.

The old story, from the Book of Judges. They'd talked
about it. Devorah in the judge's chair, predicting that a
woman would best Sisera, and the peace of Israel growing
from Yael's willingness to drive a tent peg through a man's
brain. Rachel admired Yael's courage, but she was repelled
by the violence of her act, and preferred the role of Devorah.

"You were Yael," Rachel continued. "Seducing Sisera
and killing him. Then you took your weapon and flew
away, laughing."

Her hands fluttered like wings against the plastic, her
eyes a dark and glassy sea, with something new shining in
them. Crows flying at the back of the night. Bat Kol, daughter of a voice, speaking the word of the Divine in dreams.
But Rachel wasn't an empath. She didn't have visions.

Rachel pushed herself up on her elbows. As she did so
she grunted.

Jaguar leaned toward her. "Okay?" she asked.

Rachel grimaced, but nodded. "Too many enemas," she said. "It's humiliating." She turned her head from one side to the other, light from the window pouring in patches across her ashen face. She tilted her head back, and a cry of pain escaped her. Jaguar stood, but Rachel held a hand out to stop her movement.

"I'm getting the nurse."

"No. I don't want any damn nurse. I just want to get this over with. Nobody told me it took this long to die."

"You're not dying," Jaguar said sharply.

"*You* don't know that," Rachel snapped back. "Don't *tell* me that when you don't know and don't lie to me. Nobody goddamn knows a fucking thing, and it's all so stupid and humiliating, and God, Jaguar, I'm so afraid."

In one complete and liquid movement, Jaguar sat down on the bed, pulled back the plastic tent, and held her.

*Here, Rachel. I'm here. Be still.*

She felt the pull of Rachel's resistance, saying she shouldn't be doing this, it wasn't safe. She spoke into her, knowing how to find this place easily after being her teacher and friend.

*Be still. I know what I'm doing.*

She held her, rocked her back and forth, put what she could of healing in her hands, and stroked her hair. Then, in this close contact, Jaguar understood the source of Rachel's dreams. They grew from illness. And it was illness deep enough to draw her close to the spirit world.

That wasn't right, though. She should be showing improvement. Small and steady improvement every day as she recovered from the poison Philo had injected her with. There shouldn't be illness or any dreams. No, Jaguar thought. Just no.

Holding Rachel close, she crept into the level of being that had to do with molecules and energy that moved along neurons, passing like light through membrane and skin organ. She let her thoughts pass over these places, seeking poison, erosion, dysfunction. Any problem would first make itself known as a simple block, and wellness was the hum of nothing wrong. Not broke, don't fix. She traveled the various systems, feeling the hum in heart and belly and lung and kidney and liver. Nothing wrong in uterus or ovary or breast. She made her way into the central nervous system, the buzzing wires of signal over signal, complexity of emotion and thought reduced to its simplest format and—there.

The spinal column. There. Something. Something unpleasant. It was not degenerative. Not fused. It was open and swollen. Confused and wrong.

To feel it was not to know its name, though. She took in as much information as she could, then sought a way to articulate what she'd felt in words the medical community might understand.

"Where's your pain, Rachel?" she asked.

Rachel shook her head. "I can't tell anymore. I'm stiff and sore all over. What hurt just now was my neck. My neck and head."

Jaguar sighed. A secondary meningitis, maybe. Easily fixed with a proferon shot. Maybe. She felt Rachel shift away from her, and she let her slide back down to the pillow.

"I want Alex to call my family," she said.

"I'll call them, Rachel. But you don't have to—"

"No," Rachel said definitively. "Have Alex call. You'll just get all pissed off at them. And yes, I have to."

Jaguar stroked her hair. "Okay," she said dully. "Okay."

"And—if anything—if I die, I want you to sing for me," Rachel continued. "No, don't argue. Just promise. I want you to sing 'Oseh Shalom.' I want my father to hear you sing it. Promise."

Promise. Promise to sing if she dies. The words sat lumpish and still somewhere outside Jaguar's understanding and she wouldn't give them entrance. She couldn't. She didn't know how.

"We don't need to talk about that. There's no reason to talk about it."

"And what if I get to a point where I *can't* talk? Jaguar, I had another dream, too."

Jaguar felt tension rise in her like electricity along a hot wire. She didn't want to discuss this. Didn't want to think about it. But she had thousands of ancestral voices telling her to listen to the dream because that's where truth was.

"Tell me," she said.

"It was dark and I was falling. I had a child in my hands. A little girl. I had to do something about it, but I didn't know what. I had to stop falling, but I didn't know how. I kept smelling mint. Like you. Fresh mint in someone's hand. And I knew I was dying because I could feel it as I fell. All my cells told me. It was the same feeling I had when Philo stabbed me and I knew my heart wasn't beating. I could feel it not beating and I was so afraid."

Promise. Promise to sing. Rachel felt death moving in her cells. The quiet of an unbeating heart, and visions of death.

"But you're here, Rachel. Alive. And I'm here and I won't let you go, Rachel. I won't let you die," she said, as if it was an option she'd considered and rejected. No. Just no. She wouldn't allow it. This was not to be.

Rachel smiled weakly. "You got connections I don't know about?"

Jaguar released her hand, leaned back into her own chair. "I'll deal with the devil on this one. Don't you worry about it. Just get some rest."

Rachel turned on her side and closed her eyes. Jaguar let her hand linger on her forehead. She was warm, her face mottled with fever.

"No," Jaguar whispered to nobody. "No."

Before she left, Jaguar spoke with the medic at the desk. "She's worse," she noted.

The medic nodded. "Secondary reactions. We gave her a proferon shot earlier, but it's not counteracting whatever the problem is."

"Oh. I see." She looked down the hall, as if there were

an answer waiting there, but there wasn't. "Look, I'll be away for a while. Pinkie Horton's cleared for visits, and Supervisor Dzarny will be by daily. If you should need me for anything, let him know, and he'll contact me. We're the only ones who have final code for nonresuscitation orders. Is that understood?"

"Yes," she said. "We've got that down, with both your comcodes."

"Good. And—there's something else. Have you tested for a neurotoxic meningitis?"

The medic blinked up. "Meningitis responds to proferon."

"Not if it's neurotoxic. She's feverish, and in pain. In her back and neck. Is there a meningitis that's—" She struggled for the words to express what she'd felt in Rachel. It appeared in colors and shapes. Blue, and pinpoints of light. Crescent moon. "—that works specifically on centers of consciousness?"

The medic looked confused. "We scanned for all the regular toxins, and your supervisor gave us a list of common terrorist compounds. We can search the literature to see if there's anything we've missed, but I don't know if there's anything else we can do right now."

Jaguar felt heat move from her jaw to her temples. She lifted her hand and slammed it down on the desk. The medic jumped.

"Of *course* there's something else you can do," she snapped, voice shrill and high. "You can do your fucking job and keep her alive."

She glared at the medic. The medic gaped back. She turned on her heel and walked down the hall, reaching into her pocket for the drying leaves of mint she always carried, rubbing them between her finger and thumb.

By the time she was two blocks away from the hospital and toward her next destination—the transport wings that would take her to the VR site—she was calm again.

•  •  •

Carolan leaned over Andy's shoulder, and enjoyed a view of heaven.

"How's it looking, Dave?" Andy asked, uncomfortably aware of Carolan's breasts, and uncomfortably aware that, as a professional, he shouldn't be aware of her breasts. Even better, professionals shouldn't be allowed to have breasts. They made everyone too—uncomfortable.

"Everything's go," Dave replied. "Full range of motion in all quadrants, induction levels steady, feedback in normal range, and no static jumps between human and holo-figures."

"Good," Carolan said. "You've accounted for the extra neurological burden of Dr. Addams?"

"Ye-es," Andy said tentatively. "We upped the wave correlation, like you said, and that'll bounce back any extra psi thetas she's putting out. But we can't predict holofigure trauma based on your numbers. So we'll graduate the curve by twelve along the axis."

Carolan considered. That would work, she supposed, though she was guessing about much of this. With Alex's direct order against monitoring, she had to use a smaller v-line recorder that plugged into the computer directly, where it wouldn't be seen. And she wasn't breaking her promise, she told herself. The v-line wasn't for Jaguar. It was for the induction waves around her. But she'd need stronger currents to get a good read, and she hoped the designers wouldn't question that too deeply. Best to take what they offered, and make adjustments as necessary.

"Very good," Carolan murmured. "You guys are very good."

Andy sighed. "Thanks. Oh—we put in the figures you wanted. Nuns. Women in chadors."

"Great," Carolan said. "The place needed more women. Okay. Let's see the resurrection."

Andy pressed keys and the screen faded, then showed a view of the SleepTight store, zooming in to the bed where Sardis stirred in her sleep, opened her eyes, looked around, sat up.

A man in a blue suit with a store tag on was at her side before she could stand.

"Welcome," he said, "to the kingdom of heaven."

Sardis blinked at the fluffy quilts hanging on the wall, the ruffled pillows and bedspreads.

"This is heaven?"

" 'And the city was pure gold,' " the man quoted for her, " 'The foundations adorned with every precious jewel.' Wait'll you see the rest."

Sardis turned a beatific face to him. " 'Happy are those invited to the evening meal of the lamb's marriage,' " she quoted in her turn.

The man extended his hand to her, helping her off the bed. Then he tucked her arm in his and led her forward.

"Indeed," he said. "Shall we shop?"

While Sardis strolled the Heart of Heaven mall, Jaguar wandered the Moroccan bazaar. She'd seen the formal garden and the car lot, and memorized all the points of exit from the site to the computer room. As soon as she felt comfortable in the Bazaar area, she'd head for the Mall and find her prisoner.

No, she thought. Not comfortable. Familiar would be a better word. She'd never be comfortable in this place or in this role.

She was to be an angel, sent to test Sardis before she met her God. She wasn't to leave the VR site until the assignment was finished. And no, she couldn't wear her Ray•Bans onsite. Angels didn't wear sunglasses. Not even Silver Predators, which Jaguar thought would be eminently suited to her position in the celestial hierarchy.

"Jesus, Alex. Who's the prisoner?" she'd complained.

"Sardis is, but we don't want trouble. Too many people in and out makes for bad security, and we already lost one prisoner," Alex told her.

He was right, but she'd begged off sleeping in the designers' quarters, and requested permission to stay with Marie, who ran the Animal Sanctuary within which the VR site was hidden. If she could retreat to Marie's house at night, she'd still be within the gates of the breeding complex, and she'd at least have the pleasure of visiting with Hecate and Chaos. If she could get away from the site itself, she might also be able to keep her headaches under control.

VRs, she kept telling Alex, were not designed to accommodate empaths, and the designers were not willing to take their neural peculiarities into account. In fact, they weren't sure about having humans onsite at all, and kept suggesting they should design holoteachers to deal with the prisoners. Cheaper, they said, and easier to control. Right now Jaguar was inclined to agree. Already her head had begun the low hum that signaled the presence of induction waves, of too much diodic activity, of an oncoming headache.

She picked her way through the holocrowds of the Moroccan bazaar, listening to the cries of the hawkers and the chattering of passing people, reminding herself that none of it was real. She put a hand out to a stall and picked up a ripe mango, bit into it, then quickly spit it out. There was no taste. No texture. A sense of something unpleasant in her mouth, but not a solid something. It felt like having a hair stuck at the back of her throat.

"Billions of dollars for a taste of nothing," she said, wiping at her lips. "I hope they give the prisoner real food, or she'll be dead before I figure her out."

Women in chadors floated down the long cobbled street toward her, and as they approached she saluted them. " 'And I shall free my people,' " she declaimed, " 'with an end to injustice.' "

They giggled and walked on. She shrugged and continued walking in the opposite direction. A man in robes that flowed with colors and a turban wrapped around his head called to her from behind his stall. She ignored him, and he walked out onto the path, placing himself in front of her. She saw that just at the edge of the turban two bumps protruded like incipient horns. He held a watch in front of her face.

"A watch, perhaps," he said. "Ticking to the eternal now. Ticktock. Ticktock."

"No time," she said. "Got an appointment with the big guy. Generic male deity, monotheistic type one," she added as she sidestepped him and continued on her way.

She left the bazaar area, and made her way back across the grassy knoll, toward the box and hedge of the formal garden. At the edge of the rosebushes, she paused and looked back. A peacock had followed her out of the bazaar and was wending its way toward her. She waited to see how far it would go, wondering if the holofigures were stuck each in its own particular quadrant, or if they had free mobility between quadrants. As she stood contemplating the bird she heard a voice behind her.

"Let the one who has an ear hear what the spirit says to the congregations: 'To him that conquers I will give some of the hidden manna,' " Sardis Malocco said as she walked across the lush green grass toward Jaguar, her white death robes moving softly against her in the breeze.

"Revelation, Chapter 2, Verse 17," Jaguar replied. She extended a hand. "Welcome to heaven."

Sardis took Jaguar's hand in both of hers. "I am so happy to be here," she said warmly. "Are you the angel of the congregation in Sardis, by any chance?"

"Yes," Jaguar said. " 'Become watchful and strengthen the things remaining that were ready to die, for I have not found your deeds fully performed before my God.' "

Sardis nodded solemnly. " 'Those who call themselves justice slew me.' " She leaned in close and whispered, " 'But happy is the bride called to the feast of the lamb. It won't be long now. They will be broken into pieces like clay vessels. And the fires of the dragon's tongue shall be poured upon the earth.' "

She stopped speaking and pulled back, gazed around at the softly rolling green hills dotted with wildflowers, purple, yellow, orange, and red. "Nice place," she noted. Then she held up a bag. "I've been shopping."

A small burst of laughter bubbled up from the back of

Jaguar's throat. She caught it before it escaped. "Show me."

Sardis's eyes flitted back and forth, and a light shudder rippled over her frame, reminding Jaguar of Philo. "Many wonderful items," she said, and dug in. A large straw hat, and a package of sensible underwear emerged.

"Very nice," Jaguar said.

"I thought so," Sardis agreed. "Oh—and this, which is very special to me." She ducked down to the bag again, coming up with a Bible. It bore a gold insignia that marked it as a genuine celestial publication. She handed it over for inspection, and Jaguar took it, fumbling because in her hand it lacked weight and substance. Dammit, she thought. I'm supposed to feel these things, aren't I?

She didn't have time to wonder further, however, because Sardis had more to show her. "Then there's these interesting items from our pagan past." She continued pulling objects from her bag and handing them over. First, a tallit. Then, a yarzheit candle. Pagan? Jaguar wished for a moment that she could show her real pagan and be done with it. Finally, Sardis pulled out a parchment inscribed in Hebrew and English with the Kaddish.

The Jewish prayer for the dead. Jaguar's hand shook, and the weightless, insubstantial items she juggled faded, and disappeared. All except for the Kaddish.

She held it up. Turned it over. On the back, in lurid red calligraphy, were the words to the song "Oseh Shalom."

"Where'd you get this?" Jaguar demanded.

"Why, that nice man at the bazaar. With the clocks and watches. He said it was a reminder of the wages of sin."

"Is that some kind of a bad joke?" She held the parchment high, her hand closing in a fist around it. It fizzled and then disappeared in curling smoke. She blinked, and considered her unscorched hand.

Sardis gasped, dropped to her knees, and bowed her head onto folded hands. " 'And there appeared a great wonder in heaven; a woman clothed with the sun and the moon under her feet, and upon her head a crown of twelve stars.

And she being with child cried, travailing in birth and pain to be delivered.' "

Great, Jaguar thought. Off to a rolling start, building confidence and trust. "Get up," she said impatiently.

" 'And behold a great dragon, having seven heads and ten horns and the dragon stood before the woman for to devour her child as soon as it was delivered and her child was caught up unto God and to His throne.' "

"Cut it out," she barked.

" 'And they overcame the dragon by the blood of the lamb and they loved not their lives unto death. Therefore rejoice ye heavens and woe to the inhabitors of earth and of the seal for the devil is come down unto you having great wrath because he knoweth the time is short.' "

The low hum of a VR migraine upped its volume. She could barely hear what Sardis was saying, it made so little sense, the words all sucked into a meaningless thicket of irritating sound. The words were a wall of static around her, painful to listen to, blocking any possibility of real communication.

Jaguar was caught between wanting to run away and wanting to dive in and figure this one out as quickly as possible. Anything to stop the sound, so filled with unfathomable energies. She had to remind herself that Sardis might know the antidote to Philo's poison, that it was important for her to take care. While Sardis droned on she put her hands out, touched the air around her to push away the sound. And she felt nothing.

Nothing? No resistance, and no subtle signals of the boundaries all humans carried. No energy field humming inside the boundaries.

" 'And when the dragon saw that he was cast unto the earth he persecuted the woman which brought forth the child,' " Sardis chanted, her voice thick and confused.

Jaguar moved closer and touched the heavy dough of Sardis's face, felt briefly for the surface of her thoughts.

*And to the woman were given two wings that she might fly into the wilderness, where she is nourished for a time, and times, and half a time, from the face of the serpent.*

More of the same. Words, like a wall of sound, and then a hardness, old and dynamic with kinetic accretions. Old emotions, covered with new, covered with racing thoughts that went around and around to get nowhere very fast.

She pushed a little harder.

*And the second angel poured out his vial upon the sea and it became as the blood of a dead man. And every living soul in the sea died.*

Barriers, intricate and effective. Just as Alex said. They tingled, sharply electric in the palm of her hand, and had nothing like a human personality that she could feel.

Jaguar dropped her hands and backed away. She considered this state of affairs, chewing her lip and eyeing her prisoner, who now prayed silently, lips moving as she rocked back and forth on her knees.

Sardis, fleshy and full and filled with piercing light, had no normal external boundaries. She had only a finely developed system of internal barriers, which Jaguar would have to clear before she'd make any progress. That was tricky work. It was easy to get stuck in barrier material, easy to slide into that river of confusion and drown. And barriers that strong meant she was working hard to keep something locked down, hidden. Something big, and potentially explosive. To release that too fast could mean a psychological or neurological crisis that would leave Sardis really dead.

She continued to pray and rock, muttering to the ground and to her hands and to the inside of herself where she didn't want to hear what she really had to say.

" 'But if I speak without love, I am cymbals clanging,' " Jaguar said sternly, wanting to break through.

Sardis stopped, lifted wide eyes to Jaguar.

"Saint Paul," she gasped. " 'He has the name that he is alive, but he is dead.' " She scrambled to her feet, lifted an arm, and pointed at Jaguar. " 'Those of Satan will burn,' " she said firmly.

Jaguar could have kicked herself. She'd forgotten that

the Revelation sect called Saint Paul the false God because of his views on women. And he was associated with Catholicism, which Sardis saw as idolatrous. It was so difficult to keep these theological arguments straight, to remember who hated whom, and why.

"Relax," she said, recovering her angelic demeanor. "It's—um—just a test."

Sardis lowered her arm, and tilted her head at Jaguar. "A test?"

"That's right. There'll be a few before the big day."

"Of course," Sardis said, smiling and blinking around her. "Yes."

"Yes. Tests and questions."

"Ask whatever you want," she said, waving a hand airily, and shook dirt from her robe. "I'm prepared."

"Fine. That's fine. What if I told you God's really pissed about all those children you killed."

She snorted derisively. "My God doesn't mind death. Only sin."

"Certainly," Jaguar said. "Very good answer. And what if I told you that God lives in a twenty-six-year-old Jewish woman who may be dying because one of your people stabbed her with a toxin."

"I gave her time to repent, but she is not willing, and so forth. So look, I am about to throw her into a sickbed. And her children I will kill with deadly plague, and so on."

"You seem pretty sure about that. You have no doubts? No fears?"

"Yes," she said, smiling beatifically. "Of course I do. 'For he hath judged the great Whore which did corrupt the earth with her fornication.' But," she added, " 'All will be washed clean in the blood of the lamb.' "

Jaguar asked her confusion to subside. Don't get stuck in it, she told herself. Let her spin out her threads. You can count them, but don't get caught in them. Keep your eye on the prize.

"You're doing just swell," she said. "Now, about this

deadly plague. Can you name the one used against the Jewish woman?"

Sardis stared at her blankly. "The plague of fire?"

"Poison," Jaguar corrected. "But what kind of poison?"

Sardis stared up at the sky, and showed every sign of breaking into prayer again. Jaguar put a hand on her shoulder, calling her back. "Sardis, what kind of deadly plagues do your people use?"

She turned half away, shrugged off Jaguar's hand. "Father took care of all that," she said.

Father? "You mean Philo?" Jaguar asked.

Her lips twitched into a smile and her face softened, came back to attention in the present. " 'And he showed me a pure river of water of life, proceeding out of the lamb.' "

"Yes. That would be him. Is that why he was given the—deadly plague—to use?"

"Of course," Sardis said. "No man is able to enter the temple until the seven plagues of the seven angels are fulfilled."

Jaguar let this sink in. "And the other angels, do they use the same plagues?"

"God gives them strength, and clothes them in the white linen raiment. They will meet at the gates of the city, and the one whose name is written shall bring them unto the New Jerusalem. Has Philo arrived? We boarded an aircraft together, but I don't know where he was taken."

"Do you carry any medicine for the plague he used?"

She seemed to search an interior file for the appropriate response. Then she declaimed happily, " 'My people are healed with the blood of the lamb. They'll meet at the gates of the city. The days of counting will give way to the hours of woe, and the new name shall be written on the stone.' You know," she added, nudging her. She slewed her eyes around, as if looking for someone. " 'Those that have power over waters to turn them to blood, and to smite the earth with all plagues, as often as they will.' It's all been taken care of."

Immersed in fantasy, the testers said. Sardis certainly believed in the End of Days as an upcoming event. Soon. It seemed a strange story she told herself at night, to keep herself feeling warm and safe. It certainly didn't help Jaguar learn what she wanted to know.

"You're doing splendidly," she said in what she hoped was a hearty and encouraging tone. "Tell me, does Philo have an antidote for his poison?"

Sardis blinked at her.

"Philo," Jaguar repeated patiently. "Did he have an antidote for the toxin he stabbed Rachel with?"

All blood left Sardis's face, turning it as white as her death robes. "Rachel?"

Now, what was that about, Jaguar wondered. " 'Rachel is weeping for her children,' " she murmured, " 'and will not be comforted.' "

Sardis's face twisted in inexplicable rage, and she grabbed Jaguar by the arm, shook her hard.

In her talon's grasp, Jaguar felt the stinging memory of death, sudden and shocking. She clapped her hand hard over Sardis's and held on, the motion of barrier material twisting and writhing, pinching at her hand like fire ants. Intricate nonsense. A barrage of words. Biting blips of static charge.

There, a child making noise. Barking? No. Dogs were barking. Circling and howling.

An arm reaching for her, pulling her close.

The sound of dogs barking. A child?

Brief and sharp, like glittering knives, she saw a little girl's face.

*Rachel. Such a pretty stone you brought me.*

*Rachel.*

Rachel. Jaguar remembered now. It was in Sardis's files. That was her daughter's name. Her dead daughter. This was important. Something real about Sardis and her fear.

"Sardis?" she whispered. "Is it about Rachel? Your daughter?"

Sardis shook her off roughly, backed away from her, and

the image was gone. " 'All will be washed *clean* in the blood of the lamb,' " she insisted.

Jaguar opened her mouth to say something placating, but her intent was overpowered by a clamorous, wailing cry like the screams of burning children. Sardis jumped, and took a step back.

Again, that haunting entreaty. Jaguar tried to gauge the source of it. It came again, and she looked toward the stream below them. Three male peacocks stepped out from behind the willow tree, opened their tails, and displayed the many eyes that mocked them both.

Sardis gasped. "Is that—that's not—Him? Is it?"

Jaguar threw her head back and howled out laughter to the virtual sky.

Proteus ambled down the hall toward the cafeteria, taking his time, nodding and smiling at people as they passed. Any residue of Philo was gone from his aspect, and he was glad. He'd played him for a long time, and was beginning to worry that his face would stick. Stupid worry. He could see that now.

He paused briefly at the closet where he'd stuffed Mark's body and sniffed the air.

Getting ripe in there. He'd leave right after lunch and make his way cautiously toward Sardis. He'd found out more about her, though not as much as he would have liked. Whatever program they were working on her was shrouded in secrecy. Coded, and Mark's key wouldn't access it. Idle conversations he had in the men's room, at the computers, while getting coffee, taught him that her teacher was a woman named Jaguar Addams, who had a reputation for getting it right. He didn't like the sound of that. By rumor, she was also quite the practiced empath. Even worse. Too much practice, and she could see through all his faces clear down to the original, though it had been so long since he used that one, he often forgot what it looked like.

The last time was in Israel. He'd been hired to help mediate a little argument between the Jews and the Arabs over rights to a mineral bed. Ten years earlier they were fighting over whom they were going to pawn it off on, because the senithin in it was considered less than worthless. Then, when it turned out to be crucial in the solar chips used in the newer air cars, they both claimed they'd always seen it as sacred land.

And for once, he agreed. He believed in the sanctity of money, and would make any offerings, any sacrifices necessary to propitiate the money gods. In this case, the sacrifice had been to make his own face visible to a certain woman who had certain valuable information regarding the title to the plot of land in question. Of course, he'd killed her once he had the information so he didn't have to worry about her memory of him.

Since then, he thought he'd been someone else's version of reality on a pretty steady basis. Once, when he consulted with an empath about hypnopathic techniques, he'd been warned that it was dangerous to be so far from home base for so long. He should spend a fixed amount of time in his own aspect on a regular basis. He'd killed the empath, too.

But then he thought maybe the guy was right. Maybe he did need some time off. The jobs weren't fun anymore. The work had become as rote as the lab work he did before he fixed his first viral base for an assassination, spliced his first retro-V, curled his first gene loops, implemented his first hands-on takeout, which was his favorite part.

He had all the money he could want, all the freedom he desired, and could get just about any thrill available in the world, but it all began to feel flat. A few close calls, a slip of the hand that could have cost him his own life, convinced him that he needed to reevaluate, relax. Then he met Sardis and the Revelation Sect.

She was making a live local appearance at a hotel he was staying at, and on his way to the bar he wandered past the filled ballroom where she was speaking. He pushed his way through the crowd, and heard her preaching the usual Gospel of the End of Days. A new order was near, she proclaimed, and would make itself known when the Great

Woman clothed in sun and stars met with the Son of Man to create a new family for the child whose name was written on the stone. Sardis, blowsy and sloppy in her passion, wasn't his usual type, but there was something in the situation that appealed to him. Perhaps just that it was so far from anything he believed in. Anything he'd experienced. Anything that mattered. It could be such an amusing way to pass the time while he wasn't working.

He searched her thoughts to see what aspect the Son of Man held for her. Then he assumed it, and stepped forward. By ten o'clock that night they were in bed. By the next day they were—in sect terms—married. For the next three years he lived with the sect. They were all crazy, as far as he could tell, but that didn't bother him. Most of the people he worked with were crazy. Obsessed with their particular agenda. He had no agenda except to take care of himself, and have some fun. Often, the obsessions of others helped him in that.

He encouraged Sardis in her vision of the Apocalypse and the redemption it would give her, because as long as she was full of that, she never noticed when he left the sect house to visit Nevada or New York, where any pleasure could be purchased. After a year, just before he grew sick of the whole thing, he began to see that Sardis's vision might also have something to give him. He realized that both the young women and the young men in the sect saw him as the new Father in the upcoming world, so they'd do anything he wanted. Anything. In fact, most of them expected him to have his way with them, this being proper activity for a godhead in all their known definitions of the Divine.

He didn't like to disillusion them.

He had to laugh when he thought about it. He never expected the religious life to be so much fun. And when an acolyte lost herself or himself in ecstasy to the Father, he'd take the opportunity to make sure they didn't write home any epistles about the pleasure of the New God.

They all died well, calling on their God, and nobody

remarked on their absence. People in the sect had a tendency to make sudden exits. He tried to keep it discreet, though. Especially since he was beginning to see some other possibilities for his time with Sardis. One day she came to him and told him she'd decided to put the sect money into new accounts, and to put his name on them along with hers.

That way, she said, he could carry on the battle on earth while she fought the battle in heaven. He found out she really did have plans, and a cache of weapons left over from the Serials that she'd storehoused in an empty recording studio nobody knew she owned.

It was time, she said. The kingdom of heaven was long overdue, and she'd had a vision that it was her job to move it along a little faster.

He had no problem with that. It fit in with his plans just fine. He'd improved on her weapons stock considerably with his own talent for creating interesting means of death. But then the weapons runner gave them away to the Feds, and Sardis didn't die when she was supposed to. He'd take care of that soon enough. He had all the information he needed, and a plan.

After lunch, he'd leave the building, go out and find someone else's cash card, another ID. He knew just how he wanted to do that, too. And just who he wanted to be next.

# 6

*day six*

JAGUAR BROUGHT HER COFFEE TO THE ROUND
wooden table near the sink and set it down. Marie, who
was rolling and punching dough at the counter, looked over
her shoulder, grunted at her, then returned to her work, back
curved toward Jaguar. They were both naturally taciturn in
the morning, and comfortable with few words mixed with
a lot of coffee.

Jaguar watched her hands, gnarled like old trees, as they
worked the soft white dough. Marie liked fresh biscuits,
and to get them on a regular basis she took the easiest
expedient of making them herself. On her stove a strange-
smelling dark brown liquid simmered, and Jaguar knew this
was some sort of vitamin concoction for the animals, probaby stock boiled from odd parts of beef and chicken. A
witch's brew of sorts, but effective.

Marie had been director of the Planetoid Animal Sanctuary breeding complex since it had opened, signing on
there because she said she couldn't stomach the home
planet anymore. She'd been a vet at the Bronx Zoo during
the Serials, and was there when the vigilantes went through
and burned the animals in their cages. She still had scars
on her hands and face to remember the night by.

Jaguar liked her immediately when they met, and she
chalked that up to Marie's early experience as a wildlife

ranger in South America. She'd spent many years observing the behavior of jaguars in the wild, when those cats still existed in their natural territory. She knew how to deal with all wild animals, human and otherwise.

Now that she was getting older—somewhere in her mid-sixties, Jaguar thought, though she never said her age—the sanctuary was perfect for her. It was a small operation that had no government regulations to comply with. She could run her programs as she wanted, and had a reputation for success in breeding animals others said couldn't be bred in captivity.

The sanctuary was also camouflage for many of the Planetoid program houses, since the breeding complex was closed to the public and the various habitats provided good cover. It added an extra layer of natural security to these places and to the VR site, which was last within the circle of enclosures. The VR had laser fencing around it, but interference from the pulse waves generated by the site often caused this to turn itself off. Jaguar trusted the protection of the trees more than she counted on the fence.

"Anything from Alex?" Jaguar asked Marie's back.

"Message on the board," she replied tersely.

Jaguar stood and went to Marie's telecom board, punched up the code for her message. It was brief, but hopeful.

*Idiopathic meningitis established. Medics testing for toxin-antitoxin possibilities. There's been some seizure activity, but symptomatic treatment looks good. Prognosis: cautiously hopeful. Call for details. I'm here.*

She tried not to panic over the casual mention of seizure activity. Of course there would be seizure activity. Not a problem, as long as treatment kept it under control while they figured out a cure.

Idiopathic meningitis. Meningitis of unknown origin. It could be secondary or it could be part of what Philo injected her with. Toxin-viral duplex shot? That was a trick that got popular during the Killing Times, to combine a quick-acting toxin with a slow-acting virus, but it was usually transmitted in gaseous form through an explosive, and usually the bombers chose a nicely contagious virus if they could.

Or maybe it wasn't a virus at all. Neurotoxins imitated viruses, and were easier to manufacture as a rule. They didn't require such rigorous aseptic conditions for cultivation, or the same equipment for splicing and dicing. And they were more reliable, since proferon came into use against a lot of the retroviral splices. Of course, if they knew what the toxin was, they'd try the toxin-antitoxin routine established during the Serials as a means of coping with the vigilante toxic bombs so frequently used in the cities. It was painful, and could just as easily kill an older person or a pregnant woman, but for someone like Rachel, it could work. If they knew the toxin used.

But they didn't know, and they didn't have Philo to ask. Jaguar's hands twitched to get hold of him and wring the information out of his scrawny neck. Or Sardis. Sardis should know something, if she could be brought to earth for a brief minute and get real.

Brought to earth. That was a laugh. She was in heaven, by tester's choice.

"Rat-fucked," Jaguar muttered at the screen. "It's all rat-fucked."

All they had for Rachel was symptomatic treatment. But controlling symptoms meant dealing with anything from seizures, hallucinatory episodes, diaphragmatic paralysis, liver or kidney failure, secondary lung infections, or blood depravity. Anything. Anything could happen, and nobody knew.

Prognosis, cautiously hopeful.

She replied to Alex, keying in her message:

*There's nothing cautious about hope.*

*And who was Philo before Sardis got hold of him, anyway? Where'd he get his stuff?*

She went back to the table and sat with her coffee, getting ready to deal with her day. Find Sardis, clear more of her barriers, get closer to the center. It was tedious and irritating work. The fear-of-God program wasn't sitting right, either. She needed a real program, and she'd have to establish the parameters herself. If Sardis was possessed, that meant her daughter's spirit couldn't leave. Jaguar shuddered at the thought of existing within a woman like Sardis. Part of her was fascinated by the prospect of dealing with a case of possession, which was rare, and part of her was so filled with rage, she'd just as soon wipe Sardis's face clean and get fired so she could go back to Rachel.

"Rachel okay?" Marie asked as she cut the dough into circles and put each circle on a tray.

"Define okay," Jaguar said.

"Is she alive?" Marie asked.

Jaguar nodded. Marie liked to start with the basics.

"And she'll stay alive," Jaguar added.

"From your mouth to God's ear," Marie said.

"Which one?"

"The nearest available."

Jaguar put her coffee cup down on the table and sat with her chin in her hand. "Marie, do you believe in God?" she asked.

Marie picked up the tray of biscuits and slid them into the oven, then straightened herself, pressing a hand against her lower back and grunting.

"Which one?" she asked, her deep wrinkles smoothing into a grin.

Jaguar groaned. "Hoist by my own petard. Y'know, I asked Gerry that question once, and he said he believed in all gods, and worshiped none."

"Sounds like him," Marie said. She picked up a cup of coffee from her counter and joined Jaguar at the table. "Why're you asking this?"

"I was thinking of Rachel. Wondering if I should pray to her God. But I don't think he'd listen to me. I don't think he likes women very much."

She remembered Rachel saying that her community believed their rabbi was prophesied to have a child who would be the next Messiah. Everyone was stunned, Rachel said, when he died without any heirs. The prophesy had been so clear.

Of course, Rachel said, he did have children, but they were all girls, and they didn't count either as heirs or the Messiah.

Even if Rachel's God did like women, he had probably forgotten how to hear their voices. They had been silenced for too long. And as far as Jaguar could tell, the Christian version of this God wasn't much better. How many tens of millions of women were dead at the hands of good Christians, Protestant and Catholic. And what twentieth-century pope tried to forbid the worship of Mary? Well into the twenty-first century, Christians and Jews everywhere still seemed to insist on the importance of having a God who could pee standing up.

"I'm not so sure about his tendency to kill His children, either," she added.

"I know," Marie agreed. "The sacrifice-of-Isaac thing scared hell out of me in Sunday school. But your people did the human sacrifice routine, too, didn't they?"

Jaguar nodded. "For a long time. They stopped because sacrifices were no longer being made with joy. They were only made of fear, and the gods didn't like the taste of that as much. The Mertec were supposed to learn to wander the world without fear so the gods would have something more pleasant to eat." She picked up her coffee and swirled it in her cup. "Of course, when I have to work with someone like Sardis, I can understand the joy of human sacrifice in a whole new way."

"Blood will tell," Marie noted.

Jaguar grinned. "The thing is, she's so vacuous, she's not even worth sacrificing. I mean, who could I show her head to? Where's the honor in that? And why would so many people follow someone like her?"

"Maybe she looks so big and empty, a lot of people can fill it in with whatever they want."

"Maybe. Were you raised Christian?"

"Catholic," Marie corrected. "Most Christians say

that's not quite the same. I haven't been to mass for a long time, though. Last time I went it was to hear the first woman priest preach. I'll remember it forever. She preached good.''

"What'd she say?''

"She said faith was letting God be what God wanted to be. Orishas. White Buffalo Calf woman. Jesus. Mary. The earth. She said if you didn't do that, you didn't have faith. You had fear. That dogma and fanaticism was the absence of faith.''

Jaguar nodded approval. It went along with the way she was raised, with an understanding that there were fundamental differences between the human and spirit worlds, and that difference could appear in many different ways to different people. For herself, spirituality wasn't so much a matter of faith as it was of experience. What she believed she communicated with every day. The wind. The stars and the sky they lived in. The animated spirit in stone and tree and jaguar. In the play of spirit that showed her how to use the empathic arts.

She was also taught that communication with the spirits required openness, and fear closed you. If you feared your god, it was time to get a new one, which meant that she had very little experiential basis for understanding how to run a program based on a fear of God.

"But you aren't afraid of God, are you?''

Marie chuckled. "Jaguar, I wouldn't be lying if I told you I'm not afraid of much, except maybe arthritis.'' She flexed her hand, which had grown knobby with this illness. Even with the new cartilage treatments, sometimes it got away from her. "But y'know, people want something bigger than they are. Something they can be a part of. Maybe sometimes it gets away from them. Scares them. Like your prisoner, right? You gotta hate someone like that, don't you? Or, maybe not.''

"Maybe not?''

Marie tapped the tabletop with her fingertip. "What if,''

she said, "you heard God telling you to do something. Wouldn't you do it?"

"Depends," Jaguar answered.

"On what?"

"Which god?"

Marie pointed an imaginary gun at Jaguar and fired it. "Okay, you got me. But you know what I mean. You got your own way of doing things, and it can look pretty odd from where some people sit. So where do you draw the line when your spirits ask you to do something?"

Jaguar picked up her cup and sipped at it. Marie was very good at asking questions.

How do you know where to draw the line? Even if you think you know, there was always the thirteenth thing.

The Mertec and Maya with their understanding of numbers as numinous powers, said the number 12 encompassed everything, but 13 was that which we couldn't account for. They said thirteen thank-yous at the end of every praise, so that mysterious force wouldn't feel left out. She believed in that. The thirteenth thank-you. That which she didn't necessarily account for, or see, or understand.

So how did she discern the difference between vision and madness? The Mertec said fear would lead you down the road to evil and madness and greed. Sardis, she was sure, acted primarily out of fear. She just didn't think it was a fear of God.

"I can't imagine my spirits asking me to kill someone like Rachel," she said. "Or blow up children. That's such a coward's act."

Marie sighed. "I know. Me neither."

"And I hate just about everything she believes in and stands for and is."

"Must make it hard to work with her."

"Yeah," Jaguar said, "You could say that."

A headache pounded its way from the back of her head toward her temples, where it setttled, perhaps for keeps. She winced, and pressed her palms against it.

*Rachel.*

Sardis's voice, speaking a name.

*Rachel. You brought such a pretty stone to me. What does it say? My name?*

"Need something?" Marie asked.

"No," Jaguar said. "It's just a headache. I knew I'd get them. I told Alex. Marie, I'm going to see Rachel tonight. When I'm done for the day. Will you report me?"

" 'Course not. Give her my love."

Jaguar wasn't surprised at this. Marie didn't interfere unless she saw reason to. She gulped down the rest of her coffee and stood, pressing down the folds of her long dress with her hands.

"Nice dress," Marie said.

She wore a sage-green robe modeled after the dress of the shamans in her tribe, painted with black figures here and there, symbols from her Mertec heritage. All of it was lost on Sardis. Jaguar had hoped that the color green, which had come to be associated with empaths, might shake the woman up a little bit, but so far she hadn't come out of her fantasy long enough to notice it.

"Every assignment's just another fashion opportunity," Jaguar replied, and made her way toward the VR site to start her workday.

When she got to the site, she checked in with the designers, who located Sardis for her in the mall quadrant.

She shook her head. "Do you really believe that this is heaven? A giant shopping mall? Is that really the kind of God you want?"

"Well," Andy said testily, "why not? Didn't God promise us our daily bread? And isn't God everywhere? I mean, his name's still on the legal tender. Why shouldn't He be in a mall?"

"Why not? I'll let you know what He's got on sale when I come back through."

She made her way straight to the mall, ducking in and out of stores and calling for Sardis here and there. The main corridor swelled with happy holofamilies, floating angels, and the sound of Renaissance music. Conceived in late-twentieth-century architectural style, the ceilings were domed with skylights and at either end of the mall a major department store was situated. The site designers had placed their holoGod on the third floor of Macy's, translating a former Santa's workshop into a gold-lined room they'd designed in strict accordance with Revelations description. This was where Sardis would meet her Maker at the end of her program.

Jaguar stuck her head into a Family Furniture Outlet and observed a mother, father, two children, and a dog, gazing worshipfully at two Naugahyde chairs.

"I like the red one," the little girl said.

"I like the blue one," the boy said.

"We'll take them both," the father exclaimed, and the family cried yippee in response.

Jaguar pulled out while she could and continued walking, scanning the aisles and the fronts of stores for Sardis. When she saw a crowd gathered in front of the Silky Self Lingerie store, she stopped. This, she thought, would be it.

Sardis, standing in front of a rack of bras, held up a sheer red negligee as she addressed the crowd of attentive women gathered around her.

"And he was clothed with a vesture dipped in blood, and his name is called the Word of God," she said to them.

A group *oooh* passed through the crowd, and Sardis smiled. "Yes, and the armies which were in heaven followed him upon white horses, clothed in fine linen, white and clean." She dropped the red negligee and picked up a white cotton nightgown that hung nearby.

"I'd like one of those," a young woman whispered to another, and Sardis extended a hand to draw her forward.

"Of course you would," she said. "And so you shall have one." She handed it to her, and the young woman clutched it to her breast, smiling beatifically.

"Hecate," Jaguar groaned as she watched from the back of the crowd.

"White is the raiment of the servants of the Lord," Sardis said, "after the time when the great cities of the nation fell."

"No more," Jaguar muttered, her head pounding. She shoved aside a quivering figure of ecstatic womanhood who clutched a green silk bra-and-panty set to her bosom, and made her way to the front of the crowd.

"Sardis," she said, "We've got work to do."

Sardis blinked at her, smiled at the crowd. "Carry on," she said. "Await the day. There will be a new heaven and a new earth. The name will be written on the stone."

"Right," Jaguar said. "Come on."

She led her out of the lingerie store and through the mall, not sure where she was going, or what she intended to do, but keeping firm hold of her arm as Sardis continually tried to get loose and move toward the passing figures.

"Stay with me," she said, shaking her lightly, trying to hold Sardis's brain still for longer than a millisecond. Sardis turned to her and blinked as if noticing her for the first time. "I—that is, God wants to know more about your partner. If your partner is fit for the job."

Sardis shook her head. "I—my partner?"

"Philo," Jaguar amended. "He was your partner, wasn't he?"

A smile floated across her face like a bright and fluffy summer cloud. "He was anyone I asked him to be," she said.

Curious answer. Anyone she asked him to be. "What did he do in the world? Before he came to the sect?"

"His job was anything I asked him to do," she said beatifically. Then she lost interest, and turned toward a holo-shopper. Jaguar grabbed her elbow and turned her around.

"Leave them alone," she snapped impatiently. "They're not real."

Sardis turned back to her and gaped.

Jaguar caught herself, then thought about it. Something like an idea was beginning to say hello to her. She let it take shape, not trying to articulate it just yet. A passing holoangel tried to hand her a white rose, and she shook her head at it. Not real. None of it. And Sardis needed something real. She watched it pass, then turned to Sardis, put a hand on each shoulder.

"I want to show you something, Sardis." She took a step back, but Jaguar held her. "It's okay," she said. "It's just an angel's perspective on the sacred."

Jaguar felt a vision of the mesa creep up behind her eyelids. New Mexico. That's where she'd spent her childhood before and after Manhattan. That's where her people were born.

New Mexico. The sun on the warm stone bones of the earth. The wind, and a rainbow dropping out of a cloud briefly, passing through heat and sun to red earth, then drawn back up into the sky like a veil. The pulse of the land under her feet. The heartbeat of earth. The breath of sky. The animal talk around her. Not all of the sacred was here, but certainly this was all sacred. All of it spoke in the language of the Divine.

She cupped this image in her hands and placed one against Sardis's cheek.

*Can you see this? See it with me.*

She let the feel of the wind sing through her hand and into Sardis, clearing out the old smoke of tangled emotions, of hurried thoughts and frightened visions. She moved gently, breathing gentleness into Sardis's thoughts, letting the wind do its cleansing work.

Jaguar let the image continue, and added to it. She shared with Rachel a love of arid lands, and once they took a trip together to the mesas around the village where Jaguar lived after the Serials. The memory stung like honey at the back of her throat. Too sweet. Too rich. She and Rachel, walking silently across the top of the mesa like young goddesses in the golden light. She gave the feel of it to Sardis, who closed her eyes and moaned softly.

Jaguar probed gently at Sardis's thoughts and felt the movement of pain under the first layer of barrier in her. Rough and jagged at the edges. Loud and ugly.

*Breathe, Sardis. Breathe out the old. Let it go. It's okay.*

Sardis began to twitch. "The blood—of the lamb. Worthy is the lamb that was slain," she whispered. "All the blood."

Jaguar stayed very still, remembering the inverted energy field, so potentially explosive. She could feel the jagged edges of her barrier beginning to build toward fury, and debated with herself briefly whether to push forward, or drop back.

She decided to risk it. Push forward.

*What blood, Sardis?*

No answer. Keep going. Try something else. She'd responded to Rachel's name before.

*Sardis, Rachel wants to know. I'm Rachel's friend.*

"Oh, no you're not," a vaguely familiar voice said next to her ear.

Sardis gasped and pulled away, breaking the connection. Jaguar whipped her head around and saw the face of the hawker from the Moroccan bazaar. Dark eyes. Dark hair. And, at his temples, two small protrusions, like little horns trying to sprout.

"What the hell?"

He shoved a pocketwatch into her face. "You're here to buy a watch," he declared enthusiastically, spinning it.

She took a swing at it and missed. Sardis giggled.

"Ticktock," he said, "Buy a clock?"

"Cut that out," she barked. She saw, out of the corner of her eye, that Sardis was wandering away, humming a wordless lullaby, rocking an invisible child in her arms. When Jaguar tried to grab her back, the hawker intercepted, neatly stepping in front of her.

"Slow it down, Jaguar, before you blow it up," he scolded.

She sidestepped, but he stayed with her. Back and forth. Left and right, mirroring her moves exactly. She raised a fist. So did he.

He lifted the pocketwatch to her eyes, and she lunged for it, but he stepped back quickly, putting her off balance.

She stumbled, and he grabbed her arm, twisting it painfully back and holding her.

"Buy a clock," he implored. "Save time."

"You can't do this, dammit. You're a holofigure."

"That's what you think," he replied, and with a quick jerk, he threw her onto the floor and sat on her, weightless and implacable.

"Great Mysterious," she whispered reverently.

He dangled the watch over her face. It spun, silver catching the light and light melting and writhing, shifting into the shape of a dagger, long and red and made of glass.

He held it poised half an inch from her open eye. She lay very still.

All sound in the mall, except the sound of his voice, ceased. A breathing, mechanical and distant, filled her ears. Somewhere within it, his voice spoke.

*Ticktock, Jaguar. Watch the clock.*

Her eyes filled with the blade, ears filled with breathing. Breathing, and the sound of singing in the high and distorted pitch of young voices. Singing, sucked back into breath and the machines of life in a hospital room, tangles of electric wire holding her to someone, to someone.

*Ticktock. Watch the clock.*

Eyes filled with a clock that grew larger and larger, within it reflected a hospital room, bare, sheets pulled back from a bed, no one occupying the white and newly sterilized space. Breathing that ceased.

The sound of ceased breathing.

Jaguar felt horror rise within her. Was Rachel getting worse? Had Sardis killed her, with fanaticism and cowardice and she wouldn't even accept responsibility for her actions called it all the will of God killed children and said God wanted that it was infuriating and Jaguar hated her hated her hated her beyond hate beyond rage beyond the possibility of forgiveness.

She lifted an elbow and swung it around.

No one was there.

"What the hell?" she asked.

Gone.

He was gone, and so was Sardis. Only a series of holo-figures strolled through the mall.

"Shit. That's enough for today." She pulled herself up and walked briskly down the hall, bumping into a father who had his family out shopping for free Naugahyde.

"Sorry, miss," he said.

"Fuck off," she snarled, grabbed his face, and shook it hard. At which point he fizzled and disappeared.

She frowned down into her hand, which felt like she'd burned it lightly. "Did I do that?" she asked it, but as she spoke he reappeared, shook his head, and blessed her with the sign of the cross.

"All is forgiven," he said. "Go in peace."

"Go in pieces is more like it," she shot back, turned, and walked out of the mall, across the Moroccan bazaar, and to a neatly hidden door at the wall in back of the bird-seller's stall. She opened it, went through, closed it behind her, and leaned on it heavily, staring out from under half-closed eyes down a long gray hallway to where she could see two men sitting in front of screens.

"I don't know where the hell she went," one of them said. "I thought she was in the mall with Sardis. That's where she was last time I looked."

Jaguar stopped, listened.

"Isn't it your job to keep track of her?" Carolan asked.

"Not really," the other man said. "It's our job to design and implement creative sites for the use of Teachers in Planetoid programs. *Punto*. That's the contract."

"Could the increased wave scale affect your ability to detect human presence?" she asked.

Jaguar frowned. Increased wave scale? Did that mean something? She wished she knew the language of technology better.

"I told you when you suggested it, we can't predict what it'll do. It's a nonlinear function, stuck in the heart of a dynamic system, which, as I explained—"

"Will contain her thetas," Carolan said testily. Andy

glared at her, and she sweetened her tone. "But maybe you know a better way to solve that problem. You're the experts, after all."

Jaguar felt anger rise slow and molten inside her. Problems. She could give them one of those.

"A holofigure just attacked me," she called down the hall. "Does that constitute a problem?"

Three heads turned her way.

"Dr. Addams," Carolan said, clipped and official. "What are you doing off the site?"

Jaguar strolled toward the room where the viewscreens kept track of her movements, taking the walk at a liesurely pace. "I get to leave at the end of my day, and my day just ended."

She walked up to Andy and put a hand on his shoulder. "Are they programmed to attack all Teachers, or is there something special about me?"

Andy gaped at Dave, and Dave gaped at Andy.

"Don't be ridiculous," Carolan said. "There's no attack mode programmed in."

"Then explain why a hawker at the mall just put a knife to my eye," she said.

Andy leaned forward and began punching buttons. Dave peered at her eyes, as if they held the answer. "Don't worry," he said. "They can't do anything to you. Nothing real, anyway."

"Are you sure?" Andy asked. "Everything was stable and in normal range last time I checked."

Carolan narrowed her eyes at Jaguar. "What happened?"

"I told you," she said coolly, "a holofigure attacked me. A man selling watches. I saw the same figure at the Moroccan bazaar. He followed me into the mall."

"That's not possible," Dave said. "Bazaar hawkers stay at the bazaar. The only wandering holofigures are the families, the peacocks, and the angels."

"If you need a witness, my prisoner saw the whole thing. Fortunately she's too bonkers to be disturbed by it. Or maybe she was just being polite. Tacky thing, holo-violence."

Dave turned his neck toward Carolan. "Like I was saying, we can't predict—"

"All right," she cut him off. "We'll discuss it later."

"See anything, Dave?" Andy asked. "I mean, check me here and make sure I'm not missing something."

"I think," Jaguar said, "you're all missing something." She strode down the hall and toward the exit that would spit her out at the rim of the breeding complex. Her head ached, and right now she wanted an aspirin more than answers.

As she walked she heard Carolan's voice calling. "Dr. Addams, wait. We need to talk about this."

Jaguar stood still and let her catch up, then turned to her. "So," she said, "talk."

Carolan ruffled her sleek hair, then held out a conciliatory hand. "Look," she said, "I think we got off on the wrong foot. I'd like to change that."

Jaguar's face stayed neutral as milk as she stared at the hand. "So change it," she said evenly.

"You're not being very helpful," Carolan noted, dropping her hand to her side.

She shrugged. "You want to talk. You want to change. Those are your wants, not mine."

"I don't understand," Carolan said testily, "why you should hate me."

"Hate you? You're barely in my consciousness at all, except as a bit of noise now and then."

"Then why do you treat me like I'm your enemy?"

"Because you might be. Look," she continued, cutting off Carolan's protests, "it's nothing personal. I just prefer my safety to politeness. I don't trust you, because I don't know what your agenda is. What game you're playing."

"Game? You think I'm—what, working with Sardis?"

"Put it this way: I don't know that you're *not* working with Sardis. She had a big operation going, with parts of the legislature in her back pocket, so for all I know she has the Feds there, too. And a holofigure just attacked me, which makes me even less sure of who and what you are.''

"But that's—ridiculous.''

"Maybe,'' Jaguar admitted, "but I don't know that yet, so our budding friendship will have to wait until I do.''

Carolan brought her hand to her hip, made a sound of frustration. "This isn't about Alex, is it?''

"Alex?'' Jaguar said, surprised. "What's he got to do with it?''

"You two seem pretty close. I didn't know if you were—'' She was at a loss for the appropriate verb. Jaguar, finally seeing the implications, bit back on laughter and helped her out.

"If we're fucking? No. We're not.''

Carolan's face reddened, and she stared down at her high heels.

"If you want to make a grab for him,'' Jaguar said, "go ahead. Knock yourself out. I can't vouch from personal experience, but local rumor has it he's quite good.''

# 7

## day six (continued)

ALEX WALKED DOWN THE CORRIDOR WITH BRAD
Deragon, reading over the file as he went. He stopped at
the door to the stairs, lifted his head, and sniffed the air.

"What's that smell?" he asked. "It's awful."

Brad shrugged. "Don't know. It's a new one."

Alex cast a glance up and down the hallway, which
looked clean enough. "Smells like something crawled into
a storage closet to die," he said. "When we're done, call
maintenance and have them check it."

Brad made a note on his clipboard, and they took the
stairs to the second floor, stopping in front of interview
room 23. Alex opened the door.

A pretty young brunette turned in her chair and flashed
a smile. Then she turned back to the woman seated across
from her and lifted her arms, her voice a banshee's cry.
"All—all will be washed clean in the blood of the lamb."

"Sorry," Alex said, and closed the door. He turned to
Brad. "Did you say twenty-three?"

"Forty-three, actually," Brad replied.

"Okay. Let's keep going."

This part of the building, reserved for exit meetings with
prisoners and interviews that weren't particularly dangerous, was usually quiet. Today, however, the hall was filled
with shouts and long rapturous declamations of ecstasy.

Cult members were being interviewed by Planetoid Teachers and Federal Agents. And none of them were getting much of anywhere.

The sect members swung between apocalyptic ranting and a morose silence. The testers tried truth serums, neural subconscious pathfinders, and catogenic probes, and learned nothing except that they were all obsessed with the End of Days and believed it had already begun, in grand biblical style. Poisons and plagues and fire poured upon the earth. The blood of the lamb washing them clean. But if there were any sect plans for trouble, they either didn't know or were being shielded by a bigger god than Alex or the Feds had on their side.

Alex hoped there would be no further violence, but he was uneasy resting in supposition, though he doubted these prisoners could give him anything concrete. The farmhouse where they lived was reserved for acolytes. It was a place where long-term members introduced novices to sect life so they could choose whether to become first- or second-order members. Everyone they brought in had been with Revelation for less than a year. That might be why they hadn't taken their cyanide pills like good boys and girls. The elder members who were at the siege were all dead— either blown up with the children, or victims of cyanide suicide as they were dragged out the door.

They had nobody who could tell them anything except for Sardis, and Philo. And there was no sign of Philo anywhere, now or apparently ever.

When Alex received Jaguar's question about Philo, he'd already checked the database records on him. His fingerprints, photo, DNA chart were not on record anywhere. Before Revelation, it seemed he didn't exist. No birth name. No birthplace. No previous employment. No rap sheet. Cross-checking his arrest files with preexisting files anywhere in the world didn't turn up a thing. He'd been with the sect for three short years. Before that, he was nowhere. Now he was gone.

So when Brad told Alex about two cult members who

were ready to ship back to the home planet for the rest of
their rehab, Alex decided to give them a try. They were all
he had left.

Now he was going to see a nineteen-year-old who was
with Revelation only five months when the siege occurred.
Her sect name was Corinth, and she was seven months
pregnant.

Alex stopped at room 43 and rested his hand on the code
bar. "Here?"

"Here," Brad confirmed. "Do you want me with you?"

"Only if you've got nothing else to do," Alex said.

"Yeah. Right."

Alex grinned and saluted. "Dismissed. Get out of here.
Check on that smell in the hall. And don't forget to eat
dinner tonight."

Brad ambled away, looking leisurely even if he didn't
feel it, and Alex went into the room where Corinth waited,
sitting at a table with her hands folded tightly over her
pregnant belly, her head held high and stiff. As he took a
seat across from her she lifted a pinched face to him.

"Are they all dead?" she asked.

Alex, who was pulling his chair under him, stopped in
mid-motion. "All dead?"

She swallowed. "The children. I saw them. I keep asking
and nobody will tell me."

Alex settled himself, met her eyes. "Yes," he said.
"They're all dead."

She winced, closed her eyes tight. "I didn't know. I
didn't know she would."

Alex regarded her in a detached way. "The Nazis said
that about Hitler," he noted, "though he told everyone repeatedly and in detail what he'd do. And Mayor Lester said
that about the Safety Squads in Manhattan, right after they
burned Midtown, even though the squad leaders announced
what they'd do and when they'd do it. To the minute."

She gasped, opened wide blue eyes, and stared at him.
Apparently, she'd expected sympathy from him, an attitude
he found irritating.

"Sardis told you, didn't she?" Alex insisted. " 'And her children I will kill with deadly plague.' "

She shook her head, screwed her face up to get it ready for tears. "They kept saying we had to prepare for the new heaven and the new earth. That the old would be broken by fire and plague and—I thought they meant like in our hearts. I didn't think they meant it for real."

"Nobody ever does," he said pointedly.

She lowered her head and covered her face with her hands. Alex gave her a few minutes to deal with her shame. He understood why she wanted to deny something as horrific as what she'd seen, but her denial was deadly to those children, and she had to face that. But he knew, too, that someone like her, pregnant and alone and young, was perfect prey for cult recruitment. They would gather their flock from the vulnerable, and there were so many of those after the Killing Times that Sardis didn't even have to look. In recent years she'd probably had to work a little harder, but not much. There were still the young and the displaced, people who responded to the love-bombing techniques and the total fusion with a group that cults offered. Corinth was not totally to blame. The shame still belonged mostly to Sardis. No wonder she cloaked herself in words and more words. It took a lot of words to protect yourself from that much horror.

"She took you in when you found out you were pregnant, didn't she?" he asked, a little more gently. "You had nowhere else to go." He saw her head bob up and down behind her hands. "And when the Federal Agents showed up, she told you what would happen, didn't she?"

Again, the head moved in an affirmative gesture.

"What else did she say?" he asked, still speaking softly. "What else did she tell you that you didn't believe?"

Her hands came down from her face and she lifted reddened eyes, a tear-streaked face. "Wh-what?" she asked.

"What did Sardis say about the End of Days?"

Corinth's face was young, puffy, and blank. Not a very bright girl, Alex thought. She might be okay when she got over this, though she probaby wouldn't want to think much beyond what was required for the most superficial daily living. Her memories would hurt her too much to probe them deeply.

"She just said it had started," Corinth replied. "That's all. She was going to—to heaven, and the battle had begun."

Alex leaned forward and brought his face closer to hers. "Nothing else? Nothing about what the other sect members were supposed to do? More deadly plagues? The army of God?"

Corinth shook her head. "No. Just the blood of the lamb, and worthy is the lamb who was slain. We were all sort of crazy. People dancing and singing in this strange way, like—like—"

"Like you were about to see God?"

"I guess," Corinth said. She put her hand in front of her mouth and chewed on the tip of her finger, face going blank and disinterested.

"Would you happen to remember a man named Philo?"

She mouthed the name, then blinked up at him. "Yes. Of course. He was the Father."

"The father. Could you explain that?"

"The Father. Sardis was the Mother, and he was the Father."

The father. Of course. "And you were the children?"

She giggled, an unnerving sound. "No. There's only one child."

Alex looked at her, waiting for further explication.

"The lamb. The blood of the lamb," Corinth said, as if that explained it all. Then she grew wistful. "We were sinners, waiting to be washed clean. Sardis said we had to become part of the blood of the lamb, and that would wash clean our sin. That's what they said."

"They didn't say how you were to be part of the blood of the lamb?"

She shifted in her seat, rested her chin in her hand, and stared at the wall. " 'Worthy is the lamb that was slain to receive power and riches and wisdom,' " she quoted dully.

"We had to be like the lamb to be part of the blood. I—guess she meant we had to get killed."

Alex frowned down at his clipboard, which was taking a voice record of the interview. He didn't like the sound of that. "Corinth, do you know where the sect members would go to hide? Were you told what to do or where to go at the End of Days?"

"We had to go to the Gates of the City," she said automatically. "Like it says in the book."

"Any particular city?" he asked. She shook her head. "Then, do you have any idea where Philo would get hold of a viral agent and hypomodule?"

"A—what?"

Alex sighed. "He had a vial with a toxin in it. We're trying to determine if Sardis had any more, or if any of the others might."

"I don't know anything about that," Corinth said. "I—wait. When he was in the world he worked in a lab. He told me. We were in the kitchen, and I remarked on what a good cook he was. He said that was from working in a lab. That there wasn't much difference in mixing chemicals or spices. He was very nice to new people. Very friendly."

A nice man. Of course he was. And he worked in a lab. A chemist of some kind. And labs kept employee records, which they had to file with the Feds. "Did he say where the lab was?"

"No. I mean, maybe, but I don't remember."

Two quick taps on the door interrupted her. He stood and went to it, cracking it open enough to see Brad's face on the other side.

"Busy, Brad," he said.

"You're gonna get busier," Brad replied. "We tracked that smell in the hall. It's Mark. Or, what's left of him. And he's wearing prisoner's clothes."

Alex leaned his face against the side of the door. Philo. The Father. Running around in Mark's clothes. Dammit. "Okay. I'll be up in ten minutes. Get the forensics in."

"Done that. But you need to come now. Agent Shannon's on the telecom. She's holding, and says she's gotta talk to you right away. Something came up at the VR. About Jaguar.''

Alex stifled a groan, excused himself to Corinth, and went to see what the fuss was about now.

Proteus squinted at the sun, at the tall glass spires, at the wings that moved smoothly in their patterns above him. Yonge Street, Toronto replica. Planetoid Three. Not a bad place, he thought. He'd go slow and make his way toward the VR site while he adjusted to his new aspect.

He chose something very passive and nonthreatening for the streets. Someone women would trust implicitly, and might feel a little sorry for. Someone men would be willing to help out.

He made his way to the corner NetHelp directory and got in line. The man in front of him was getting information on public transit, and he was taking his time. Proteus stood very close to his back, just so that the man would feel his breath. He finally turned and might have said something rude except that Proteus grinned broadly and meaninglessly. The man shook his head and walked away.

He coded in Mark's ID for the last time, requested parks-and-recreation information, and examined the map that appeared. There was a park about half a mile from the Animal Sanctuary. Grace Park. He liked that. And from the description, he'd be able to find a suitable spot for his business. He flipped off the screen and walked on. He stopped at a hot-dog stand and got supper, lingering over it, sitting on a bench and eating slowly while he waited for the sun to set. He needed some light to see whom he was picking up, but then he'd need dark for the job itself.

And, as it turned out, his timing was perfect. He entered the park just as the evening was turning purple. He looked around at the benches, the high shrubs bordering a pond, the trees and the wide stretches of grass and flowers. He noted where the shadows fell, where the people would tend to group, where the isolated spots would be.

Then he smiled.

There she was, sitting on a bench tossing the crumbs of her sandwich to the birds just as if he'd wished her there. He knew she was the right one because she was small and pale, not too good-looking but with a certain frail appeal to her delicate features and her blond ponytail in its light blue holder. Young. She couldn't be more than eighteen.

He sat next to her on the bench, and she jumped just a little, hid the motion with another toss of the crumbs. He groped around for her thoughts and found them, amid confusion. *A man . . . liked men, didn't like them, was frightened by men only was here to help Aunt Sue set up a store didn't like the Planetoid wanted to go back to Cheyenne where Ricky was probably already looking at other girls . . . always wondered what it would be like to have a man would it hurt would it feel good . . . friends said it was so good and he wasn't bad looking was he . . . couldn't quite tell maybe he was a pervert one of those mutoids how could she know what should she do.*

"Beautiful," he muttered to himself. "Just beautiful."

A virgin. Anxious virgin. Easy to fuck, and easy to kill, and transparent as glass. Her ID card wouldn't help him since he couldn't take on a female aspect, but she might have a cash card, and if he managed her death right, the authorities would continue to look for a crazed cult member named Philo who no longer existed. And certainly she'd be fun.

Her young eyes would hold unguarded answers to the questions he always asked a kill in the final moments: How does it feel? What's it like to face the ultimate reality? The only reality. The only real power. The reason behind everything.

He knew there was a reason for everything, because his mother always told him so.

When she was killed, her murderer cut off all her fingers, strung them on a thread, and mailed them to him. He was twenty-six and relaxing under a foreign sun at the time, new at the game, going under his birth name still. He'd just

sent out a very big check to his mother so that she could
get the hell out of the cities, which were about to fall apart.
It was the beginning of the Killing Times, and her death
was unnoticed in the general violence, but he knew it was
a specific and well-targeted hit, aimed at him to avenge a
job he'd recently completed.

Everything happened for a reason, she always told him.
God has a reason for everything, even if we don't know
what it is. He thought the reason for everything was death.

For instance, when he started working with the Safety
Squads, gave up his name and a lot of money to go un-
derground, a lot of his cohorts thought he was nuts. But he
had a reason, and it was all about death. A lot of people
died from the bombs he made and sold, and their deaths
were only a way of covering the kill he would make on the
man who killed his mother. There was a reason why everything happened and it almost always had something to do
with death. Either avoiding it, or enjoying control of it for
a brief moment.

Killing this anxious virgin would help him both avoid
his own death and enjoy hers. It would also give her the
biggest thrill of her life. Maybe the only thrill. Too bad
she'd never get to giggle about it with her anxious virginal
friends.

He turned a kind and fatherly aspect her way.


"I don't know how you work with her," Carolan said.
"You must have the patience of a saint."

"Hardly," Alex said. "It's just that I know her. I know
her ways. And she'll be like that with you until she feels
she can trust you. Right now she can't, and why should
she?"

When he arrived she was bent over the computer in her
hotel room, working with the incoming data from cult
members. She'd asked to meet here, where they could talk
in private. She seemed to think it was a matter of delicacy.
She didn't know Jaguar, who had left two angry messages

on his telecom, telling him she was sending a memo on the incident to Paul Dinardo.

He'd gotten the messages after he talked with Carolan, went to officially identify Mark's body, and found that not only his clothes were gone, but all his papers. Ident card, cash card, the works. Philo now had access to all parts of the Planetoid system that Mark did, if he knew how to use what he found. And though he gave all indications of being crazy, Alex was beginning to think that nothing in this case was quite what it appeared to be.

Alex was more concerned about that than he was about Jaguar right now. For Carolan the formula was reversed. Philo was a nut, but Jaguar could hurt the system.

"She said it held a knife to her eye," she said, trying to work him into something like shock.

"Did she mention why it did that?" Alex asked laconically.

"No. Just that it did. Alex, is she okay?"

"Hardly ever," Alex interrupted. "But she's not given to imagining things. Unless . . ."

"Unless what?"

"VRs give her headaches. She has a hard time, even with short-term exposure to the induction waves," Alex said. "She's been there—four days? I don't know how that might affect her. What do the designers say?"

Carolan looked away from him. "We've discussed the possibilities, and they're looking into it."

Alex straightened up and gazed down at the top of her head. "That's pretty vague."

"It's complex," she said. "You probably wouldn't understand."

"Try me."

She pushed her chair back from the computer and twisted around to face him. "I barely understand it. Something about the difficulty of accommodating your teacher's proclivities. I thought you'd be more concerned about her state of mind, the way she's so hostile to me."

That was pretty clear, he thought. She wanted his support. And she wasn't used to the normal tensions of Planetoid work, which often resulted in a show of temper. She didn't know enough not to take it personally.

"I'll go talk to the designers tomorrow, okay?"

"Okay," she said, "I suppose."

"What else do you suggest, Carolan? I told you she's unconventional, difficult. Everything you've heard about her. It's all quite true. And you requested her."

"I know," she admitted grudgingly, "but I didn't expect to have to deal with it firsthand."

"Hurts, huh? I'll talk to her about it."

She turned grateful eyes up to him, her smooth face a pleasant kind of eye candy, and held out a hand, which he took briefly and released. "I really appreciate that," she said. He found her gratitude warming, her touch pleasant. She swung her arm over the back of the chair and let it dangle, close to the region of his thigh.

"This world you work in is so strange, and you seem so"—she paused, and chose her words carefully—"so capable of remaining calm in spite of the passions flying around you. I want to understand how you do that. And why."

He frowned. "Data for your files?"

"No," she said, standing up and coming close to him. "Data for me." Tentatively, she lifted her hand and ran two fingers over his cheek, down his neck.

He raised a hand in the gesture of the empath and touched her forehead. "You want to know about that?" he asked. "The touch of the empath?" She turned her face up and he noticed that he had to bend down to her instead of looking directly across the way he did with Jaguar, found that making such comparisons so automatically was troubling, and dismissed the thought. She was Carolan. She was a smaller woman. She wanted something from him.

"I want that, and more," she said. She took his hand in hers and slid it to her lips, pressed them softly against the skin of his palm, then pushed it back to her forehead.

He caught his breath. He wanted to speak the ritual

words into her, bring himself into her mind, her being. Carolan Shannon, see who you are. Be what you see.

But he couldn't. That was reserved, somehow. Not for
here and not for now. Not for her. Instead, he stroked her
face, feeling the pull of desire and a swirling of wanting
that wouldn't go away because she could never satisfy it.
There would be an unlimited supply of longing with her,
because she wasn't what he wanted and he didn't know
what he wanted beyond this feeling of desire. Didn't know
where the pull would lead him, and if satisfaction of it was
the answer, or if the answer lay in the feeling itself. With
his hand on the soft skin of her face, moving down her
neck and stroking, he was just a man and he wanted a
woman. Nothing abnormal in that. Just healthy. Just real.
No fantasy. No impossibility here.

Not real, though. Not the really real. But dammit, what
did that matter? The really real was a philosophical pos-
tulate, and he wasn't about to wait his whole life for what?
For what? He wasn't waiting for anything. Philosophical
postulates had nothing to do with the aching of desire. She
was good to hold. A good woman with a clarity of intent
that you wouldn't lose yourself in. An orderliness of passion, if that was possible. She knew what she wanted, and
the reasons for wanting it were easy to fathom. Nothing to
get lost in, get tangled in. Just pleasure.

Something normal and healthy and real.

He would enjoy himself here.

"Lovely," he murmured into her hair. "Carolan.
Lovely."

The hospital window faced west, and Jaguar stared out of
it at the sun, which was going deep gold and slipping down
as late afternoon turned toward evening.

She'd stopped at Marie's to get something for her headache and call Alex, who wasn't in his office or apartment.
She left lengthy and vituperative messages for him at both
places, telling him that she was taking the rest of the day
off and didn't want to be interrupted. She had to think.

She'd lain down, meaning to close her eyes for a few minutes to let the herbs work, and promptly fell asleep for two hours. She woke with rage at the back of her throat after a dream of watching Rachel being swarmed by flies that licked at her desiccated flesh, with Sardis standing over her and laughing.

She got up and went directly to the hospital, where she found Rachel asleep. The tent was gone, but Jaguar didn't touch her. She didn't wake her. She wanted only to see her, listen to her breathe, know she was alive.

The door opened, and a medic entered, walking softly. He ran a scanner over Rachel's sleeping form, made some notes on his chart.

"How's she doing?" Jaguar asked, keeping her voice low.

The medic started. "Oh. Dr. Addams. I didn't see you there." He looked down at Rachel, then nodded to the door.

Jaguar followed him to it and out into the hall, where medics walked past them on soft shoes and doors to rooms opened and shut silently The absence of sound in the hospital always astonished her.

"More seizures today," he said, checking his chart, "but we've got her on some new meds. We're hoping they'll call a halt to that."

"How long before she's out of here?" Jaguar asked.

The medic's uncomprehending stare was her only answer.

"How long?" she repeated.

"Look, Dr. Addams, I don't know what you've been told, but right now we're just trying to stay on top of the symptoms. Whatever she got jabbed with, it's ugly and it's invasive. It'll be touch and go until either we find an answer, or her system is able to clean itself out, or . . ."

Or what? Jaguar was about to ask. Or what? But her mind shut down on the words, wouldn't say them. Wouldn't acknowledge the possible answers. No. Just no.

"No," she said to the medic. "No."

She resisted the urge to shake his stupid face into better

shape, and instead pushed herself back into Rachel's room and closed the door between them. She leaned her cheek against the cool wood, listening to the sound of his footsteps retreating down the hall.

"You shouldn't be here," Rachel's voice said softly, and Jaguar turned to it.

Her eyes were glassy, pupils dilated, but she seemed clearheaded.

"Then let's pretend I'm not," Jaguar said lightly, walking over and sitting down next to the bed. "Do you need anything?"

Rachel gave a good imitation of a smile, and mouthed a no.

Jaguar reached over and brushed a hand against her forehead. "This is hard, isn't it?"

"Not too bad," Rachel said. "My legs hurt from the seizures, but there's not a lot of pain. Only, I feel so strange. As if I'm floating away, and I can't stop the motion."

"Just grab a hand," Jaguar said, taking one of Rachel's. "I'll make a good anchor."

Rachel squeezed lightly, then rolled onto her back and closed her eyes. Jaguar let the minutes pass, waiting to see if she'd fall back asleep. She leaned back and closed her own eyes, and wasn't sure if she was dozing when she heard Rachel speak again.

"What do *you* need, Jaguar?" she asked.

She was startled by the question, and the tone of voice Rachel used. As if she knew something.

"If I say nothing, would you believe me?"

"No," Rachel said. "I know—I mean, I have these dreams. They're so real, and when I wake up, I seem to know things."

"What things?" she asked, trying to keep her tone casual, free of concern.

Rachel pushed herself up on her elbow and stared past Jaguar, as if she asked someone far away a question. "That you're troubled. About the case. Is it going okay?"

The case. Sardis's tangled mind. Attacking holofigures. VR headaches. She didn't come here to bother Rachel with that. "I've had worse," she said. "I'm making some progress."

"You're lying, aren't you?"

Jaguar sighed. "Are you sure you're not an empath?"

Rachel laughed, a sound Jaguar liked to hear. "I don't need to be an empath. I have what's called good people skills."

"That's why I keep you around. I count on you to make up for my deficiency in that area."

Rachel turned serious, eyes large and looking through Jaguar. "Is that why? I've always wondered what it is I give you. You seem to need so little."

"I need you," Jaguar said intently.

"Why? Someone to boss around?"

Jaguar winced. She knew it wasn't true, but it hurt to think Rachel might believe that. Being someone's boss stole your capacity for independent action. She never wanted to be or have a boss. Maybe she just wanted family. A sister of any kind not to own or control, but to belong with, and belonging was a different proposition from ownership.

"Rachel," she said, gently as she could, "that's bullshit."

Rachel blinked twice, and broke into a peal of laughter that was loud enough to make the medic stick his head in the door.

"Now, ladies," he said patronizingly, "some of us are trying to have quiet time."

Jaguar, baffled, held her hand palm up to Rachel. "What? What'd I say?"

"It's not what you said. It's how you say it. Like you're trying to throw your knife at someone in a kind way."

"Well," Jaguar said, "it *is* bullshit. I never wanted to boss you around. I'm a lousy boss because I don't trust anyone else to do it right except me. So I always end up doing it myself."

"I know," Rachel said, her laughter dissolving into quick breaths and a tired smile. "I'm just pissed off that I'm here, Jaguar. Pissed and scared and here you are to take it out on. I want my regular body back, and that's the truth."

"That's why I need you around," Jaguar said. "Because you're honest. Because you're real."

"I wasn't," Rachel said, "until I came here."

"No. You always were. You just needed someone to notice and say okay."

"You see people where they're real, Jaguar. That's your talent, I think. Even if it gets everyone pissed off at you." Rachel let her head drop back down on the pillow. "But you can't see Sardis, can you?"

Jaguar leaned over and rested her arms on the bed, smoothed Rachel's forehead with her hand. The laughter, just that little bit of exertion, was enough to wear her out.

"Don't worry about Sardis," she said. "It's not important."

"Yes, it is," Rachel insisted. "You have to—see it through. That's one of the things I seem to know, Jaguar. Maybe that's why I keep dreaming about her. About you." Her voice grew dreamy, wisps of words emerging slowly from her. "Didn't her daughter Rachel die in the Serials?" she asked.

Jaguar started. How did she know that? And how did she know her name?

"Did you read her files?" she asked.

Rachel opened her eyes and turned them up to Jaguar. "You told me."

Jaguar smoothed her face. "Right," she lied. "I forgot. Look, you know me. I'll figure it out. And you should be resting."

Rachel closed her eyes again and rested a hand over them. "I want to talk. I'm afraid if I stop talking, I'll never start again. I'll go to this wordless place, and I won't come back."

The wordless place. The Mertec had a term for that.

House of No Words was the best translation. That was
where a spirit went prior to death, as the body prepared to
die. A way station of consciousness, where it adjusted to
silence, the wordless language of the spirits. Jaguar rejected
that idea without exception. No. Just no. It wouldn't be.

"I keep telling you," she said, "I got a deal with the
devil on this. If you try to get away, I'll drag you back."

"No," Rachel said. "There's some things even you can't
manage, Jaguar. They're just out of your hands."

Jaguar would have protested, reassured, done whatever
was necessary to reject that idea, but Rachel rolled onto her
side and curled into her dreams. Jaguar waited until her
breathing became regular and slow, then she rose and left
the room.

The Planetoid had a small, efficient, and unobtrusive police
squad whose duty was twofold. First, they were to assist
Planetoid officials in carrying out programs for prisoners
and whenever possible ensure the safety of Teachers and
team members. Second, they were to engage in all the regular duties of police, such as keeping bar brawls to a minimum and making sure the wings that sped overhead were
in the right traffic pattern. Most cops considered Planetoid
work easy, since they weren't directly involved in appre-
hending criminals or investigating criminal behavior. That
was left to the prison officials. They were more like security
than cops, walking or riding unthreatening beats. It was a
friendly sort of a job that got you out among people.

Dan O'Brien, the cop on the beat for Fourth and Yonge,
enjoyed his work here immensely. As he strolled down the
clean streets of the Toronto replica, he nodded and smiled
at people, helped a mother who was struggling to juggle a
toddler and groceries as she tried to tie a loose shoe, gave
directions to a man for the museum. He had another half
hour, then he'd be off duty for twenty-four hours. Not too
shabby.

He crossed the street and walked the sidewalk that circled in toward Grace Park. He liked to walk this area. It

was quiet and green and neatly kept. There were specimens of the great oak, with its twisted branches silhouetted like many-fingered hands against the sky. Right now the lilacs were in bloom, their rich scent filling the air. He stopped at the point where the path wound off toward the gently rolling lands of the park, looked down it.

Nobody around. All quiet. All well.

A rustling in the bushes to his right caught his attention and he turned that way. Then another sound, like a sharp cry.

He listened. Yelping dogs? Sounded like one or two.

He walked down the path, toward the bushes the sound came from. As he spread back the branches, two yellow dogs looked up at him, eyes all pupil in the darkness. One of them pulled back his lip and growled, showing sharp little teeth.

"Git," O'Brien said, stomping on the ground. "Git away."

They turned and tore away, tails between their legs. He walked around the bush to see what they'd been worrying.

Something that looked like a heap of old clothes. A sweater. He squatted down, pulled at cloth, saw, at last, what he was pulling at.

"Fucking hell," he said, pulling back, standing up, stumbling backward and away. "Fucking hell," he repeated, then he swung toward the nearest tree and returned the remnants of his supper to the earth.

# 8

*day seven*

THE TONE OF HIS BELT SENSOR JARRED ALEX
from sleep, causing Carolan to roll away from him on the
bed.

He made his way out from under the covers, found the
sensor under the heap of his clothes at the side of the bed,
and punched in the code for his message.

Body in the park. With sect markings.

He crouched on the floor reading the message, trying to
make sense of it as his consciousness crept sluggishly from
dreams into the day.

Day. It was day. He blinked, looked around the room,
realized he wasn't home. The pale and ineffective light of
pre-dawn washed through windows that weren't his. He'd
been dreaming about cliffs, and jumping off them, hands
reaching to grab for something, body following hands
through space.

Not his hands, though. Not him, flinging himself into that
abyss. Someone else. Someone he had to be with, stay with.

He shook himself and stood, looked down at Carolan's
sleeping form, and sighed. He was right about one thing.
He'd enjoyed himself there.

He put a hand on her shoulder. "Carolan," he said gently. She stirred, opened an eye, and stared at him blankly.

"I have to go. Cop found a body in the park. It's Philo's work."

"Why?" she asked.

"I don't know," he replied, not really sure what she was asking.

Maybe she didn't know either, because she simply replied, "Oh," and closed her eyes. Within a minute, she was sleeping again.

He dressed quietly, left the hotel, and took his wings to the park, where two uniformed policemen were consulting with a man in civilian dress. It was Paul Dinardo.

Alex walked over to them, noted the roped-off area and the blanket that fell over the contours of a body. He shook hands with the uniformed policeman and then nodded at Paul. "Up early, aren't you, Paul?" And obviously, there only to guard the body, see that it wasn't taken away before Alex had a chance to perform his own version of a post-mortem.

When Alex had been a Teacher, Paul had seen him bend over a body and gather the information he wanted in his own way. Alex had long ago learned to run his hands over a scene and read what information might be left pulsing in the energy around it. In that case, his ability had led to the identification of a murderer. Paul never mentioned anything to him about it, partly because he never said the word *empath* out loud to anybody, and partly because he respected the boundaries that Alex himself preserved around his own psi capacities. Unlike Jaguar, he was discreet in his use of the arts. Paul approved of discretion, and so here he was, silently making sure that the body stayed *in situ* until Alex arrived.

"Yeah," Paul said, "and where've you been? We couldn't find you at home, or in your office, or even at the hospital."

"I'm here, Paul. My belt sensor's been working all night."

"I never had to use it before," Paul commented.

"You're always home or at your office, or else doing something crazy with that Addams woman."

Paul was right. He spent far too much time working, or alone, or—at any rate, it was about time he made some changes.

"You found me," he said now. "What's up?"

"See for yourself," Paul said, kicking the blanket down from the face of a young woman. "We held her for you."

Alex took a breath and knelt down on the ground, thinking maybe Carolan should see this. She forgot that those who accepted the privileges of the empathic arts also had to take on the burden of feeling. Empaths didn't just listen. They felt the living and dying experiences, the bloodcurdling fears, the rivers of grief that humans could cause each other.

He rocked back and forth on his heels, letting her wide eyes tell their stories to him. She was young. Very young, and she hadn't been dead long. He passed a hand over her face, feeling around the edge of her. Choke marks on her neck. Not enough to kill her. Just enough to keep her quiet. And there, carved into her forehead, the numbers 666.

He shook his head. "Philo," he said.

"There's more," Paul said, nudging the blankets down with his toe. Alex saw that a plastic covering had been secured at her belly, where skin had been unskillfully ripped open, and what was left of her bowels protruded from the rip.

Alex stared at it, and moved his hand back and forth about an inch above the plastic.

Shock. He could feel her shock in his skin. Shock, mingled with pleasure.

*a poet he said he was a poet I thought he was it feels so good what he's doing the reason he says there's a reason always a reason why God does what he does always a reason but I don't like it all the blood all the blood all the blood God says when it's your time God God God something's happening all the blood all the blood why don't I die is that me my body what's he doing why don't I die.*

*why don't I die*
*why don't I*

He pulled the cover back up, and took a minute. Pressed his fingers against the inside corners of his eyes and closed them.

"It's a bad one, Paul," he said.

"Yeah. A bad one. You need more time?"

Alex nodded. More time. He ran his hands over her eyes again, letting them linger there. He wanted something on Philo. Something that told him what Philo planned to do next. Where he was going. Where they could find him.

But he couldn't feel anything of Philo at all. Strange. He supposed it was possible that her emotions were so powerful they wiped out any trace of his presence, but it didn't feel like he was being overwhelmed. Philo was simply not there. Not a trace of him.

Alex pulled his hand back. Picked the blanket up to cover her and then hesitated. He lifted the young woman's left hand.

"The tip of her left index finger is gone," he said. "Cut off clean. That mean anything to you?"

Paul leaned down, not too close, but close enough to see. "Weird," he said. "I got no clue."

Mark's hand had been missing a fingertip, too. But there was something else familiar about it. A story he almost remembered.. Alex let her hand drop and stood. "I'll run it through the computers. And let's get a DNA read from the semen. I want to know who the hell Philo is when he's not Sardis's backdoor man."

"If you say," Paul replied. He turned to the officers. "You can take her away now."

"I'll want some people tracking Philo between here and the Animal Sanctuary. Pass around some pictures at the sanctuary and in the immediate vicinity. And you'll need to double security measures at the VR site. See if they can keep that damn laser fence working."

Paul turned back to Alex. "You think he'll get that close?"

"I think," Alex said, "he probably already has. I'd like to make sure he doesn't get any further. Can we get some Feds on it? They're crawling over the place like flies. We might as well use them."

"Sure," Paul said. "I'll call some people."

"Thanks, Paul. I appreciate you waiting for me."

"Forget it. I probably owe you one." He pulled his coat tight around him and walked away.

Alex stood in the almost empty park and looked around. It was damn early. He could go back to Carolan's and warm up before he went to work, he supposed. Or, he could go home and take a shower. He was about equidistant from each point, so it wouldn't matter in terms of time.

Then he realized he was actually closest to the hospital. He could stop in and check on Rachel's progress, make a few calls from there to be sure the area around the sanctuary was being secured properly. That's what he'd do. He'd see Rachel. Then he could call Jaguar and let her know about the body in the park.

He'd started his day with murder, so he thought he could afford to take it easy. After all, what else could go wrong?

Andy Spodris chewed on a tuna-fish sandwich as he logged into the computer his observations for the program so far.

"Teacher J. Addams interfaced with prisoner, monitors steady for C-activity, for neurocardial response, *and* no lapse in triangulation of thetas. The Teacher, incidently, is making diddly-squat progress with the prisoner," he said, chewing as he spoke. He knew that Dave hated it when he listened to a log that had chewing in it, so he made it a point to include one every so often. It was Dave's job to get his reports in order for the Governors' Board so they could update their own files and decide on protocol for the VR system.

He swallowed, and said more pointedly, "Recommendation—design should include holoteachers, which are more amenable to program instructions."

He read out the pulse rates for each sector, then shook

his head. He'd insisted on putting them down nearer the normal range, no matter what the pretty Federal Agent said. She just didn't get it.

The VR was a dynamic system, and it responded to feed-back loops. Small changes in input could bring large and maybe disastrous output shifts. Overloading wave correlations was just stupid. But Dave was all excited about Ms. Shannon and her breasts and her connections with the Feds. He wanted a job on the home planet, Andy knew, and saw her as a ticket in.

"Dammit," he said, "lucky for them I'm here."

He switched the screen to a quadrant that hadn't been visited by humans yet, and spent a minute admiring his handiwork. The main celestial hall was truly beautiful. Walls of gold inset with jewels, just like in Revelation, and a quality of light that hadn't yet been seen by earthly eyes.

He'd modeled it after electropulse readings of the Aurora Borealis over a glacial sea, and flooded the main room with it. This was where that Teacher was supposed to lead Sardis at the end of her program. The Big Reward. The Payoff in the Sky. God of the Mall. It made sense to Andy. He'd never had enough space to put his stuff in, or enough money to buy the stuff he wanted, and he sincerely hoped that heaven would give him both.

Andy was particularly fond of his God pattern. That flowing beard, that white robe, those piercing blue eyes, so like his own. It would scare the hell out of the prisoner. He thought he could probably even keep the Feds from messing with it, though they seemed to want to mess with everything else. Upping the induction waves.

Since they'd done it, he was beginning to see holes in the Ciliated Neural Web. Very small holes, easily repaired with programming tweaks, but they were appearing in a random scatter formation. And if he counted from today to yesterday and the day before, they were showing a gradual increase in occurrence, which he hoped didn't indicate a fast path to turbulence.

Just keep fixing it, Ms. Shannon told him. And Dave

agreed. Nobody listened when he said they shouldn't have an empath here in the first place. Nobody heard a word he said. So he kept plugging the holes. Only now he was seeing bulges as well as holes. Something he had no clue how to explain. Something he'd never seen before, and didn't want to see again.

After this assignment, he'd take his portfolio to the home planet, too. He could get a better job in the home-entertainment industry, doing R&D for a corporation that appreciated his talents. Let Dave work for the Feds. It wouldn't be half as much fun or pay half as well as Adult Home VR.

He rocked back in his chair and watched the holobreeze ripple the silvery leaves on the holotrees.

Then he blinked, frowned, leaned forward.

What was that?

A blip?

Static?

It looked like a figure, just for a second there. But it couldn't have been. It wasn't anything he'd created, at any rate.

"View section eight, full screen," he said to the computer. The image enlarged, and the blip enlarged with it.

It was there, and it was gone. Damn that Halpern, he thought. If he put something in there without saying, he'd be in deep shit.

He looked around the room. Where was Halpern anyway? Out to lunch, or in the next room checking on the monitors the way he was supposed to?

"Halpern," Andy called out the door, "Halpern—get your ass in here. We gotta talk."

The next morning Jaguar found Sardis in the Moroccan bazaar, preaching to a group of men in turbans. Her voice rose and fell with studied intonations, mellifluous and pleasing, but the men didn't seem pleased, and that surprised her. Weren't the holofigures supposed to respond positively, no matter what?

She walked over to where they stood in front of a stand of fruits and vegetables, and listened. Sardis, seeing her approach, acknowledged her with a nod and continued speaking.

"And we know this to be true because of where it is written, worthy is the lamb that was slain to receive power and riches, and wisdom and strength, and honor and glory and blessing. Now this very lamb, slain in God, will rise up against Babylon, slaying the fallen whore."

One of the holofigures nudged Jaguar. "Don't care how a whore falls down myself," he whispered, "so long as she don't charge too much for it."

Jaguar blinked at him and took a step back. As she did so she saw another holofigure firmly grasp a handful of rear end from a passing angel, who yelped, jumped, and fluttered away.

"What the—" Jaguar looked up at Sardis. She seemed sublimely oblivious to the man who stood in front of her, vigorously rubbing his crotch.

"Trouble in paradise?" a voice whispered in her ear, and she whirled to see a handsome man, dressed in tight black pants and a red silk shirt. He lifted a pocketwatch and it swung slowly in front of her face. He leered at her and with one hand slicked his dark hair back over the two horns protruding from his forehead.

Before she could say a word, he bowed gracefully and retreated into the crowd. She glanced back at Sardis, back at the crowd, back at Sardis. She pointed herself toward him and, kicking a cluster of peacocks out of her path, went after him.

She kept him in sight through the open market, where his red shirt bobbed like a buoy through the holopeople. From there, he dodged across the open field that led to the formal garden. She sprinted to catch up with him when he stopped to prance for her on the wildflowers, but then he darted across the meadow and ducked into the entrance of the garden maze.

Jaguar ran after him, into the maze itself, where she

stopped and caught her breath, then surveyed the vista before her. Boxwood towered over her head, creating curving rows of walkways that spliced in and out of each other in some way only an aerial view could make clear. And the man she was chasing was nowhere to be seen.

"*Rat* fuck," Jaguar said sincerely. Now what was she supposed to do? He could've picked any one of these holes to fall into, and they could chase each other there endlessly, wasting time. Wasting energy.

She dropped down onto the grass, found the sensation of holohedge disturbing against her back, and pushed herself away from it. Angels drifted by in pairs, deep in conversation that she couldn't quite hear. Angelic conversations were always just a little out of her earshot.

At least, she thought, the programmers had an eye for landscape. She might as well enjoy it. She walked ahead, turning at the first opening in the hedge, hoping casually to lose herself in the greenery, wondering if anyone would notice she was gone. Statuary of mythic creatures and buxom ladies stood along the boxwood walls of the labyrinth. More angels drifted by. A peacock opened its tail and gave its piercing plea for sex, sex, and more sex.

She bent down to pinch off a leaf of the mint that grew at the edge of the tall boxwood. When she brought the crushed leaf to her face, she smelled nothing.

"Irritating, isn't it?" a voice said.

She wheeled around, and there he was, leaning on a leering stone figure, his horns, white as his teeth, catching pieces of the hololight and tossing them back to her. In his hand he held a pocketwatch that he waved back and forth in front of her.

Just what I need, she thought. A holodemon.

David Halpern leaned over Andy's shoulder and stared through thick glasses at the VR viewscreen.

"There," Andy said, "west quadrant, number fourteen."

"Cute," David said, looking at the holodemon that was

talking to the Teacher in charge of this assignment. "Something new?"

"I don't know," Andy said petulantly. "I didn't put it in."

"Yeah? Who did, then? You think Georg fucked up an angel? Or maybe Sally slipped it in? She's been going on about that women's stuff, lately."

"Cut the shit, Halpern," Andy said, bringing the quadrant up to full screen. "You've been moaning about how you didn't get to put anything fun in. So if you wanna play a joke, okay. But you could screw the system with a new figure. You know that."

"What? You think I put it in? No way. I don't even like holodemons. They're too swishy for me. But then," he added, "you cut the pattern for them, didn't you?"

Andy turned his thin face to David and glowered. "If you didn't put it in, who did?"

They turned back to the screen and stared. As they did so the holodemon turned to face them, as if he knew they were watching. He leered, pulled his pants down, and exhibited a member of impressive proportions.

"Jesus," Andy said.

"I don't think so," David replied, gawking.

The holodemon pulled his pants up and went scampering up the garden maze just as Jaguar came into view.

"I think," Andy said, "someone better check on this."

"I'll call Agent Shannon," Dave said, moving toward the telecom.

"No," Andy said. "Absolutely not."

Dave stopped his motion, hand caught in reaching forward.

" I want someone from the Planetoid to see this," Andy continued. "They write our checks, not the Feds, so we better cover our butts with them. Besides, it's appearing as a bulge, not a hole, so I think it's something different. I think it's that Teacher."

"Andy," Dave said, "what the hell are you talking about?"

"Hypothetical retrojection," he said.

"But—that would—I mean, if you're serious," Dave sputtered.

"I'm serious. I think it's that damn Dr. Addams, and I want her supervisor to know about it."

"I said," the holodemon repeated, "irritating, isn't it—the way the mint doesn't smell, and the breeze doesn't feel, and the prisoner doesn't fear God?"

She stared at him coolly and said nothing.

"You're wondering," he said, pushing himself away from the statue and walking over to her, "how I know that. Aren't you? Come on, Jaguar. A little common courtesy wouldn't kill you."

"Common," she muttered, "is right." She saw him grinning and realized what he'd just said.

"Now, where have you heard that before? You and Alex, right? Am I right?"

"What are you?" she demanded. "And what're you doing to the holofigures? They're all whacking out."

"Whacking off, last time I saw them," he amended. "Fun, isn't it? But back to the important question. Who am I? Hmm. Let me see. How about . . ."

As she watched, his face melted and re-formed, his body shortening and thickening, until he was the standing image of Nick, once a coworker of hers, now deceased. Her red glass blade stuck out from the center of his chest.

"Maybe I'm a ghost," he suggested.

She frowned slightly, but showed no other sign of disturbance.

"Have you got a spare bit of reaction?" he asked. "It isn't easy doing that, you know. Try this one, then." He lengthened and narrowed, his hair going salt-and-pepper, eyes going dark. Alex. She smiled.

"Well, that got something more than a passing yawn from you. Try this." Curves formed on him, and his hair grew out long and dark with streaks of gold. Eyes of green gold. A dress, green silk, painted with ceremonial signs.

She looked down at her own attire. A perfect replica.

"Pretty, isn't it? You really are quite lovely, you know. Your hair," he said, walking over to her and touching it lightly, "your hair is like liquid tiger's eye. I know that you receive many compliments on your eyes, all well deserved. But your hair, my *dear*. What magnificence."

"Does this," she asked, "tell me who you are?"

"Well," he said, "if you can't take a hint, it's not my fault. Your mind must be growing dull through overuse. Better take a rest leave." He shifted back to his original self.

"I was trying to," she said. "They wouldn't let me."

"Mm. I know. And you're getting nowhere with this woman, and the VR is giving you a smashing headache. You can't even wear your Ray•Bans here, and wave induction screws up your signals so you can't tell what's real, and you just want to go back to Rachel."

Jaguar started slightly.

"Oooh. Success." He clapped his hands together.

"I suppose," she said, "you're working for the Feds, hoping to drive me crazy."

"Don't be stupid. *You* called me up. To help you hold on to Rachel." He tilted his head to the side and held an open hand to his ear, as if listening for something. She heard the sound of her own voice, speaking familiar words.

*I won't let you go, Rachel. I'll deal with the devil himself on this one.*

"Who are you?" she demanded.

"Well now. You claim to be a heathen. How about you call me Baal."

She laughed. Baal. Lord and husband. Not a chance. "I'll never call any man that. Nor any holodemon."

"Careful dear. The nether gods are always listening. What makes you think I'm a *holo*demon?"

"This is the VR. What else would you be?"

"There are more things in heaven and so on, if you don't mind hearing that tired old horsie whinny. There." He waved a hand at her. "That's given me an idea. Call me

Rider. It's not my name, but it's what I'll be doing to you."

She scowled at him. If he was something the Feds came up with, she'd be better off ignoring him entirely. If he was a system anomaly, she couldn't do anything to fix him, but she could waste a lot of time trying to figure him out. She should go back to Sardis, make sure the other anomalies weren't getting any worse.

"Hop on, then," she said. "Give it your best." She stepped around him and continued walking quickly through the maze.

He skipped after her, calling out. "Wait. Jaguar. I have to tell you. Something important."

She stopped and let him catch up. When he reached her, he leaned over and touched her arm. She felt the light pressure of it, and a soft sensation of touch, unlike human touch, seeming to come from under her skin rather than from the surface of it.

"I'm you," he said.

She looked from his hand to his smooth and grinning face. She pulled her arm away and took a step back.

"Is that what you ran so fast to tell me?"

"Yup. That's it."

"Anything else?"

"Oh, lots. But first you have to accept the basic premise. The VR messes up your signals, so you can't touch, can't feel, can't trust, can't know. But you're such a strong empath, you're sending your signals *into* the system, and it has generously responded to your mental effluvium by ever so sweetly spitting out exactly what you asked for."

He flourished with his hand, and bowed so deeply that his horns brushed against the toes of his shiny black shoes. "*C'est moi*," he said, coming up for air, "A ret-ro-jection. Plain and simple."

She put one hand on her hip and tapped a foot.

"I can prove it, too. I know all about you. How you were raped after you watched your grandparents murdered in the Serials at the cusp age of eleven and all that jolly old news. No fears left to face—or maybe there is just one little residual, but we won't go into that right now. Too tedious. So garden variety.''

"Anyone could know that," she noted.

"Oh? But there *isn't* anyone else who knows it, except for Alex and Clare Rilasco. You haven't even told Rachel.''

He melted into a prone position, and became Rachel, lying in a hospital bed. Her voice emerged from his mouth, whispery and distant. "Is that what I give you? I've always wondered, since you seem to need so little.''

She could feel her fingers curl into her palms, nails digging in, and she assumed her face showed it because in a minute he was himself again, standing and giggling unprettily, covering his mouth with his hand.

"Christ Almighty—''

"Shh—not so loud. He might hear you. Then we'd have to spend hours listening to Him go on and on about love and making those pithy little comments. I swear there's nothing worse than a Jew with a cause to push. Now," he concluded, "what were we talking about?''

"The basic premise," Jaguar said, her voice uncommitted to any emotion or thought. "Look, if I'm dealing with the devil, it's only to save Rachel. So how're you gonna help me do that?''

Rider waved a hand in front of his face. "Dry as dust around here. Let me put it this way. Because of my form, I can get past those barriers you can't, though truly I know only what you know, though you don't know you know it." He preened happily. "Wasn't that nicely said?''

She waited to see if there was more.

"Boy, you aren't much on small talk, are you?''

"Not," she said, "much. I have a job to do and it's on my mind.''

"*Ye-es*," he squealed. "Making Sardis face her fear. Christians and pagans, at it again. The meeting ground is bloodied by history, and slippery in consequence. Add the interference of the VRs and you've got a recipe for disaster. But she knew that when she gave you the assignment, didn't she?''

"She?"

"You know," he said, and assumed the shape of Carolan Shannon. "An attractive woman. So competent, and never confused by complexities the way you are. You're a trouble magnet, my dear, and she's a magnet for order and law. You're a lightning rod, and she's an iode transfer line. She's structure, and you're chaos. Or is it Hecate? I always get those two cats mixed up. Which reminds me, there's something else, too."

He took a prancing step closer to her, cupped a hand to her ear, and whispered, "It's the numbers, my dear."

Jaguar frowned at him. The numbers? What did that mean?

"The numbers," he repeated, nodding portentously. "Like the Holocaust of the Jews. The burning of the witches. The genocide of the Native Americans, and the slave ships and, of course, the Serials. How many people died in that one?"

"About ten million."

"Yes. You not among them. Feel guilty about that?"

"No."

He sighed, and checked his nails, picking at a cuticle. "You have the most logically based emotional system I've ever seen, my dear. It's a damn shame. What *do* you feel guilty about?"

She thought about it. "I feel guilty about Rachel."

"You made her look away from Philo. And you were trying to save her at the time. The implications are stunningly complex, but right now you just don't get it." He pranced around her, chanting softly in singsong voice, "Jaguar doesn't *get* it. Jaguar doesn't *get* it."

She stood still and closed her eyes, stifled an urge to scream. He was worse than Sardis, with all those words slipping through her like beer through a drunk's bladder, but it had the feel of something real. Or, at least, the feel of something instead of a total absence.

"I don't get it," she admitted. "Can we move on?"

"Not at all. Not until you accept me into your heart, and profess your faith in me."

"I believe," she said, "you're the most irritating holo-figure I've ever had the displeasure to meet. I guess you must be real."

"Not just real, sweetie. Really you. Irritation and all. Only, I can see more."

He held his hand up to her face, and embedded in the palm she saw an image of a Semitic man, raising a knife over a little boy. It dissolved, and became a crucifix, blood-ied man hanging from it. Then an image of Jaguar, her knife poised at a man's chest, ready to plunge.

"Your people believed in sacrifice, too, didn't they?" he asked.

"They did," she admitted.

"So does Sardis," he said pointedly. "So does Philo. Keep that in mind."

With that, he dissolved from her vision.

She was left alone, the mint she was unable to smell or feel crushed in her hand.

" 'What is *real*?' the Velveteen Rabbit asked the Skin Horse," Alex read. " 'Is it when you have sticks coming out your side, and you buzz and whir?' "

"No," Rachel answered. "It's not like that. Not at all. But it hurts to be real, doesn't it?"

Alex put the book down. "Sometimes," he replied. "Sometimes it does."

Rachel's flushed face smiled up at him from far away. She was drifting, sometimes able to respond coherently, sometimes not. Her fever had spiked in the night, and she'd had five more seizures. The medics thought they'd have to go in with an EEG cap, but for no apparent reason, the seizures stopped. She had been sleeping when he came in, but woke immediately from a dream that she wouldn't tell him about. She asked him to read to her. From *The Vel-veteen Rabbit*.

She dozed as he read, but when he put the book down she woke and began talking in a rambling way about her

childhood. About her family. Had they arrived yet? she
asked him. Not yet, he told her. Then what about Jaguar
and Sardis? Were they coming soon?

Not for a while, he told her. She should rest.

Then she came back to herself and laughed at what she
had just said. Even when she was this sick, he liked her
laugh. It was easy and open, like her eyes. Alex knew that
Jaguar had put in quite a few hours to peel away the ac-
cretion of fear and pain that hid that openness. She had
done a good job, he thought. Rachel was probably the most
pragmatic and centered of his workers. She had a way of
working that was easy, relaxed. All problems could be
solved without a crisis, and she'd just go her way, solving
them. He hoped she would stay on the Planetoid when she
got well. If she got well.

The panic *du jour* was the indication of encephalitic
swelling, and the Cerebral Activity Chart decline. Parts of
her brain seemed to be going to sleep, and they didn't know
if that was permanent. They weren't damaged. Just—asleep
was the only word they had to describe the reading for
activity in those sectors.

They advised Alex to continue reading to her, being with
her. It would help maintain her connection with the world,
maybe keep her from slipping into a coma. As long as she
wasn't overstimulated or overtired, it was important to have
friendly faces around her.

They were still cautiously hopeful.

Like the Feds were feeling about Sardis. They'd passed
the three-day mark with no sign of trouble on the home
planet, and everyone was breathing sighs of relief. Now
they had only to collect their data and tidy up the remains.
They could take their time searching out the other sect
members, and let Jaguar do her job with Sardis.

The Vermont house members were being dealt with
slowly and laboriously, but they had no new information to
offer, so work with them was off the emergency list. The
Feds had sent up more of their own people to deal with the
overload, which he was grateful for. They'd contain the area

around the sanctuary with efficiency, quiet, and politeness. These latter three characteristics were their hallmarks, and it made them easy to work with. They stood in marked contrast to Planetoid workers, who tended toward the eccentric, probably because they were usually ex-prisoners, or people who were desperate to get off the home planet, plagued by the memory of trauma suffered during the Serials. No wonder Carolan had a hard time with them.

A medic, tall and cool and frosted from her delicately styled hair to her discreetly buffed nails, entered and looked around the room.

"Alex Dzarny?" she asked.

He closed the book and stood.

"Telecom. For you. Somebody who sounds like they're having a bad day."

"We've got to stop meeting like this, Paul," Alex said into the viewscreen. "People will talk."

"Yeah, and every nice thing I ever said about you I'm taking back. The VR designers just called, squawking like old hens. She's done something," Paul said. "Damn witch in the machine. Can't you keep her under wraps, Alex?"

Alex laughed. He didn't have to ask who Paul was talking about. Jaguar was in trouble on the VR. "Is this the place where I get to say I told you so?"

"If you do, I'll fire you. You got nothing more important to do right now than get over there."

The viewscreen went blank, and Alex flipped the telecom off. He stood and thought about his next move—whether he should call ahead to the VR for more details, or just go—when the medic's voice asked for his attention again.

"Supervisor?" she asked courteously, and he turned to her.

"Someone else want to yell at me?" he asked.

"Maybe," she said, smiling coolly, "but it's not me. I just wanted to let you know we've made a little progress tracking Rachel's problems. It's a nanosyringe. Neurotoxic amino acid. Looks like a retrosplice in it, too, but we haven't coded it for radical dilodes yet."

Alex held his hands palm up. "That's a little over my head, ma'am," he said.

"Hmm?" she inquired politely.

"I'm an English speaker," he explained.

"Oh. Sorry," she said. "Technobabble gets to be a bad habit in my profession. Nanosyringes are made of amino acids designed to target specific cells—neural membranes in this case. You can pack them into a syringe, or a pill, and once they're in the bloodstream, they'll float around until they find their target cells, which they'll access through naturally occurring ion channels."

"Oh," he said. "Right. We call them T-and-Vs."

She tapped her nose. "Exactly. Toxin and virals. The nanosyringes are partial virus splices that attach to the victim's own DNA to reproduce themselves, and they float in a base of quick-acting toxin—a paralytic in this case. Since the toxin didn't kill her, the rest of it had a chance to move in. It's an interesting bit of work. Real popular with terrorists because it's relatively easy to make. No live viral or bacterial material, no tricky cultures and so on."

"Does that mean you know how to take care of her now?"

The medic assumed a look of concern and regret, which Alex took as not a good sign. He was right.

"Actually, it tells us we can't do much more than we are doing. Nanos are a bitch to clear out, if you'll pardon me. We'll code the specific chain this guy used and try for a nanoline to break it up, but that'll take time, and—well, how much time we have depends on how strong she is."

"Okay," Alex said. "Okay. So, what do you do?"

"Like we're doing. Keep her quiet, treat problems as they occur. I wish I could find a med she'd respond to for the seizures, and I'd be happier if her CAC would lift, because if it doesn't we'll see all kinds of systemic problems starting." She clucked softly and shook her head genteelly, gestures Alex had come to associate with the medical profession. "Well," she said, "there's one consolation. Now that we know what it is, at least we have a clue what to expect next."

"We do?" Alex asked. "What's that?"

"The worst," she said.

When Alex returned to Rachel's room she was awake, almost coherent.

"Sorry," he said. "No more time for reading today."

"Is it Jaguar?" Rachel asked, looking a little frightened.

"How'd you guess?"

"I dreamed about her last night. We were walking someplace very dark, and then she let go of my hand and we were falling, but apart from each other. It was—dark."

"It's okay," Alex reassured her. "She's not in trouble. She's just making trouble, as usual."

The tension left her face, but she remained serious. "Alex, don't tell her how sick I am."

"Rachel, I can't promise that."

She licked her dry lips, and her glassy eyes grew wide. "Then don't let her leave Sardis. And don't you leave her. She's always so alone. Don't let her be so alone."

"I won't," he said soothingly. He didn't want her agitated. "I'll take care of it."

"Don't humor me, Alex. I've known you a long time and—just because I'm sick doesn't mean I'm stupid."

"Okay. You're right. I'm sorry. But she prefers to be alone, Rachel. You know that."

"You're so used to her, you forget to see her sometimes," she said, but she leaned back into her pillow and closed her eyes. "Don't leave her. You know how she is. What she feels is always bigger than her. It gets away from her."

He smiled. "That may be the truest thing anyone ever observed about her."

"It's how she is," Rachel murmured, drifting now. "And she'll drive you crazy with it. Tell her I said not to worry about me. Tell her she's doing the right thing."

• • •

Alex stopped on the way to the VR to check in with Marie at the sanctuary. She had a good eye for trouble, and was protective of her animals in the breeding complex. No trouble, she told him. But if he expected any, she'd take precautions. She glanced toward the glass-front cabinet in her living room, which held three shotguns. She preferred them to the newer laser weapons, she said, because their sound was so much more satisfying.

That taken care of, he went to the VR site and was admitted to the computer rooms, where Andy and Dave spoke in unison in a rush at him.

"Hold on," he said as he made his way toward them. "I know there's been trouble. Just show me what you got."

He leaned over Andy's shoulder, watching as the designer pointed to the viewscreen.

"We saw it—what, yesterday late?" Andy glanced to David.

"Yeah. Yesterday." David squinted at the image of the VR site. "Wait. Is that him? No. Just another angel. How come you put so many angels in, Andy?"

"It's heaven, David. That's why." They continued to peer at the screen, which showed four different quadrants of the site—the maze, the mall, the car lot, and the Moroccan bazaar.

"Hey—what's that? Oh. Damn peacocks. Why'd you put so many peacocks in, Andy?"

"I *like* peacocks. My heaven'll have lots of peacocks."

"Look," Alex interrupted. "Maybe I don't actually have to see the holodemon. Maybe you could just explain to me what it means that you've seen it."

Dave pushed his chair back from the viewscreen and swiveled it around to face Alex. "Well," he said, "it could mean a number of things. Viral infection of the system is one."

"Not," Andy interjected. "I checked."

"Okay. Then, sabotage is another possibility, but that's

unlikely. Our security system's intact and reporting no problems.''

"Except for all the holes," Andy said, pointing to the readout, where white space intruded in a random pattern over what, to Alex, looked like a picture of butterfly wings.

"Shut up, Andy," Dave said, and glared at him. "You're the one who said it isn't that."

Andy clamped his mouth shut tight and glared back.

"What," Alex asked, "are you talking about?"

Andy and Dave exchanged glances. Andy hissed out breath through his teeth and then pursed his lips. "You deal with it," he said to Dave.

"Deal with what?" Alex asked.

Dave rolled his eyes at Andy and then turned to Alex. "Andy's got this bug up his ass about Dr. Addams. He thinks she's created a hypothetical retrojection. He says she's a—you know." His eyebrows wiggled up and down while he gestured mysteriously with his hand in front of Alex's face.

Alex requested patience from the nearest available deity. "You're saying that Dr. Addams's psi capacities are affecting the VR site," he translated.

"Andy's saying that," Dave said. "I'm banking on tracking interference. Something simple and stupid. But empaths scare the piss out of Andy. He's afraid they'll break into his mind and steal it for nefarious purposes, though I think they'd be sorely disappointed at the take."

"You're a real shit, Dave," Andy commented sourly. He took off his glasses and fiddled with the earpieces, cleaned them on his shirt, and returned them to his face. Then he turned to Alex. "I know what I'm talking about," he said. "She's a problem for the system."

So, Alex thought, what's new? "She might be," he admitted, "but not intentionally."

Andy snorted.

Alex sighed. "Look," he said, "psi capacities—the empathic arts—they're just ways of utilizing energy, like you do here. The neural system has a charge, and empaths know how to read it, work with it. Really, it's not that different than utilizing light waves or sound waves or induction waves. It's just human energy, highly evolved.''

''That's what I told him,'' Dave interrupted. He punched Andy on the shoulder. ''C'mon, Andy,'' he said. ''Evolve.''

''That's not the point,'' Andy replied, attitude and chin held high. ''The point is, those particular energies can have an effect, and it's possible that what we have here is a hypothetical retrojection.''

''Retrojection?'' Alex asked.

''Hypothetical. They haven't been proven to actually exist.''

''Well, if a retrojection did actually exist, what would it be?''

''Hypothetically, it would be a psychic outpouching. Look, if I explain it, I gotta explain it from the start. What do you know about VR sites?''

''Probably as much as you know about the empathic arts,'' Alex said. ''So assume I'm blissfully ignorant.''

The comment was lost on Andy, who took a sanctimonious tone and began preaching his gospel. ''Okay,'' he began, attempting to look down his nose at Alex from a sitting position, which gave him a peering appearance, like a meerkat or a llama. ''Virtual Reality systems currently use a combination of holofigures and CNW—Ciliated Neural Web. The holostuff gives nice sharp images, easily controlled, and the CNW relays tactiles, visuals, olfactories— the works—via induction waves.'' He undulated a thin hand in Alex's face. ''Through the air. It operates on a generative influx schedule that mimics the pulse of outgoing and incoming neural messages in the central nervous system. With me?''

''Attached at the hip,'' Alex said.

''Good. What people forget is that the CNW is a dynamic system, and we have to account for input from human users. That's why we're always fiddling with the program, and have to keep a watch on it. As long as we do that, there's no problem, unless you have a system overload.''

"Caused by what?" Alex asked.

"Telecoms and ovens," Dave chimed in.

Alex looked from one designer to the other, waiting for an explanation. Andy gave it.

"The wrong kind of equipment onsite can interfere with the CNW," Dave explicated. "We had problems with convection ovens in the dining hall, and telecoms. Since then we found that any transmitting equipment can be trouble. We have containment procedures now, but we're still learning how this works. Or doesn't work."

"But they don't makes holes," Andy said pointedly. "System overload makes holes. We already got those, and now we have bulges, too, and that's a retrojection."

Dave rolled his eyes. "Just get on with it, Andy."

"Right. So what makes a retrojection?"

"Theoretically, induction sensitivity generates neural hyperplasia in a subject, which starts a feedback loop. See?"

"No," Alex said. "I don't."

"Neither does anyone else," Dave interjected. "That's why it's hypothetical."

Andy glared at him. "Put it this way," he said. "A retrojection happens when the subject puts information into the system as well as receiving it. The psyche starts pushing out information of its own, and the stronger the output, the stronger the image. It's a psychic outpouching, human in origin. Is that clear?"

"Yes," Alex said. "I'm afraid it is. But is there any way of telling who the human source is? Could it, for instance, be the prisoner?"

"No way of knowing for sure," Dave said cheerfully. "The thing doesn't even exist as far as we're concerned."

"Well, can a hypothetical retrojection have a negative effect on the rest of the system? Can it create these holes you're worried about?"

"Theoretically?" Dave asked.

"Theoretically," Alex assured him.

Dave twisted his thick neck around and grinned up at Alex. "We haven't got a hypothetical clue."

# 9

''ARE WE SECURE?'' CAROLAN ASKED KARL MAD-
den, whose bland eyes regarded her from her telecom
screen.

"Do we need to be?" he asked.

"Yes."

He punched the code into his telecom and disappeared
in brief static, then reappeared, leaning in toward the
screen, ready to listen.

"Go," he said.

"I was to meet with Supervisor Dzarny this evening for
a social interaction," she began, watching him carefully for
a response. Nothing more than a slight shift in his focus
told her he understood, but she was used to reading very
subtle signals from him. "He called to cancel a short time
ago, and also to let me know that anomalies have been
cropping up at the VR site."

This time the reaction was sharper, clearer. He raised
himself in his chair.

"What anomalies?"

"The appearance of unscheduled holofigures, and unprogrammed behavior on the part of scheduled holofigures."

His upper body relaxed, and the hint of pleasure twitched
at the edge of his lips. He was expecting this? Pleased at

it? She was prepared for him to be coldly angry, to blame her.

"Have they located a cause for the malfunction?"

"Alex—Supervisor Dzarny didn't say, but one of the designers complained from the start about having an empath onsite. He believes she affects the system negatively. I've—um—expressed my agreement with his opinion."

Madden nodded. "They think it's Addams. How does our equipment register the anomalies?"

"Sir," she said, holding her hands out, "That's partly why I called. I'm using a v-line for discretion's sake, and it works fine as long as the induction waves are set higher than normal, but I'm afraid that's compounding the problems onsite."

"You're afraid it is, or you know it is?" Madden asked.

Reluctantly, she took a stand. "I know it is. I've seen the shift that occurs with the induction waves up, and when I add the load of the v-line, then the designers start seeing holes in the web. We *are* affecting the CNW, and I don't know how bad it'll get."

Madden turned his face away from the screen, away from her. He was in his office, so she knew he was staring at a picture of his grandfather, which he would consult at difficult moments.

"All right," he said, turning back to her. "Starting tomorrow, I want you to follow a graduated schedule of increase that puts functions to close-top range within five days."

Carolan shook her head, not to deny his request, but because she didn't understand. "But, sir, with that schedule, we could—we could reach turbulent levels of malfunction and the whole system could start breaking down. The designers are obviously worried about it, too, or they wouldn't have called Supervisor Dzarny."

"And you're afraid you'll end up catching the heat for it, aren't you, Shannon?"

She noticed that he was really smiling now. They'd always spoken in an almost secret language, and she would have to decode all his words as she heard them. Today he was speaking outside the code, as if he didn't need to hide with her anymore. Her ass was on the line in this. He recognized that without dodging. She supposed that was good.

"Yes, sir," she replied. "Supervisor Dzarny forbid me to use any monitors at all."

"Think about this for a minute. What happens if the VR site blows? The prisoner is without a program, the Planetoid has to explain to the senator in charge of their funding exactly what went wrong, and in the middle of it all sits a woman who is not only known to be an empath, but to regularly use the empathic arts in her work. Which is still not code behavior. Standing right behind her is a computer designer who says she affected the site. And standing right behind him is Supervisor Dzarny, who supports Dr. Addams without question. Now, with all that in mind, what do you suppose will happen next?"

Carolan felt her heart begin to beat a little harder. Sardis would end up in their hands. The funding for new VR work would end up in their hands, because their equipment would be the only record of what happened. Alex would probably be actively seeking another job. And Jaguar would be far away—either back on the home planet, or on some Planetoid doing her own time.

A plan. It had been planned from the start, and she didn't see it. Madden put all the intricate little pieces in place and then watched them play themselves out. He had to expend very little effort, and he was getting everything he wanted.

"Sir," she asked politely, "have you ever been tested for psi capacities? Adept capacities in particular?"

For the first time since she'd gone to work for him, she saw him laugh. It wasn't much of a laugh, really more of a chuckle, but it was the first. It made her feel, somehow, safe at last.

"I'm not an adept, Shannon. I'm just damn smart. Turn up the volume on their equipment and ours. Five days to the top. And placate the designers. You're good at that sort of thing. That's one of the reasons you're on this assign-

ment. By the way," he asked, "how are you getting along
with Supervisor Dzarny?"

She hoped the warmth she felt in her face wasn't a blush.
She blushed too readily, she thought. It didn't look good
in an agent. "We seem to have a lot in common."

"That's good to know," he said, "since you may end
up spending more time together in future. Good work,
Shannon. Keep it up."

The telecom went dead, and Carolan stared at it, taking
time to absorb and process all she'd just learned. In a little
while, she thought, she'd check in with Alex again. See if
he wanted to come over for late dinner after he was done
at work. He'd be tired, and maybe discouraged, but she
could help him with that.

In fact, she thought, it would be her pleasure to do so.


At the VR site, the program had created a rich and deep
night. Alex went immediately to the stream at the foot of
the formal gardens. He knew Jaguar was still on the site,
and he thought that if there was one place she would enjoy,
it would be the great willow that overlooked the stream.

He found her there, sitting by the edge of the clear running water. He stood some distance away and observed the
set of her back as she dabbled her feet in the water.

Without turning around, she spoke. "Hello, Alex. Heavenly night, isn't it?"

She pushed herself to her feet, turned to face him. He
saw that she wore the blue stone jewelry and soft green
attire of the Mertec medicine people. Chant signs were
painted in black and silver on the shimmering stuff of her
dress, which fell in folds around her hips, her breasts, her
arms and legs. He had forgotten she was qualified to wear
the ceremonial dress of her people, and he had forgotten
how much power there was in it. The power of beauty,
stopping time and motion. She was stunning and he felt,
momentarily, stunned.

"What's the matter," she asked when he remained im-
mobile, "does it make me look fat?"

He walked over to her. "Actually, it makes you look like yourself," he said.

"Someone around here has to be," she replied. Then, keeping her voice scrupulously blank of emotion, she asked, "Are you here because Rachel's dead?"

"No," he said quickly, reassuring her. "She's—no, Jaguar. It's not that."

The rise and fall of her shoulders was the only indication that she'd been terrified, and now was relieved. By the time he reached her, she'd twisted her mouth into almost half a grin. "Okay," she said. "So what've I done now?"

"Maybe," he lied, "I just came by to say hello."

"Sure," she said. "And bureaucrats like art, too. That's why they spend zillions of dollars on this kind of crap."

"Now what's your complaint, Dr. Addams? Look around. Great green grass, beautiful night, beautiful clear stream." He picked up a flat stone and flung it out, watching it skim across the stream. VR stones always skipped so nicely. "What could possibly be wrong?"

"It's not real. Not any of it. Not even the damn screaming peacocks."

He laughed. "Jaguar, didn't you ever have an imaginary friend?"

She crossed her arms and scowled at him. "What of it?"

"Nothing, except some of the most real things in the universe are imaginary. What we think and imagine is as real as what we hold. You know that."

"But this isn't even imaginary. Some technopop bureaucrat brat with a two-week psychology seminar under his belt manufactured it. It's *manufactured*, not imagined. And they can't manufacture a god for Sardis when they don't know what's in her soul. What you name as sacred, what you see as divine, is a reflection of your own soul. Like this."

She touched the edge of his mind briefly, showing him the image of Rachel, dancing at the edge of the Galilee, a drum in her hand, bright skirts swirling around her. She was singing to her God. Then the scene shifted, and he saw

Jaguar greeting the dawn on the mesa, sky bending down to touch earth around her, the white stone bones drinking the light. She stood under a curve of stone smoothed by centuries of wind and an ancient sea, speaking with her relations.

She was right. Technology was simpler than imagination. It could manufacture VR sites, but it couldn't do the work of the spirit, envisioning and participating in the divine. That took imagination, supremely real. Still, it took imagination to get to VR technology in the first place.

"Jaguar," he said, "the whole Planetoid system is manufactured from what someone once imagined. If you object to the VR on the grounds that it's manufactured, you're writing a philosophical check that reality can't cover."

She picked up a stone and flung it into the stream, splashing water up onto their feet. "Cover that," she snapped at him.

Alex stepped back. "Whoa. I'm not the enemy. Not even a little bit."

She subsided, contented herself with kicking at the ground. "Sorry, but I've had enough intellectual constructs and abstract Gods. I want something I can touch more than this." She held out her hands, grabbed around at air. "I want to be able to *feel* something."

Alex frowned at her. "What do you mean?"

"I mean," she said, "I can't touch anything so that I really feel it."

He shook his head. That wasn't possible. The VR had tactile sensation built in, as well as smell, taste, hearing, and visuals. An empath like Jaguar might resent the absence of emotional resonance, but she should get physical sensation.

He stood in front of her and brought his fingers to rest on her eyelids. "Close your eyes," he said. "Now put your hand out."

He bent down and scooped up a handful of sandy earth, which he poured into her hand.

"Tell me what that is," he said.

"What do you mean?" she asked.

"What I just put in your hands. What is it?"

"You didn't put anything in my hands."

Dammit, that wasn't right. He took a step over to the water and scooped up a handful of that, then went back to her and cupped his hand over hers, letting the water run through.

"What do you feel now?"

She gave him a small and tight-lipped smile. "Your hand, Alex." She curled hers around it.

He paused, and stared down at her fingers twining over his. He noticed, not for the first time, that her hands were like her, long and lean and strong. He knew that if he leaned down to breathe in the scent of her skin, it would be of mint, sharp and clean.

He lifted his free hand to her face. Her hair was tied back in a long braid, but a strand had broken loose from the twining. He took it between two fingers and rubbed it lightly before brushing it back into place, pressing his palm against the side of her face. She breathed in hard, and seemed to hold her breath.

All motion in him was temporarily suspended as his entire being expressed surprise at the gesture he'd just made. At how good it felt to make it. Then he dropped her hand and stepped away from her. She opened her eyes, moved back to the edge of the stream.

At least, he thought, she could feel what was real. Maybe a little too much. He stared at her back, cleared his throat, let his hand stop tingling, and got back to business.

"So you still perceive—um—normal touch and—so on?"

"Yes," she said, keeping her back to him. "Absolutely."

"Well, that's good. I mean it indicates . . . a good indication."

She shrugged and looked at him quickly over her shoulder. Her face was strained, muscles in her neck and jaw holding tension. She shifted from side to side restlessly, which was unlike her. She was normally still as a cat in the sun, unless she was in absolute motion. Her movements were never unnecessary, and hardly ever indicative of uncontrolled nervous energy.

Skittish, he thought. He didn't blame her, either. He stayed well back.

"Can you hear all right?" he asked.

"Sort of. I have a hard time with the angels, but the peacocks would wake the dead. What Sardis says blips in and out, but that's because I'm listening to her center, and she's talking off the top of her head. You know how that works."

He did. In empathic work, if you were listening hard to someone who was lying, either to you or themselves, their words sometimes disappeared in a fog of meaningless babble. But that was normal. At least for empaths.

"Taste and smell?"

"Nonexistent."

Interesting that her perception was disturbed most in the earliest senses. And none of it applied to Sardis. Her empathic ability was interfering with the system, her particular psi capacities operating through those older functionings of the senses. He had no trouble, but he wasn't using the arts and she was.

"Jaguar," he said, "I don't know if this has anything to do with your perceptual problems, but the designers think you've done something to screw up the VR program."

She turned to face him, and knitted her brow. "I have? What?"

"You don't know?"

"Haven't got a clue. What could I possibly do to it?"

"There's only one thing I can think of, offhand."

She uncreased her forehead, and blinked at him. He meant the empathic touch. "That messes up the program?"

"You have any other suggestions?"

"Tell me," she said, a light growing in her eyes, "how badly does it mess up the program?"

"Depends on the strength of the empath, I suppose. Nobody really knows, since they can't officially acknowledge empathic work. My best guess is that empathic pulse waves interrupt the regularity of induction current. I was sent to tell you that whatever you're doing, you should stop. Are you," he asked, "feeling well, Jaguar?"

She brought her attention sharply back to him. "Well? I told you, Alex. VRs give me headaches. And Sardis makes me sick to my stomach. I almost wish I could find out more horrible things about her, just to confirm my bad opinion of her. Another rotten thing to know about myself. It's not helping my headaches any, believe me."

"I'm sorry, Jaguar," he said sympathetically. He was a Teacher before he was a Supervisor, and he remembered the difficulty of trying not to dance in other people's shit, or let them dance in yours, while conducting a difficult program. "If it's making you sick, I could probably have you pulled. Since there's no reason to panic about cult violence, someone else could take her."

"No," she said.

Alex was surprised. He would think any excuse would do to drop this one. "No?"

"No. I can't. Not yet."

"What is it? And don't hold back on me, either. Last time—"

"I'm not. It's just that I promised Rachel I'd see it through. She's been dreaming, Alex."

Rachel. She told Alex to make sure Jaguar stayed. She was wandering in dreams, and Jaguar would listen to them. She was trained to listen to dreams.

"Do you know anything about Sardis's daughter?" she asked unexpectedly.

"Sardis's daughter? She died in the Serials. She was shot. Random kill. What's the interest?"

She turned eyes that looked slightly fevered toward him. "It's as close as I've gotten to anything real with her.

There's something there. It fills her. And it fills me with loathing.''

He ran a hand through his hair and considered. The something undefinable hidden under the tangled mass of fabrication and illusion. That was why he hadn't fought the Board's decision to send Jaguar in. He knew she would feel it, too.

"You rule out possession?" he asked.

"Not yet," she replied. "I can't get far enough in to tell. And I swear this VR is making it harder. It helps her maintain her illusions. It all needs to be changed. The whole damn program.''

She made a sweeping gesture with her arm, vehement and final.

"You sound rather apocalyptic yourself, Jaguar," Alex said. "All will be changed in the wink of an eye."

"What we do here needs human contact, with someone real. That's how people heal, Alex." She took a step away from him, turned her face toward the speckling of stars that arched over their heads. Abover her, Alex could spot Sagittarius rising, and Jupiter riding high.

"Her daughter's name was Rachel," Jaguar said softly.

Instinctively, he reached for her, then just as swiftly pulled back. No more of that, he told his arm. It could be habit-forming.

"You're not telling me everything about how she is, are you?" she asked, turning back to look at him.

He took in breath and let it out. "The medics found out that Philo used a nanotoxin. T-and-Vs.''

"Shit," she said. "That's serious material, Alex. Where'd he get hold of that?"

"Good question. One of the sect people remembers him talking about working in a lab, so I'm running a computer check on that. In the meantime the medics are doing their best.''

She folded her arms across her chest and stared out across the stream, into the distant illusion of night. Closed.

Traveling far from him. Not wanting him to know where she was going.

"We have to hope for the best," he tried.

"No, we don't," she said. "Not unless we have a plan to make the best happen."

"How about trusting that we aren't the only ones who can make it happen."

"Yeah," she said. "Right."

Okay, he thought. That went well. But if he couldn't help her feel better, at least he could try to get her to behave sanely. "Jaguar, I don't want you leaving the site because you're in a panic about her," he said. "She's getting good treatment, and there's nothing you can do."

"I don't have to leave the site to find her, Alex," she said, arms wrapping tighter around herself.

Was she considering making empathic contact with Rachel when she was this sick? She wouldn't, he thought, and immediately corrected himself. She would. And it would be very dangerous if she did.

He stepped in front of her and made a face like thunder. "Don't. Just don't even kid about that," he said. "It's high risk and you know it."

To be empathically enmeshed in a mind as ill as Rachel's was pure folly. Empathic contact took energy, and to hit Rachel with that right now could send her right over the edge. Then it would be too easy for them to stumble into a Death Walk. Too easy. And too difficult to pull out of it. Alex had once been called on to do a Death Walk, and even though he had help, even though he came out of it in one piece, it was touch and go throughout. His body responded to the death it walked with, feeling it as his own. If he hadn't let go in time, hadn't known the rules of the landscape, hadn't had a partner to remind his body it was alive, he would have simply slipped away in the wake of someone else's death, like being caught in the downpull of a sinking ship.

"Jaguar," he repeated, "don't kid about it. I've done it, and—dammit, you know better."

"Don't worry," Jaguar said lightly, "I'm not kidding."

"Clever," Alex said. "And while I admire your witty use of language, I want you to promise me you won't try contact with Rachel. It might kill you, and it would almost certainly kill her."

"And mightn't it save her?" Jaguar said harshly, lifting her chin high and showing him a determined jaw.

"Haven't you done enough saving for the time being?" he said testily, and immediately regretted it when he saw her wince. Still, if it would keep her from falling into a Death Walk, it was worth her acrimony.

She said nothing.

"Point taken?" he asked.

"Dead on," she replied. "Through the left ventricle."

"Good," he said. "That's where it should be. And you should be with your prisoner."

Jaguar threw him a quick, false smile. "Welcome to my hell. Stuck with Sardis until I figure out if she's mad, or if I am. She's possessed by God, and I'm stuck with a holodemon. Do you suppose that's Christian justice visited on a poor pagan? Or is he just my imaginary friend?"

She held her hand up and looked at it, spread her fingers to let the virtual moonlight seep through, then closed them.

She saw it, then. The holodemon. The designers were right.

"Not imaginary, Jaguar," he said. "The designers saw him, too. That's what I meant about messing up the system."

She twisted her neck and gaped at him, waiting for him to explain. He obliged.

"Retrojection?" she said when he was finished. Then she grinned. "That's what Rider said."

"Rider?"

"He calls himself Rider. He's the holofigure who attacked me earlier. Alex, do you think he's something the Feds are throwing at me?"

"Paranoia," he reminded her, "is the illusion that your

enemies are organized.'' He was about to say more, when his belt sensor buzzed, indicating a call, which he read, and put away.

''You were saying something about paranoia?'' Jaguar noted when he was done.

He rolled his eyes at her. ''Jaguar, don't start.''

''Oh,'' she said, sweet venom in her tone, ''so that *wasn't* Agent Shannon?''

''All right. That's enough.''

''She got you recruited yet?''

''Jaguar, will you let go of it?''

''You know, Alex, the Mohawk have a prayer they say when they go on a journey. They ask that they not be seduced from their true path by the things that glitter along the side of the road.''

''Let it go,'' he said testily, feeling her keen ability to toss him from unexpected gestures of affection to tingling anger in ten words or less. He had learned to anticipate discomfort in their conversations, but not to keep it away.

''Please,'' he said more calmly. ''I am not recruited, she is not recruiting, and the holodemon is not a Federal conspiracy. It's you, Jaguar. Keep the empathic work contained.''

She groaned, threw her hands up in frustration. ''I can't change the program, I can't work the program, and I'm stuck inside the program. How about you let me take her out of here and show her something real?''

''Like what?''

Jaguar glared, stabbed the air in front of her. ''Like Rachel,'' she said.

Alex glared back. ''Don't get any ideas. And don't leave the site. In fact, you should be careful going back and forth between here and the sanctuary. Philo's in the area.''

He filled her in on the most recent developments in that part of the assignment. The dead woman, her body marked for the beast with its triple six. The carved-out belly.

''I've got the area secure, and the laser fence is up and

running," he added. "I don't think he'll manage to get through."

"Laser fence," she said disdainfully. "They can't keep it working. The VR site drains it or something. Why don't they just put up an old barbed wire. Something you can feel when it rips you to shit."

"I'll speak to the Board about it," Alex said, ignoring her pique. "Look, are you serious about wanting a different program for Sardis?"

"I am. She doesn't need more illusions, and her fear isn't of God. Or it's of a different God than the testers manufactured for her," she said.

"You have suggestions for where to take her?"

"I have a few ideas, but mostly they start with taking her out of here."

"Okay. Work on alternatives. I'll see what I can do. But you know it'll take a lever bigger than your ego to pry the Board loose from their toys, so while I'm building it, stay put and be careful."

"Thank you," she said. "I appreciate it. And you be careful, too."

He tilted his head at her, and she wiggled her fingers here and there around him as if distributing fairy dust.

"Of the things that glitter," she said, grinning.

"Jaguar, we have enough fantasies going without you adding to the load." He turned and walked away, leaving her to consider the illusory stars.

"I may manufacture conspiracies," she muttered at his retreating back, "but I know a woman on the make when I see one."

She kicked at a stone, watched it plop into the stream without feeling it, then expressed herself further by making a fist and slamming it into the willow tree.

She felt nothing. Not even the satisfaction of pain at her own stupidity. The bark on the tree wavered, re-formed itself, and was still.

As she stood watching it a sound caught her attention.

Singing?

It was singing, and human, she thought. Close, but not too close. Not holopeacock, or virtual wind. It had to be human, because of all the animals in the world, only humans sang off-key.

She followed it away from the stream and toward the boxwood maze. There, just at the entrance, was a proud oak, its branches spreading toward the sky, and its base broad enough for a small army to rest against.

Sardis sat at the base of the tree, eyes closed, arms wrapped around herself. Jaguar stood less than ten feet away, silent, listening.

*The green sea is rough, and shadows do darken. The ship it is rocking, and billows are high.*

A lullaby. Very flat. As Jaguar watched she moved her arms as if she stroked something she held there, lovingly. She spoke to it, softly. Too softly for Jaguar to hear, and she didn't want to move closer, didn't want to disturb this moment. This was the first time she'd ever seen Sardis not enmeshed in her Scriptures.

*Over the cold water, whatever our way be.*

She slowly put her hand out in front of her, held it there, listening with her skin, feeling the movement of emotion in her fingers and cupping it in her palm. There was something here she could feel. Something.

*Child of my love, to save you shall I.*

Something empty. Big as the universe, but empty and cold. Too much cold. Somebody was cold. Somebody. And it was so sad.

Jaguar sensed the opening and allowed her thoughts to flow into it, spoke to Sardis subvocally.

*You couldn't save her, Sardis.*

Sardis gasped, opened her eyes, blinked at Jaguar. Neither woman said anything for a moment, and then Sardis smiled.

"Happy is the bride," she said, arms cupping nothing, moving back and forth, rocking a cold and empty nothing.

"Called to the marriage feast of the lamb. Soon. Soon. Soon."

Sardis got up and walked away. Jaguar let her hand drop, and felt sorrow pour out of her, from the tips of her fingers to the millions of blades of unreal grass.

# 10

PROTEUS STOOD UNDER THE LEAPING PANTHERS and sauntering elephants scrolled in ironwork in the arched gate of the Toronto Animal Sanctuary. He was just where he wanted to be.

And in case anyone saw him at the park, he'd changed his aspect slightly. Now he resembled his memory of the librarian at the library his mother used to take him to when he was a boy. He could still remember the look of shock on the man's petulant face when she'd cursed him soundly after he suggested that something more subdued than *In Cold Blood* would be appropriate for her son. He was about twelve at the time, he supposed, but he remembered it quite clearly.

He strolled inside the gates and followed the meandering path around the small mammals, toward the atrium. That would be a lovely place to spend the afternoon. Maybe he'd stop in the gift store and see if they had any books for sale. He could sit among the birds and read—another fond memory from his childhood. Bringing the Hardy Boys mysteries to the Washington Zoo atrium and sitting and reading while his mother worked on Saturday afternoons.

She was a secretary at the school he attended during the week, but to make ends meet after his father left, she took on weekend work, cleaning out the bathrooms at the zoo.

She'd get real tired, he remembered. Working her fingers to the bone, she told him. He promised her that someday he'd change that for her, but then she was murdered. Her fingers made into a necklace while all hell broke loose in the streets of the cities and he was drinking daiquiri on a foreign beach.

Her fingers. Something about fingers. He held his hands up and looked at his own. There was something he needed to remember about fingers.

A woman with a child came up behind him, bumped into him. "Sorry," she apologized, tugging at her child to make him stop staring.

"Why's that man staring?" the little boy asked.

"Shh," the mother said. "He's not hurting anyone."

He watched them move away, and then realized he was holding his hands up high, just the way Sardis did when she blessed the crowds who flocked to see her. He shook himself and chuckled.

"I'm not getting enough sleep," he muttered to himself. "Bad news."

He continued following the path, and tried to focus. After the kill last night, he'd stayed up late until he found a man about his size for a nice quiet kill, an ID card, and a clean shirt. It took half the night for him to find the right man, more time to dispose of the body, find a place to change, attend to details. He didn't finish until dawn.

Even so, he'd checked himself into a hotel and tried for sleep, but it had proved elusive. Too much on his mind, and the adrenaline from two kills in a night still flowing in his blood. Before noon he was out of his room and on the streets again. Now, of course, he was groggy as hell, feeling a little down, a little maudlin.

After the atrium, when the sun started setting, he'd find a place near the VR entrance and hole up, get himself rested before he began the next leg of the mission. He wasn't short of time yet. At least he didn't think so, though time seemed to slip away from him here in a different way than it did on the home planet. But his calculations told him he had—

four days to go? Five? He wasn't sure how home planet time differed from Planetoid time, if it did.

A chill wind came up and caught him at the back of the neck. Or maybe it felt colder because he was tired. But the bird atrium was close by. The songs of the birds would revive him, remind him of happier days. If he believed in life after death, he'd believe that's where his mother's spirit had gone.

But he didn't. He believed in taking care of business and taking care of himself in a universe that seemed largely indifferent to his presence. Anything else made a good story, but was self-delusion. Three years with Sardis hadn't changed his opinion on that at all. On the contrary, everything he knew about her confirmed his opinion. Self-delusion was her stock-in-trade for the sect and for herself. It was crucial to her livelihood and, he thought, to her life.

Once when they were fucking she wanted him to talk to her. He preferred not to notice her presence during sex, to think of the act as a sort of masturbation, but she liked it when he talked to her about God, about the new heaven. That day, he'd had it with the new heaven, so he pinned her down by the wrists and looked right at her.

*It's all a lie, Sardis. You know that. All a lie. You're fucking everyone just the way I'm fucking you and you know why you're doing it, don't you? C'mon, Sardis. What is it tell me say it go on you can say it you know it's all a lie a bunch of crap you're making up c'mon Mother, it's all crap but what's the reason for it, what's the reason, Mother? Might as well tell me who will ever know and I won't tell and there's no one else not your family not your daughter they're all dead all dead even your little girl.*

She got one hand loose from his grasp and clawed at his face, drawing blood. She was a strong woman, and he had to work hard to regain control. He gave her three good rights to the jaw, and her eyes rolled back in her head, but he kept going.

*C'mon, Mother, there's a reason for everything tell me*

*why you're fucking everyone and does it feel good like this
is it good for you.*

She stayed out for two hours, and he thought he had a
dead woman on his hands. And then it was three days—
she just lay on the bed and stared at the ceiling. He told
the rest of the sect she was deep in prayer, and he changed
the sheets when she pissed and waited to see what would
happen next.

It was a good time, in many ways, because he consoli-
dated his own power base with her people, and began to
formulate his own plans.

When she finally came out of it, she seemed to remember
nothing that had driven her into that state in the first place,
but that was his first understanding that there were certain
topics best not mentioned around her. Never again would
he try to take her delusions from her. She could keep them,
as long as he got to keep the cash.

And he would. He was very close to that right now. A
little rest, a little more work, and he could get out of here.
He shrugged himself deeper into his shirt, trying to warm
himself from the inside out, pointed himself toward his destination, and walked on.


Jaguar sniffed at the air in the food court, and smelled nothing. A man walked by and threw a Styrofoam cup into a
transparent garbage can, where it immediately was transformed into a dove that rose up in a flutter of flight. She
watched it fly toward the skylight and disappear.

"Nice touch, guys," she said, knowing that if the designers had their monitors turned her way, they'd hear the
compliment. Unless it was lost in the hollow echo of con-
verging conversations that always filled the food court.
Words she could never distinguish. Conversation that came
to her ears like ambient, erratic noise.

She pulled up a chair at a table next to a pizza stall and
plopped herself into it, lifting her bare foot and rubbing it.
She'd been looking for Sardis all morning, without success.
She couldn't tell if the woman was being deliberately elu-

sive, or if she was just busy gathering holoconverts. All Jaguar knew was that her feet hurt, and her head hurt, and the low thrum of happy families around her was making her sick to her stomach. Thousands of years of evolution, she thought despondently, and we still can't get away from malls.

"Ever kiss a holofigure?" a voice whispered in her ear.

She jumped to standing, knocking her chair over in the process, and made a face when she saw Rider was laughing at her.

"I can't imagine anything more unpleasant," she said. She put the chair right, then straightened herself and walked away.

"Really?" he said, hanging back while she walked on. "I can. How about this?"

She heard the sound of a child screaming, and then an explosion. She spun around to face him.

"Handy thing, being a holofigure. And let's not forget this, either."

He assumed Alex's face and form, his hand lifted to an invisible other, his fingers mimicking the gesture of gently fondling a lock of hair.

"Goddammit, cut that shit out," she said, striding over to him, not sure what she meant to do, but sure she meant to do something. He had no right to trespass on that moment. No right to make it public, make her think about it, throw it at her in this meaningless and intrusive way.

"That's none of your business," she hissed in his face.

She heard Rider's voice speaking inside her. *Private fantasy, admittance for only one? I don't think so.*

He pulled her face to his and kissed her hard.

Stunned by the move, it took her some moments to remember to fight. She raised her hands and pushed him away, but he held her fast. Over his shoulder she saw Sardis, and a gathering crowd of holofigures, all of them gaping at her.

"And she teaches and misleads my slaves to commit *fornication* and to eat things sacrificed to *idols*," Sardis bellowed. The holofigures huddled behind her, shielding their eyes.

"Whore of Babylon," a woman screamed, and promptly fainted.

"Uh-oh," Rider said, breaking from the kiss and resuming his holodemon form. *"In flagrante."* And with that, he whirled Jaguar around and shoved her so that she fell directly into the shocked cult leader, the two of them stumbling onto the marble floor in a tangle of arms and legs.

"Oh, dopey me." Rider giggled, and reached out one hand to each woman, grasping them by the arms, lifting them and pushing them closer to each other.

Jaguar drew in breath.

Something. She felt something.

Dark. No. Shadow. No. Like a shadow, but filled with something. Something. Big. Powerful. Then, underneath it, a scream. A child, screaming. Words. What? What was it?

She pushed at it, and it receded, then heard the whisper of Rider's sardonic voice.

*Soft beats hard, dearie. Or have you forgotten your tai chi?*

Dammit. Damn him. She felt his static surrounding her, and breathed deeply, letting her breath carry her into stillness.

Carried into stillness, and the images played within her, she falling into them. Falling through the barrier. Through and into and carried with them, in mad and uncontrollable motion toward the center where—

A tunnel, long and dark. At the end of it, a young woman, arms stretched out to a laughing child. A little girl. A little girl with dark curls, laughing, holding something, running to her.

A young woman, laughing, arms outstretched, calling her.

*Rachel, what is it? Oh, you found a pretty stone. Let me see.*

Jaguar felt a gasp of pain. Little girl. Rachel.

Her mother held her. They laughed. The mother looked

over her shoulder, and laughter became terror, face collapsing into a horrified *no No NO*.

Then—a great scaling wind filled with electricity. Something. Whistling of bullets.

Jaguar couldn't see, felt herself tossed around in a cover of electric fire and wind surrounding her so she couldn't see, though she tried to stay with it, tried to see, she was tossed by the scaling wind, tossed out, crying, *no No NO*

*Let me see.*

A name tossed from voice to the wind of passing bullets. The center where Sardis's voice spoke, saying, *All will be washed clean in the blood of the lamb the blood of the lamb*

and wild laughter melting into Rider's voice saying

*I told you so.*

Jaguar stood still, clutching Sardis to her, Rider standing nearby, laughing.

He released his hold.

Sardis stood and pushed Jaguar away, brushed herself off, then spit out, "And her children I shall kill with *deadly* plague."

Having said her piece, she turned and ran away.

Jaguar stood and twisted back to Rider, who was grinning from ear to ear. She caught his chin in her fingers and pushed hard, letting her eyes pierce his.

Static. Slicing and sharp. She held on. More static.

Then, the smell of mint.

"Don't you get it yet?" Rider said, slapping her hand away. "Or *won't* you get it yet? Oh well. Ticktock said the clock and Jaguar's still as dense as a rock."

"What the fuck are you? A holofuckup? A Federal game?"

Rider looked shocked and slightly pained. "Of course not. I told you, I'm pure Jaguar."

"Then why do you act like such an asshole?"

"We-ell," he said, and then held a hand out to ward off the clenched fist she raised. "All right, I won't go there.

Far too easy. Let's just say I'm your ego in dissension with your self.''

Jaguar lowered her fist and pursed her lips, tried to work through this thorny thicket. "That's ridiculous. I can't live in constant self-contradiction.''

"You've managed nicely so far.''

"Thanks. A million.''

"You're welcome. It is pretty amazing what the human frame can contain and sustain. Look at Sardis. The weight of the world inside her. And a dead little girl on top of it. Not to mention the kids she blew up. And all her flock, counting on her. Await the day,'' he cried. Holofigures paused, murmured agreement, echoed his words, and walked on. He took a bow.

"Look,'' she said, "the last thing I need is some badly dressed part of my psyche playing paranoid songs in my ear. Sardis isn't the Antichrist.''

"Of course not,'' he agreed. "Whoever said she was? She is a projection of the world soul, at its whining worst. A common lunatic with good media coverage. She is the stupidity of evil.''

"Then what? If I called you in to save Rachel, just do it.''

For the first time since he'd pranced his way into her life, his expression softened into sympathy. "You care about her. I would go so far as to say you love her. Now, why is that?''

"Because she's worth loving, Rider. She's a good human being.''

"That's nothing special. So are millions of other people, and you don't love them.''

"I don't know them. I know Rachel.''

She didn't know a million other people or their lives as they woke up in the morning and ate breakfast and put on clothes and loved and fought their way through their days. She knew Rachel, though. She knew Rachel preferred wearing scented oils to perfumes, and that she washed her hair with herbal shampoos and liked classical music. She knew Rachel as a distinct life, and would go far to save her.

"I suppose. But when you think about it, Sardis has saved so many lives, put so many people on the good path in spite of that little problem she has with incendiary tendencies. What's Rachel done in comparison?"

She ran a hand through her hair. Why did he have to make her think about such irrelevancies just when she was ready to strangle him? She supposed that's how he stayed alive—through distraction. And how to explain what made someone like Rachel special. Because she was real? To be authentically yourself took a certain greatness of soul. "I don't know, Rider. It's—it's a quality of light about her. A quality of her being. She's real. And that's actually pretty rare. So tell me how to save her."

"What if I told you that you'd have to trade her in for about a few million other good people?"

"What?"

"What if I told you," he repeated carefully, "that to save her life you'd have to let a few million people die? Would you do it?"

"No," she said. "I mean—I'd want to, but—why the hell are you asking that?"

He nodded sagaciously. "Just as I thought. You'd throw yourself in front of a train, but not a lunatic child killer. Well, it's not easy being us. Listen, dearest. I love you, too. I have to, because you're me. And since you're me, I can't lie to you. So what I'm about to tell you is the absolute truth. The most important truth you need to save Rachel. Listening?"

"Hard as I can," she said.

He flourished with his hand, made a trumpet sound, and announced boldly, "Do what you're best at. Don't let go."

She waited. Nothing else happened. "That's it? That's the fucking lot? Rider, eat shit and die young." She wheeled away from him, but he got hold of her arm and held her back.

"Now, now," he remonstrated. "You know better than

that. Every curse you send out comes back to you three times. Wish only pleasantness on your enemies. Speaking of which, there's one very close. Can you feel him? He's pulled here by a longing for death. The only real friend he has. Trustworthy forever.''

He brushed his hand over her eyes, and in the darkness of her own eyelids she saw a figure. Philo, but not Philo, moving from shadow to shadow. Moving toward her. Not his face. Not his aspect. But it was Philo, moving through the zoo.

Was that real? Was he here?

"You can't tell anymore, can you?'' Rider said. "Poor Jaguar. And the clock ticking. Maybe you should go see Rachel. She's real. Real as death, right?''

"She's not dying,'' Jaguar hissed.

"Close enough for government work,'' Rider said. "She lingers in the House of No Words. Perhaps she's waiting for you to come and say good-bye.''

House of No Words. That was a Mertec term. If he knew it, then he must know her mind. But Rachel wasn't dying. No. Just no.

"Go,'' Rider said, putting his face in hers. "If you don't believe me, go see for yourself.''

She pushed him roughly away and began to walk down the long halls of the mall. Before he was out of view, she turned back around to face him one more time.

"Just let me get a hand on your programmer. That's all. Just one hand.''

She heard him laughing for some distance as she pounded ungracefully away from him.


"Besides disemboweling her, he cut off part of her finger,'' Alex said. "And he did the same thing to Mark. Cut off the tip of the finger. I've got it in the computer to see whose bell it rings, but I wish I could remember, myself.''

Carolan put down her fork and stared at the small sausages on her plate. "Maybe we could defer this conversation until after we eat?'' she asked.

Alex paused mid-chew and stared where she stared. They were eating a delicately seasoned omelette with fragrant herbed potatoes and tiny sausages, which he'd prepared for them as a quick late dinner.

"Sorry," he said. "It's on my mind."

"That's okay," she said, forcing up a smile and taking a sip of wine. "I already figured out that you're obsessive about your work. I expect it's on your mind a lot."

He shrugged. It was the truth. "But this is even worse than usual, you understand. We've got VR breakdowns, a murderer loose, and we still don't know what happened to the rest of the Revelation members. It's all getting too messy for my taste."

She reached across his small dining-room table and ran her fingers back and forth across his wrist. "They'll find Philo now. At least you've got a clean trail. As far as the VR site goes, the experts are doing their work and I'm there to help. If we can block Dr. Addams's signals a little more thoroughly, I think it'll be just fine."

Alex shook his head. "I'm not convinced it's just her. Dave keeps checking for possible equipment interference, and my sense is that anything she's doing is secondary to that."

"Equipment interference?" she said, her hand stopping its motion, resting on his wrist. "He didn't mention that to me."

"I guess it's common," Alex said. "They have to do periodic checks to make sure there's no leak from transmission outside the site to inside. So he told me."

"Oh, that," she said. "Of course. But they can manage it, Alex. That's the point."

"I suppose," he said, forking up potatoes and chewing hard, as if he could at least work his jaw harder, if nothing else. "But then there's the disappearing cult members and Jaguar says Sardis is still talking about the Apocalypse."

"Of course she is. She thinks it's real, and we've made damn sure she keeps thinking that. That's her program. But it's not ours, is it? Besides, isn't it possible that Dr. Addams is just a little nervous, given her past.''

"She's not nervous," Alex said. "I am."

Carolan laughed, a silver liquid sound washing over him as it had the first time he'd heard it.

"Did I say something funny?"

"No, but I am laughing at you. So intent. Finish your food and come sit on the couch with me."

He allowed her to take his hand and lead him to the couch, sit him down. It was pleasant to be cajoled back into good humor, even if it wasn't working. She stroked the back of his neck with fingers as light and soft as her laughter.

"Still tense," she said. "You're not convinced. And I won't try and convince you."

"You won't?"

"Not at all. I'll distract you." She pulled him to her and kissed his eyes, his face, his neck.

"Pleasant distraction," he murmured into her hair.

"This isn't all of it," she whispered. "I'll give you something else to think about, too. Like a better job."

He pulled back, held her by the shoulders away from him.

She smiled warmly at him. "I wanted to tell you sooner, but I didn't have a chance. My boss likes your work. He asked me if you'd be interested in coming to work with us. On the home planet. Research and development." Her smile broadened. "With me."

Alex, the Adept, considered his options for a response, and where each might lead. No was one option. Yes was another. Then there was maybe, or I'll think about it. Somewhere in the back of his mind, he heard Jaguar laughing, saying she told him so.

"I'm flattered," he said carefully, "though it's quite a surprise."

"Well, think about it. You could be making a big difference to how people view the empathic arts, and doing a lot of good in the world."

What they'd talked about already. An opportunity to create changes in attitude on a broader scale, and he could do
it working with her. He imagined himself in an office with
her, going over reports, stopping occasionally to touch the
light that touched her hair. Going home at night to look at
the lake—no. He wouldn't be doing that. He'd be on the
home planet. Did he want that?

"Carolan, I wasn't considering a job change."

"Maybe the right change didn't come your way before
now. This one brings you home. Don't you ever miss the
home planet? This is such a strange place to work. So isolated."

He worked and lived on a sky island, and was subject to
all the same kinds of island fevers, made worse by the fact
that the whole system was created to accommodate criminals in their rehabilitation. To live on the Planetoid was to
be a Planetoid prison system worker, even if you were a
service provider running a restaurant or working in a hospital.

"It's strange, but I've been happy here."

"Past tense."

"What?"

"You just used the past tense. You've *been* happy.
Maybe you're ready for something a little different. Start a
family, or have a home. Don't you ever want that? A sense
of normalcy? A family and a real home?" she asked. "This
doesn't seem quite the right place for it, somehow."

She moved her hands slowly over his face as she spoke,
and he found himself staying still so as not to disturb that
motion. It was sweet, and kind, and pleasantly normal. Did
it feel like home? Is that what she was to him?

Home. Did he miss that? Normalcy. What was that, anyway? Children—did he want children? He knew married
people who were raising families here. That was bound to
happen as the system developed, and measures were being
taken to accommodate it. One of them was to strictly reg-
ulate the number of children on the Planetoid, but the waiting list was short. Most people transferred back to the home

planet when they made the choice to have children. And
did he want to raise a family here? Did he want children
at all?

Once he thought he did. Long ago, before Manhattan.
Before the Planetoids. Wife, family, a house. A job that
didn't consume his thoughts. A job that had limited hours
and limited risks. A job where the people weren't all ref-
ugees from disaster, one way and another. A woman like
Carolan, so shining and clear in her eyes and her thoughts
and her needs. Nothing of the tangled complexity he had
to deal with in prisoners, in team members, in Jaguar. Nothing of the tangle of emotion Jaguar inspired in him. Though
he really couldn't blame her for that. It was his emotions
that were tangled, after all.

"I know it's a big decision," she said. "Maybe we can
arrange for you to spend a few weeks at the R-and-D center
and learn more about the job. Just think about it for now.
That'll distract your mind. I'll take care of the rest of you."

When she kissed him again, he wrapped his arms around
her, and all other worries were forgotten in the remaining
activities of the evening.


As night fell Proteus wound his way around the back of
the animal cages, toward an obscure path that led to the
breeding complex. He followed it, his mind taking accurate
and complete pictures of the area he walked through. Another of his talents was being able to retain internal map-
ping of any given location after traversing it once. This was
simple. A winding path through woods. Obviously, it was
a circle around an internal area. He could see the glow of
lights at the center through the tree cover. It was at least a
quarter mile in. Maybe half a mile. Lots of good low brush
in between.

The path itself wound past the backs of houses, through
a wooded section, out into a clearing.

A hundred feet or so beyond it was a high network fence.
He stopped and put his hand up to it, felt the spark of laser
wiring. This must be it.

Peering through it, he could see the dim outline of cages, and a house. That was a bit of a surprise. He didn't think they really had animals back there. More importantly, somewhere beyond this point was the VR site. But how could he enter these gates?

" 'And we shall gather at the gates of the cities,' " he muttered. Tired. He was really tired. He couldn't even tell what aspect he was wearing, he was so tired. The best thing he could do was find a place further in the woods and get some sleep. When he woke up, he could reconsider his position, decide what to do next. Right now he could barely decide which foot went in front of the other.

He looked around, saw that there was ample brush coverage on either side of him. He chose left as a good direction, and followed it until looking back toward the gate showed him mostly shadow. Then he lay down and let the night deepen around him, felt sleep carrying him away.

He was falling into a pretty dream about birds and books when the crunch of steps over gravel brought his consciousness racing back. Instinctively, he sat up, then crawled forward, his body and eyes fully awake before his brain was.

When it caught up with the rest of him, he could see— someone. Someone approaching, from the inside of the fence.

A woman. Tall and slim. Dressed in a light green dress that shimmered in the moonlight. No distinct facial features. Did he dare risk getting closer?

He had to.

He moved as swiftly and silently as he could, hoping the sound of her footsteps would cover the sound of his own movements. The woman paused, looked around, shrugged, then walked on.

But in that moment, when the moon shone on her face, he recognized her. He'd met her when they had him in custody. She'd put her foot on his throat and held him down.

"Dr. Addams," he whispered. "Teacher assigned to Sardis Malocco."

He risked creeping a little closer. Close enough to see her do something at the gate. Close enough to see the gate open for her. She walked through, right past the place where he crouched, and she kept walking. Pretty woman, he noted. Nice legs.

When she was out of sight he sighed deeply, satisfied beyond measure. Luck was with him. What went out would return. And when she came back, he could deal with her—maybe the way she'd dealt with him. He allowed himself the pleasure of imagining his foot on her throat. His fantasy took him to some interesting places, and he let it until at some point an idea intervened.

If he could get rid of her, it would take some days to replace her, he was sure. Some more days for a new Teacher to get up to speed with Sardis. And if Sardis was as difficult a case as the other Planetoid workers indicated, it would be some time before someone less talented than Dr. Addams got through to her.

After that many days, it would all be over anyway. In fact, by the time they got her another Teacher, it would already be too late. There couldn't be more than a few days left before the people on the home planet moved.

Which meant he didn't even necessarily have to worry about getting inside the VR. Sardis's fate would take care of itself. Once the shit hit the fan on the home planet, nobody would be inclined to rehabilitate her anymore. They'd be too busy wiping up the mess she left behind. And if she was discreetly sent on to be with her flock, he didn't think anyone would mind.

Dr. Addams would return. If not tonight, then surely first thing in the morning.

All he had to do was find a good spot in the bushes, and wait.

When Jaguar arrived at the hospital she found Rachel's room empty. She stood staring at the unoccupied bed, paralyzed by a moment of pure panic. She might have stood there all night, afraid to ask anyone for information, except that a medic came in and told her they'd moved Rachel to CCU for closer monitoring.

Still shaking, she made her way to critical care and found Rachel's room. She was sleeping, and Jaguar pulled a chair over to her bed to watch her, just for a while. Rachel slept small and curled in on herself in a time before adulthood, before childhood, before birth. Jaguar saw that there were books on the table nearby. She ran her hands over them, and felt the warmth of recent touch. Alex had been reading to her. She glanced at the monitors that lined the walls and read what she could decipher. Brain waves were running high to theta, indicating stress and fever. Heartbeat was steady, but slow. The medic said her kidneys were struggling, and Jaguar noticed the monitor for blood gases, which she couldn't read accurately. No dialytic implants yet, though, and that was good.

Jaguar sat and considered, her hands clenching and un-clenching on the arms of the chair, as if she were trying to stop them from some movement they wanted to make of their own accord.

She wanted to touch Rachel. Wanted to make contact. Didn't know if she could do it without waking her. Didn't know if there was a real reason for it. The last time she'd made empathic contact, it was to look for answers that might help the medics. This time—would it be her own hunger for a reassurance that didn't exist? Her own need to do something—*anything*—like the impulse that led her to slam her hand against the window and distract Rachel in the first place? Or was there something helpful she could do?

Rider said the House of No Words. The place where the spirits roamed with you, where words were no longer nec-essary. Jaguar wanted to know if Rachel's spirit was wan-dering there, learning the place she'd inhabit when her body no longer supported her.

Rachel stirred, turned over, and gasped. Her mouth opened and closed, pulling for air. Jaw and teeth clacking, legs going rigid. A seizure. Jaguar braced herself and stood, glanced at the monitors, which went on an unchanging course.

Her legs relaxed, the rattling of her jaw ceased, and her breathing returned to normal. Whatever it was, it had passed. Jaguar let a hand rest on her head. Inside her was the soft chiffon feel of drifting spirit, drifting thought. All seemed calm No words. Just a play of images, of memories that overlapped and joined with the present in a dance of dreaming.

Rachel, at a store, trying on a hat. Jaguar standing with her, laughing.

Jaguar, at Rachel's apartment, singing to welcome in the Sabbath queen as Rachel bent over the candles, their flames lighting her dark eyes.

Then a spinning dance, Jaguar rising from the center of fire, flame in her hand. Rachel rising above her. Jaguar chasing her through the sky, and the sky becoming a well of darkness that they ran through together, flying and flying deeper into it as if up were down and they descended then fell, fell uncontrollably, Jaguar reaching for her and she falling faster, defying the laws of physics and Jaguar reaching for her, Rachel always just out of her grasp.

"No," she whispered, pulling her hand back.

Rachel stirred, opened her eyes. "Jaguar?" she said hoarsely.

"Yes," she confirmed. "It's me."

"Mm. Is it time? Is she here yet?"

She? Who was she? Rachel was talking fever talk. Delirium.

"No," Jaguar said. "Not yet."

"Okay. I'm going to sleep for a while. Call me when you need me?"

"I will."

Jaguar realized how tense she'd been when she felt herself relax. She continued to stroke Rachel's forehead thoughtfully. She didn't like Rachel's dreams. Wanted them to be different.

The dreamscape she wanted for Rachel was an old

woman, rocking her to health under a glowing moon. The shaded forms of great cats, of the little bear and the great She-Bear, walking in slow circles around her, there to protect and guide. The birds that loved her, fluttering soft wings to keep all warmth flowing toward the sleeping human, to keep the spirit in the body. The earth sighing, breathing up strength to her daughter.

This, she wanted to give to Rachel. This dream in her hand. This, which was hers, of her people, of her land, of her life. She opened her fingers and touched Rachel's thoughts, hoping to share these visions, offering them to her. Immediately, the door was closed against her. There was no opening except into Rachel's own dreams, her own spirit wandering between here and there. Jaguar couldn't impose her wishes in this place.

She couldn't talk here. She could only listen.

She pulled her hand back and rubbed it as if it had been wounded, wrapped it around her shoulder, and felt the chill of this separation. Cold and numb. Cold and numb.

The door opened, and a medic walked in, made a clucking sound with her tongue. "You shouldn't be here," she whispered at Jaguar, and held a recorder up to the monitors.

Jaguar let her hands drop into her lap, shrugged. "She's—she seems worse," she said, keeping her voice neutral.

The medic clicked off the recorder and brought her attention back to the humans in the room. "She'll get worse than this," she said cheerfully, causing Jaguar to hate her without reserve. "But if we can manage the symptoms, keep her quiet, she'll be okay." She patted Jaguar on the shoulder, and Jaguar resisted the impolitic move of pulling back from her touch.

"You're a Teacher, aren't you?" the medic asked unexpectedly.

Jaguar nodded.

"Listen, I've had some people calling for a Supervisor Dzarny all evening. Paul Dinardo, I think he said he was.

Wants Supervisor Dzarny to call him. He's the tall hand-some polite one, isn't he?"

"That would be him," Jaguar said.

"Mm. I guess this guy's been trying his home and his office and his belt sensor. He said I was to tell him that especially. Can you get a message to him?"

Jaguar thought. She could stop in. Maybe he forgot to leave his belt sensor on. She'd get some pleasure out of waking him up with a message from Paul. And she could find out if he'd made any progress in getting Sardis moved. More and more, that seemed to her to be the right move.

"I can," she said. "I'm going that way anyway."

Jaguar decided to leave her car and walk the city blocks between the hospital and Alex's apartment. It felt good to be out walking at night on her own, with no holofigures trailing her, no peacocks screeching voices in the wind. Nothing here but intermittent traffic, a man walking a dog, music drifting down to her from someone's apartment in a building high above. She moved her arms in wide arcs around her, feeling as if she hadn't really moved in days. Without the constant pressure of induction waves flooding her, she could loosen up and let go of the noise in her own head, which was beginning to resemble the constant back-ground babble of the VR.

She walked, and let the voices pour through her and out of her, so that by the time she ascended the stairs and slipped the lock on Alex's apartment door, her mind was still.

She stood just inside, listening for a moment. It was dark and quiet, the hum of sleep folded within soft shadow, squares and elongated triangles of sweet light smoothing the planes of floor and wall.

She walked to the center of the living room and listened more. If Alex was here, he was asleep.

She looked to the left down the hallway, which split on one side toward his kitchen and the other side toward his bedroom. She walked toward his bedroom, pausing at the door, then softly lifted the latch and pulled it open, stepped inside, stood still.

Moonlight spread calm over his sleeping face, and over the face of the woman who slept next to him.

Carolan, her face softer in sleep, sleek hair tousled on the pillow. She lay on her side, facing the door, with Alex curled on his side against her back.

Jaguar stood very still, listening to the concord of breath under moonlight, feeling the twin pulse of two resting bodies, dreams spinning themselves out in hidden places.

Her mouth moved to form the name Alex, but she allowed no sound to emerge. She found that she had lifted her hand and it was reaching out, over Carolan, toward him, feeling for his dreams and a way into them so that she could wake him gently, quietly, without waking his partner. He turned his head, drew a hand across the pillow toward Carolan's hair. Jaguar felt his dreams, slow and soft, thoughts on a warm breeze tossing here and there. He mumbled something, words indistinguishable. Then he said a name.

"Jaguar," he sighed out.

She pulled her hand down to her side and backed out of the door quickly, shutting it behind her, slipping like moonlight down the hall and out of the building.

Outside, she stood in shadow, at the side of the building, and breathed, something she wasn't sure she'd done all the way down the elevator. She took a moment to gather her emotions in, ask herself a pertinent question.

What do you name this feeling?

She let it run through her body, find a place to rest within her. It had too many moving parts, included too many complicated structures of thought and habit. To untangle it all would take too long, and she didn't have the energy for it right now.

Name it sorrow, she told herself, and get back to work.

She shook it off and walked back to the hospital to get her car and go back to the VR.

●   ●   ●

Alex, who felt Jaguar's presence as normal and right, was awoken abruptly by a sudden sense of her absence.

He started, opened his eyes to see Carolan's eyes staring back at him.

"Jaguar," he said, with feeling.

Carolan blinked. "What?" she said. "*What* did you call me?"

Alex bit the inside of his lip.

Suddenly it promised to be a very long and unrestful night.

Jaguar drove back to the Animal Sanctuary, where voice and print scan allowed her to pass through the first gate after hours. It would take voice, card, and print scan to get her through to the breeding complex.

She walked the path between sanctuary and breeding complex, which grew smaller and less manicured as she traversed the half mile between. She stopped and looked up for the moon, and couldn't find it. Cloud cover had moved in since she had left Alex's, or else the moon was setting. It was getting dark. She was tired, and would be glad to get to sleep.

She stopped at the gate and pressed her finger at the code bar, then pulled her card out of her back pocket, inserted it into the slit.

"*Panthera onca*," she said into the voice receptor, and heard the click of locks releasing. As she lifted her head and looked down toward the house where she stayed with Marie to see if any lights were still on, she heard the sound of movement behind her.

Behind her.

She twisted around and saw someone disappearing into the bushes. A man. Philo? No time to ask that. She charged in after him, leaping a small shrub, feet pounding the earth.

Where?

Somewhere straight ahead. She maneuvered through tree and shrub, catching her shirt on branches, ripping it, just keep moving ahead. Just keep moving ahead.

When she'd gone as deep into the side woods as she could without losing vision, she looked around, listened. Which way? How far in was she?

First she heard nothing.

Then the sound of breath, fast and shallow, behind her.

As she flicked out the knife at her wrist and whirled on him, all she saw was a piece of wood winging out from the side. All she felt was the impact of heavy wood against her cheek. And as she fell all she heard was the sound of a shotgun breaking through the quiet of the night.

She didn't know how long she was stunned, but she was aware that time had passed, and events had shifted around her. As she lay on the ground she saw, next to her face, a pair of old leather work boots, heavy and stained with a variety of dung.

"Marie?" she asked them.

The shotgun barrel was visible now, and then a hand, and then Marie squatting beside her.

She peered at Jaguar's face. "You're gonna have quite a shiner. You want a medic?"

Jaguar groaned, pushed herself to sitting, held her head in her hand. This certainly wouldn't help her headaches any. "No. I'm okay. Did you get him?"

"I missed. He headed into the woods. I called security. They'll get him before morning."

"Okay," she said, and stood up. Marie put an arm out when she wobbled, and Jaguar used it, leaning heavily. "I should go look with them."

"You should go get an ice pack," Marie said, walking her through the undergrowth and the trees. Maybe, Jaguar thought on the third stumble, Marie was right. Call it a night. Let security deal with it.

"You want me to call Alex?" Marie asked.

"No," Jaguar snapped.

"Ouch," Marie said. "*I* didn't hit you. Don't bite *my* head off."

"Sorry. Only—I don't want you to call him. I'll call him

in the morning and let him know. There's nothing he can do right now, anyway. Security'll handle it.''

They approached the gate, and Jaguar stopped.

"Marie," she said, "did you leave that open?"

"The courtesy of closing doors wasn't on my mind," she admitted.

Jaguar turned the swollen side of her face toward the old woman. "Are you sure he headed out through the woods?"

Marie frowned. "I see what you mean."

She shook her head. "Notify VR security, just in case. I can't see how he'd get in the building, but this guy seems to be born lucky as well as vile.''

Which was as astute an observation as she'd ever made, because at that moment Proteus stood behind a tree near the laser fencing, watching people come and go through it.

Guards, he thought. Guards everywhere. Dammit. He wanted to kill that woman, and he would have, if that fucking old lady with the shotgun hadn't shown up. Bad luck. He didn't like that. It made him nervous.

Now killing Sardis was a necessary task. He wouldn't risk a second attempt on her teacher, and he didn't dare leave her in that teacher's hands. He couldn't risk her giving the game away when he was so close to his goal. He had to do it. He was exhausted, and still had a delicate job to finish. Bad luck. He didn't like it.

He rubbed a hand to his face and felt for the aspect of it. The same he'd had in the zoo, he thought. Maybe he needed a new one. He wished he could trans-sex his aspects. He'd turn his face into Dr. Addams's and breeze through the gates to Sardis. He wished he'd had a chance to finish her off. He suspected she would die well, and he was sorry to miss it. And all his wishes meant nothing, except bad luck.

Or, maybe not. Maybe killing Dr. Addams wouldn't have been enough. Maybe he still would find it necessary to kill Sardis. Funny, how often it became necessary for him to kill women like her. To kill them, and cut off their fingers.

At least one finger. In fact, sometimes he did that without being aware of doing so. He'd wake up and find fingers in his pockets. Or just a fingertip, as he did after killing that woman in the park, though he had no memory of cutting it off.

In fact, he'd told himself specifically not to do that, and not to come inside her. Lopped-off fingers was Proteus's signature, and although nobody knew his real name or face, he didn't want to establish DNA tracks. He didn't think it would matter if they knew who he was, except that often knowing who someone was told you enough about how they'd move that you could get in ahead and stop them.

And he'd come too far to be stopped. Planned this for too many years, spent too many years sleeping with Sardis—an unpleasantness he'd rather forget—to fail now.

No. There wasn't any such thing as bad luck. There was only bad planning, and he hadn't fallen prey to that sin yet. He was focused, but flexible. Always had a backup plan in his pocket, and this was no exception.

He walked carefully and quietly down the row of trees, out of the line of immediate action. He'd find a place to be still in, a place that was quiet and dark. He'd get some rest and think through his moves. Sooner or later a lone guard would pass him, and then he could get a uniform.

Once he got a uniform, he knew he'd be able to pass the next fence.

If he believed in God, it would be very clear to him that God was on his side.

# 11

THERE WOULD BE NO READING FOR RACHEL TODAY.
She was in and out of consciousness, more and more of her brain falling into a sleep that the medics couldn't understand or stop. Her condition was deteriorating, they said. Nothing they could do that they weren't doing. It was just all falling apart. Deteriorating.

Alex called her family and told them. She's deteriorating. They didn't understand. Did that mean she was dying?

No, he said. Just getting worse. Then he realized how stupid that sounded. Not that it mattered, since her father wouldn't see her, and wouldn't let her mother come to the telecom. It was a sin for a woman to be viewed that way. If Rachel died, they'd allow for a Jewish funeral, but that was all.

"Look," Alex said grimly, "Rachel's one of the most morally upright people I've ever met, of any religion. If you care, you raised a wonderful daughter. And she loves you. I suggest you come and see her while you still can."

He was going to cut off the communication, call it hopeless, when a hand pushed Mr. Shofet aside, and a woman appeared. Same eyes as Rachel.

"I'm her mother," she said quietly. "I'll come and see her. Tell me how."

At least some of her family was on the way. It was the

best he could do. That and sit by her and hold her hand. It gave him plenty of time to think.

Mostly he found he was thinking about Jaguar.

He had to tell her about Rachel. He supposed he'd use the damn term, too—deteriorating. He didn't want to tell her that.

And he had to find out what she wanted last night, why she appeared at his bedside and disappeared so quickly. It wasn't a dream, he was convinced. Her presence was too unmistakable. Her absence too stark and real. Which meant that she'd seen his sleeping partner, and he didn't really want to hear what she had to say about it. Though why she should say anything was beyond him. She slept where she pleased, with prisoner or partner, and God help him if he criticized.

So why did he feel vaguely guilty, as if he'd been unfaithful?

Stupid. That was stupid.

And it was even more stupid to put off talking to her based on this stupidity. He'd call her, apprise her of Rachel's condition, see how she was doing with Sardis. Then maybe he'd call Carolan and invite her to lunch. She deserved a little extra attention.

She was, naturally, upset at being called another woman's name. Naturally. But she'd taken his explanation well. It was just his concern about the case Jaguar was on. That made sense. She'd gone back to an easy laughter and fallen asleep with a smile, her only comment that his real wife was his work on the Planetoid, and maybe she could seduce him away from that union.

Not something he wanted to hear, but at least it gave them both the chance to back out of a tricky situation with courtesy. Still, he knew the courtesy was precarious at best. If he gave her a definite no to her job offer, it might dissolve into acrimony.

Beyond that, he had a pile of paperwork, and he wanted to get a lot further ahead with the check on Philo. He'd done a complete scan of laboratories, and found no match for his DNA file, or his prints or history. Of course, if he'd worked in a lab before the Serials, those records might have been destroyed. But the total absence of information was suspicious.

He had in his mind to see if he had results from another computer check. Something he meant to do that his memory had waylaid because his workforce was so stretched, because he was so busy with Carolan, because his life seemed to be one continous distraction. He tapped a finger against his teeth, and this cued his memory. The fingertip. He wanted to see if the computer turned anything up yet. That was it. A long shot, maybe, but worth it. He'd attend to that first, as soon as he got in to work.

No doubt about it. Between Jaguar, Carolan, and his job, he had a day to deal with. He stroked Rachel's hand, whispered a good-bye, and left, the possibility of emotional dissonance rumbling all around him.

As he opened the door to his office and took a step inside, he heard a voice calling his name down the hall. He stuck his head outside and saw Brad Deragon walking swiftly toward him.

"What?" he asked gruffly.

"Thought you should know," Brad said. "There was trouble at the breeding complex last night. An intruder. There's this, and the rest's on your computer."

Brad handed him the message and disappeared down the hall.

Great way to start off, Alex thought. He took it to his desk and sat down, opening his computer. As the report scrolled onto the screen his telecom buzzed and he reached for it.

"Alex," Carolan purred. She was excited about more than the prospect of seeing his face.

"Something?"

"We got a big fish on the line. A sect houseleader and his family. Want to take a quick trip to the home planet?"

He paused on the edge of a yes, then glanced at his computer. So much to do here, how could he leave?

He scanned the report quickly. An intruder. Sometime
around midnight. The area was secure, extra guards at the
VR. No sign of security breach at the VR. No big deal.

"Are you with me?" Carolan asked.

He clicked his computer off. "With you," he said.
"When do we leave?"

"Now. The Bureau's shuttle's warmed up and waiting.
Get your gear and meet me at the station."

When Proteus woke up, it was to the sound of singing birds,
the sight of sharp sunlight in his eyes, and the feel of a
boot kicking at his backside. He'd slept longer than he
meant to, but he needed it.

"Get up," a rough voice said.

He blinked up from his spot under the tree and saw a
burly security guard pointing a weapon at him.

He pushed himself up on his elbow, slipped, and was
prone again.

"Get up, dammit," the guard repeated.

He pushed with both hands this time, made it to sitting,
but when he tried to stand, his legs went shaky and his feet
couldn't find the ground. He slid back down.

"Christ," the guard complained, and slung his weapon
over his shoulder, put a hand down to pull him up. "Weak
as chicken shit," he commented.

Proteus grabbed the hand, and jerked hard. The guard
landed facedown, and Proteus leaped to his feet and kicked
him in the face hard, once, twice, three times, and again
and again and again until he couldn't tell where the face
was at all, just something to kick at and keep kicking.

The guard lay still.

He stood over him, nudged at him with his foot, then
squatted down and took his weapons, cards, and belt sensor.

He had everything he needed now. He knelt down and
began undressing the guard. The rest should be easy.

The next time Jaguar saw Rider, he was sitting cross-legged
under the willow tree near the stream. A stick of incense

burned in front of him and he ommed conspicuously. As she walked toward him he blinked at her, then giggled.

"What?" she asked.

"Nice shiner," he commented, hopping to his feet and putting his face in hers. He pulled back, and a similar patch of blue appeared on his own cheekbone. He brought a hand up to touch it. "Not much of a fashion statement, though. Clashes with the dress. Hurt anywhere else?" he asked.

"No," she said flatly.

"Liar," he said, and then a grin took shape on his face. "Your night was not half as pleasant as Carolan's, though just as busy."

"I don't know what you're talking about," she lied.

"Oh, yes you do," he said. "But you didn't catch them actually *at* it, did you? You walked in on that postcoital snuggle, right? I can't quite tell, given the state of your emotions."

"My emotions are not in any state."

"They are in many states. There's jealousy pricking your pride, which is duking it out with denial, which is dancing on your ego, all topped off with a lot of confusion as to why you feel any of that. I ought to know, since I have to feel it, too."

"Rider," she said, "I'm not playing this game today."

"Goody," he replied. "Then let's play this one instead." He held up a hand, shifted to become an older and more contorted version of Sardis, and declaimed theatrically, "Woe, woe, woe to those still on the earth, for the plagues of the seven angels have begun."

He took a small bow and became himself again.

"Go on," she said to him. "I know there's more."

"You sure do know it. Otherwise, I wouldn't. Or is it the other way around? Well, no time to figure that out. Ticktock went the clock. Ticktock, Jaguar. Ticktock."

He circled her, went to the back of a willow tree, and leaned against it, poking his head around the side and winking at her.

If this is me, she thought, then maybe I should forget

about Sardis and just shoot myself. "You keep insinuating that I'm running out of time. Is that about Rachel?"

He pressed his thumb against an invisible buzzer. "Wrong. Next contestant."

"Then is it about Sardis? The Apocalypse."

He produced a cigar from the air and handed it to her. "Got it in one."

She tossed it aside. "Thanks. I don't holosmoke. But if you're a projection—"

"Retrojection," he corrected.

"Retrojection of my psyche, how do I know that isn't just one of my subconscious fears, a holdover from my experience in the Serials."

"Or," he suggested, "perhaps your anger at Sardis makes you *want* to see her as that kind of monster. Or even worse, maybe you don't care if all her people blow themselves up, since they're the ones who hurt Rachel. Maybe that's *your* fantasy."

"Exactly. And how do I know which answer is right?"

"Tricky," he agreed, coming out from behind the tree. "This all must distress you terribly."

"Thank you for helping me feel my feelings. So what do I do?"

"To find the truth," he said ponderously, "you must live in the truth. And to live in the truth, you must make room for the truth to live."

"I don't do Zen," she replied acidly.

"My dear," he commented, swinging around to her and tweaking her chin, "what choice do you have? Sometimes Zen does you."

She worked herself up to a slight boil, ready to hiss and spit steam at him, then, suddenly, turned the fire off. There wasn't any point.

"Rider, can't you just *tell* me what it is?"

Rider's ephemeral hand rested on her shoulder. "I already have. Repeatedly, directly, clearly as any young demon can. You just don't want to believe me."

"But you haven't told me anything I don't know already."

"Ye-es. Your point is . . . ?" He waved a hand around, inviting her to roll out an answer, but she didn't. "There," he said. "Sheer contrariness on your part."

"I'm not being contrary," she insisted, and ignored Rider's deep groan. "Okay. Okay. I know this about Sardis. She has a messianic complex, caused by whatever it is that makes someone want to be God."

His mouth turned up in a wry smile. "You ought to know that. Absolute power and all."

"Absolute power's an absolute pain in the ass. I like to be in charge of my own life. Not everyone else's."

"Except when you want to protect them. Like you do with Rachel, whose price is above rubies and who shall find a woman like her et cetera because she's so real. You're a great lover of that item called the truth, that's for sure, and relentless in pursuing it, even when you have to beat it out of your own hide. Right now, of course, you'd like to beat it out of Sardis."

"Would that work?"

Rider laughed. "Can you beat your way through a wall of words? Beat your fists against an illusion?"

Jaguar considered this. Sardis manufactured her God to suit some need Jaguar didn't understand, then built great walls of words against anything that reminded her of the lies she told herself. It was typical of fanaticism. Typical of those who had more fear of their God than love. She would insist that others believe with her, too, because deep down she knew it was a lie. But beating against that would only put Jaguar outside of Sardis's system, a faithless enemy, a devil in the battle for heaven and earth. It would go nowhere fast.

What Jaguar really needed was a way to find out why Sardis needed the illusion so desperately. What purpose it served.

"Maybe she's trying to save someone, too. In her own way, that is." He winked at her, tilted his head coyly, and pointed up the hill, toward the formal garden. "She's up there," he said.

And with that, he dissolved.

Last night, she remembered, he had appeared in her dreams, and he was laughing at her.

"This is ridiculous," she said to herself through clenched teeth, taking a kick at the holotree.

She walked hard toward the formal garden, and just outside the maze she found her prisoner, deep in conversation with an angel, two peacocks nearby calling out their strident song. Sardis spoke with animation in her voice and face, and the angels nodded solemnly at her. Jaguar approached, and they stopped talking. Sardis drew herself up tall and pointed at Jaguar.

"Jezebel," she said sternly, "who calls herself a prophetess but teaches and misleads my slaves."

So. She was still angry.

"Get real," Jaguar replied. She reached out a hand and placed it firmly on one of the angel's faces.

Something. Electric and stinging. It ran through her hand, up her arm, and seemed to scamper directly along the neural pathway to her brain. It hurt. Electric and unpleasant. Then—a man with glasses. A computer. Wires buzzing.

Dammit. Just a designer.

She pulled her hand back and rubbed it against her leg as the angel fluttered, dissolved, and was gone.

"Did I do that?" she muttered. Her hand tingled uncomfortably. Maybe the computer nerds were right and she was blowing this place all to hell, so to speak. Right now that seemed like the most pleasant thought she'd had in a long time. She turned back to Sardis, who gaped at her, eyes wide, pupils dilated.

Fear, Jaguar thought. The angel dissolving frightened her. Her fanaticism was based on maintaining illusions to protect her from a reality she couldn't face. Not possession. Not madness. Plain, ordinary denial. And while Jaguar couldn't see any way of getting her off the VR site yet, suddenly she felt the pleasant itch of another possibility moving under her skin. But first she had to win back Sardis's trust.

She moved closer, put an arm on Sardis's shoulder. "I've frightened you," she said placatingly. "What you saw—the demon attacking me with lust—that frightened you, too. But weren't you expecting the battle in heaven to be as difficult as the battle on earth?"

Sardis's lips moved, repeating the question to herself. She shook her head. Then her eyes became pensive and liquid.

"Is that what this is? I wouldn't be afraid, if I knew that."

Go slow, Jaguar reminded herself. Don't rush in. What Sardis carried in her could explode if she punched a hole in it. She'd have to rein it in, let this develop. Pray to any god she could find that Rider didn't show up and blast her work to bits.

"But you don't know, do you?" Jaguar said, keeping her breath even, keeping her eyes with Sardis. "There's something very deep inside you that makes you afraid."

Sardis gazed at a distant point over Jaguar's shoulder and spoke with a quiet fervor, her voice deep and low. "I *am* afraid. Here, where all is possible. Where the lamb can receive all blessings, it could still fall apart."

"How would that happen?" Jaguar asked.

Sardis sighed. "If the people won't follow the lamb to the end of days, washing their robes white in the blood. If they won't do what they promised because I'm no longer a shepherd among them. Then everything I've done has been in vain."

Jaguar could feel the stirring of Sardis's muscles under her hand. Skin rippling in fear, fear building to terror. She took a chance and spoke into the surface of her mind.

*Hush, Sardis. Breathe. Breathe with me.*

Sardis sucked in air, let it escape her with a hissing sound.

Better. Back to work. Stay subvocal.

*Sardis, what have the people promised to do?*

Sardis shook her head mournfully and Jaguar felt waves
of grief running through the woman. She couldn't keep her
eyes focused on Jaguar. There was too much pain, and its
momentum pushed back into her illusions. She needed
some reassurance. Something reassuring.

*Philo will be true, Sardis. Tell me what Philo promised.*

She said nothing, but the wave of grief dissipated, and
Jaguar felt images move through her. She sat with Philo in
a large kitchen, bent over a small black box. He pointed to
a part of it, and she nodded gravely. Then, unexpectedly,
Sardis unclothed, holding her breasts to him, and he bent
a face to them. It was Philo, but not Philo. Like Rider
showed her. Philo, but not his face.

"Philo?" she asked out loud, and Sardis started, and
smiled at her as if she'd just noticed her presence.

"They're prepared," she said, brightening visibly. "And
they will act. The blood of the lamb will wash us all clean.
If you want everything, you have to be willing to give
everything up. Who would have life must relinquish life.
As I did."

She patted Jaguar on the cheek and drifted back, away
from her. Gone, Jaguar thought. What should she do? Push.
Don't push. Move forward. Hang back. Her instincts had
consistently failed in this case. But she was onto something
here.

"And the others?" she asked, moving with her, staying
close to her face, her eyes. "They have to give up their
lives?"

"More than their lives."

"More? What's more than your life, Sardis?"

"The name will be revealed when the hour is fulfilled,"
she intoned.

"What hour, Sardis? What name?"

She raised glittering eyes, shifting them back and forth
as if checking for eavesdroppers. She brought her face close
to Jaguar's. "That would be telling," she said, and she
giggled.

The peacocks cried out their piercing song, and Sardis,

laughing, threw her arms out wide, standing like Christ cru-
cified for all to witness. Jaguar brought her hands up and
pressed the palms against her temples, blocking out the peacocks and the laughter.

When she looked up, Sardis was gone.

Her head throbbed and the world around her shimmered
with virtuality.

## home planet—Los Angeles

The house looked quiet. White shingles and black shut-
ters around the windows. Petunias in the window box. No
dog barking. No sign of movement or life inside.

Carolan and Alex waited inside the mobile unit, peering
at it through the telescopic lens.

"Anything?" Alex asked.

"Not a sign. Are you sure there's someone in there?"
Carolan asked the mobile unit driver.

"We saw them enter at seven-fifteen this A.M., and nobody's come out, so I guess they're still in there, unless
they got a tunnel, which we ain't equipped to account for,"
the Sassy sergeant said. "Mind you, I would've had a team
go in soon as I saw 'em, but we had orders specifically to
wait."

He cast a disapproving glance at Carolan.

"Well, we won't find out by sitting here." Alex stood
and reached for a vest. "Coming?"

"But—you're going in?" Carolan asked. "Why?"

"Because," Alex said, "that's what I'm here for."

She laughed. "You came to help supervise."

"No. I came to see what's in there." He slipped the vest
on and realized he was sweating. It was hot in L.A.

"Alex, let the Sassies go in. You don't have to."

"I want to see for myself," he said with finality. "Do
you want to join me, or not?"

She chewed on her upper lip, bent her eyebrows down.
"What's your plan?"

"I'll ring the bell and, when someone answers, stick my

foot in the door. If no one answers, I'll see if it's open. If it is, I'll walk in. If it's not, I'll get a Sassy to convince it.''

She smiled, shook her head. "Sorry. I don't usually take on this kind of duty, so I'm not sure of the routine."

"I know," he said. "And you don't have to come with me. But I want to see for myself what's in there, or who."

He turned to the sergeant. "You got enough backup?" he asked.

"Two guys in the next yard. Another van around the street at the back. That's enough."

"Then let's go." He put a hand out to Carolan. She let her shoulders lift and fall, then stood, put on a vest, and followed them up the short walk to the front door. He stopped them at the door so he could listen. He didn't have the gift of clear seeing, as Jaguar did, and he wished for that now. All he saw was a door. All he heard was nothing.

He pressed the doorbell. No response.

He knocked on the door, waited. No response.

He turned to Carolan and indicated the door latch, motioned that she should stand back, just in case they were playing any more wiring games. He pressed his ear against the door to listen for any unusual hum or buzz that would indicate wiring, and heard none. Slowly, gently, he lifted the latch, and without any protest, it clicked, and the door opened.

"Okay," he said softly. "Okay." He gave the sergeant a nod and went inside.

The house was perfectly empty.

No furniture. No cartons. No curtains on the windows. No sign of anyone ever having lived here. The sergeant assumed the proper stance, weapon out, and went through the rooms, but Alex knew he'd find not a living soul. He could feel the absence of life all around.

"Dammit," he muttered to himself, "we missed them."

He looked to his right and left, getting an idea of the layout before he walked through. Behind him he heard Carolan, who lingered just inside the doorstep.

"Anything, Alex?" she called.

"Chicken's flown the coop," he said. The sergeant came clattering down the stairs, and confirmed that.

"I'll check the yard," he said.

"Okay," Alex replied. "I'll walk through and see if I can find anything helpful."

"Don't forget the basement," he said. "Access through the kitchen."

Alex headed for there, noting the absence of meals eaten recently. How long had they been gone? Check the obvious first. Was there food in the cupboards, the refrigerator, which was still turned on and humming. He walked to it, put his hand on the door to open it, then paused. Not smart. Bombs were too easily rigged to go off at door openings.

He checked the front panel and saw that it had a window function. He pressed the box that dropped away the insulation sheath, making the insides visible. There was nothing on the shelves, except a cake box.

A white cake box, with a red light on the top. He stared at it. Saw the timing mechanism. Saw the wires. Saw the time.

"Jesus," he said, and his long legs took him out of the house without pause.

"Carolan, get away from the door," he yelled as he ran for it. He had no intention of slowing down, even when he saw her still standing there, gawking. He just threw his arms out and took her along, tumbling the sergeant with them down onto the ground, rolling toward the curb, the van, as an explosion rocked the property behind them.

The house went up in flames after the explosion, and it was many hours before the cleanup revealed the charred bodies of two adults and three children, tucked away neatly in the basement in the white linen funeral robes of the Revelation sect. The fire would have killed them, but they were already dead from cyanide.

Carolan's immediate superior, Karl Madden, met them at the site shortly after the firefighters and medics arrived.

He went first to Carolan, put a hand on her shoulder, and surveyed her.

"You okay?" he asked.

"Cuts and abrasions," she answered. "No major injuries."

He released her, and walked toward the smoldering rubble, where Alex and a group of others stood, considering what they thought might be the remnants of a timing device found in the basement with the dead family.

"Looks like it," the bomb squad captain noted. She turned to a younger woman at her left. "See anything special?"

"Partek fusion wires. Nothing melts them. They usually indicate a preset, but that's pretty complex. Who knew how to use that?"

"Someone did," Alex said. He touched the frayed end of a red wire cover. "And they've known it for a long time. People use Partek because you can set it up to a month ahead and walk away. It's got a no-escape clause."

"No way of telling if they got it right, though. Not with this wreck. Those people want you?" the captain asked, tilting her head toward Carolan and Karl, who walked toward the group.

"Afraid so," Alex said, standing and straightening himself. He walked out to meet them, and Carolan introduced her to Karl.

"Carolan's said good things about the work you're doing up there. We'd like you to spend a few more days with us if you can, tracking down the others. We could use your help."

The Feds, admitting they didn't know everything. Now, that was a wonder.

"I'm beginning to be concerned," Carolan joined in. "If sect members intend to blow themselves up around the country, innocent people could get hurt."

"I think they already have," Alex commented, nodding toward the stretcher that had the children on it.

Carolan shifted uncomfortably. "Will you help?"

"What about Sardis?"

"Let her be," Madden said. "I hear your teacher's having a hard time with her, and we aren't likely to learn anything valuable soon. We need to go through the files and track these people down. Once we do—"

"Once you do, you may end up with another scene like Vermont," Alex cut in.

"If you have any other ideas, we're willing to entertain them," Carolan said.

"I do. I have an idea that I should get back to the Planetoid."

"What for?"

Now, there was a good question. What for? A sense of urgency impelled him to grab the small and very swift shuttlecraft that had gotten him here and fly it back himself. He needed to get back. Why? He couldn't do anything about Sardis. Couldn't do anything there. He'd be much more useful here. But the nagging wouldn't quit. Something to do with a shadowed form, crouched on a cliff, ready to leap. Something to do with someone needing a hand. Hands pulling and reaching.

"Jaguar may need me," he said.

Carolan's lips tightened into a thin line, and Alex heard the intake of breath that indicated speech withheld. He thought he knew what she'd say, if she felt free to speak.

"There's no shuttle," she said, voice as tight and compressed as her lips.

Interesting. The switch between seduction and entrapment came very fast with this group.

"There's a shuttle," he said. "We rode it here, and we'll ride it back. It's fast, and it's available. Now."

Carolan dug at the earth with her toe. "I don't know if Karl'll let it go back right away. He may need it for something."

"Why don't we ask him?" Alex said, smiling at that man who stood next to him.

Karl looked both uncomfortable and displeased. He frowned at Carolan and shook his head.

"If Supervisor Dzarny needs to get back, he can take the shuttle. In fact, maybe both of you should go and see if you can get anything out of the cult members you have there. Anything that sounds like it might relate to this incident."

Alex understood that he was asking Carolan to stick close to him. Keep it going with him, nice and easy. Don't push him too hard, but stay with him.

Karl slapped Alex on the back, signaling that they were two men who understood each other, and weren't these women capricious? Alex was suddenly sorry for Carolan, having to work in that environment.

"You two figure out your game plan," Madden said. "I'll go talk to the bomb squad."

He strolled away toward the house. Alex looked at Carolan, who was plainly distressed. "If you're coming with me, let's go. I'm ready now."

"No. Wait. Alex, this is stupid. Must we go back right away? There's so much to do here."

"I look after my people," Alex said. "You said it was an admirable trait."

"Not when there's all these lives at stake, Alex," she said. "You could do more good here than you could chasing after a fantasy of—"

She closed her mouth again.

"A fantasy of what, Carolan?"

"Of a madwoman. Two madwomen, if you count Sardis."

So that was how she read it. And it was entirely possible that she was right. It might be his fantasy that he could do anything to help Jaguar. His fantasy that somehow she was on the right track, and she would need him. It was possible he just liked to see it that way. Or, the Feds might be nurturing the fantasy that they could straighten this all out through the normal procedural routes. That might be their wishful thinking, as well as a way of keeping him around.

And right now nothing would tell him the truth about that. He wondered if he could still pray to those Mohawk spirits. Please keep me safe from the things that glitter along the side of the road. Please teach me how to recognize them when I see them. And would they tell him what he already knew? That the truth is something you feel at the center of your being, where only the sacred can speak out loud. That he did know, if only he trusted himself to listen beyond words.

"I think," he said, "I'll have to prefer my fantasy to yours right now."

She furrowed her brow, put a hand on his arm. "Wait," she said, taking a step closer to him and searching his face as if the answer was written there. "I don't understand. You're not her lover, are you? You said—"

"We're not lovers," he said decisively.

"But you'd like to be her lover?"

"I'd sooner take her namesake to bed, to be honest. It's not about that, Carolan."

"Then, what?"

Other people had made suggestions about him and Jaguar. In fact, he'd heard it often enough to wonder if there wasn't some truth in it. But this urgency to return wasn't about that. It was different, and difficult to explain because it came from the Adept space, which told him only that he needed to get back. Fast.

He peered skyward through the knives of light that slanted down through the trees. "Carolan," he said, "I wish I knew."


Proteus crossed the security line without incident and walked toward the large building, where he could see people going in and out. It was early. A man and a woman were emptying recycle bins outside a door, and he nodded at them as he passed.

"Hey," she said. "Nice day, huh? At last."

He blinked around at the sun. There was warmth in the air. They were right. He smiled, waved, moved on. Then he had an idea.

He turned back to them. "I'm looking for Sardis," he said. He patted his weapon.

"Security assignment?"

He nodded.

"Go through there," the woman said. "Someone inside'll point you right."

"Thanks," he said, and headed for the door she pointed to.

Once he was through, he saw a long hallway with doors on either side. He walked down it, going slowly. No hurry. None at all. He'd assumed the aspect of the guard he killed, and had all his identification in his pocket. He'd be fine from here on in.

Most of the doors had glass windows and led to offices. Then, down at the end, marked with a sign, a door with no window.

SITE ENTRANCE QUAD 4—APO

Authorized Personnel Only. That, he thought, would be him.

He put his hand on the door, pushed the bar lock, and nothing happened.

He stood contemplating it. Probably he had the right key card on his belt, but he didn't want to look stupid fumbling for it. Best to try to get a visual match first. As he examined the lock the door opened and a woman in a nun's habit came through, tugging at her long black robes, pulling them off.

"Damn, this stuff is hot. Can you believe they used to make women *wear* these?" The robe came off over her head, revealing a uniform similar to his. "Next shift?" she asked.

He nodded.

"Only handheld weapons. You knew that, right?"

He nodded again, and patted the pocket that contained the weapon he'd taken from the guard.

"Okay," she said. "They'll check you on the other side.

It's a warm day. Pick a better costume than I did.''

And with no further fuss, no further words, he went through the door, and found himself on the other side of heaven.

# 12

*day ten*

JAGUAR HAD A MES-
sage from Alex that read, simply, *call me*.

She punched in his home number and he appeared on
the viewscreen almost immediately, as if he'd been waiting
for her call.

Without preamble, he said, "I just got back from the
home planet. A sect houseleader killed himself and his family."

She pushed herself away from Marie's desk and swiveled
her chair, giving him her profile. He could see her jaw
working hard, her hands resting uneasily on the arms of the
chair.

"Shit," she said. "How?"

"Partek bombs, with a no-escape function." She would
know what that meant. A time line.

She shielded her eye with her hand, as if covering it for
private thought. "What do the Feds say?" she asked.

"They're looking for houseleaders, but not fast enough.
I want to know if Sardis has a plan."

"I saw something," Jaguar said tentatively. "Bombs.
People sitting around a table making a bomb."

"You made contact with her? What else?"

"Nothing. Just that. I need to move her further along

first. She's all barriers, Alex. All her energy's inverted. If I go too fast, I'll lose her.''

''Are you sure?''

''Sure? I can't tell what's real with myself, much less with her, so what I can tell you about her is beyond me. Dammit,'' she added even more cryptically, ''I'm starting to sound like him.''

Alex regarded her patiently.

''Start again,'' he suggested, ''and say something different.''

''It's just the holodemon. Rider. He talks that way. He says his form lets him know things I can't know except through him. He keeps hinting that we're running out of time.''

''Do you believe him?''

How to tell the truth in the land of illusion? ''For all I know, the Feds put him in to test my reactions.''

Alex considered. It was a possibility, he supposed. ''Tell me this,'' he said. ''Do you like him?''

She turned her face farther away from the screen. ''Funny you should ask that. He drives me crazy, but not the same way Sardis does. She makes me feel like I'm chewing on aluminum foil. Rider—I guess I do like him.''

Nothing wrong with her ego, at any rate. She even liked the parts of herself that drove her crazy. ''Then it's not the Feds, Jaguar. You wouldn't like anything they put in. Get what you can from him. If Sardis has a plan, you have to move faster.''

She nodded, ducked her head down. ''Is that all?''

He stared at her profile. Something funny here. She wasn't arguing for a program change. And she looked—actually, he didn't know how she looked, because he hadn't seen her whole face once since the conversation began.

''Jaguar,'' he said, ''look at me.''

She raised an eyebrow, but stayed in profile.

''Turn your head to the right. *My* right, Jaguar and don't fuck around.''

She swiveled around so that he saw her full face, the

welt on her cheek and eye. "It's a love bite, Alex."

"Someday," he said, "I'll explain to you about love bites, and how that is *not* one. What happened?"

"So he hit me," she said petulantly, "I was— distracted."

"*Who* hit you, Jaguar?"

"Philo. At least, I think it was Philo."

"What do you mean, you think it was Philo?"

"It smelled like him, but he changed his face. I think he's a Protean Changer. Didn't you get my report?"

The report Brad gave him, that he never finished reading. "When did it happen?"

"Two nights ago, pretty late. I was on my way back in from seeing Rachel. And you can dispense with the lecture about leaving the site. Assume I've already heard you give it."

Poised on the brink of a few well-chosen words on that very subject, he stopped completely. Two nights ago. After visiting Rachel. After stopping at his apartment. She was distracted.

So was he.

"Where?" he asked.

"As you can see, just below the eye. Okay. On the path between the sanctuary and the breeding complex. Marie scared him off with her shotgun and notified security. Of course, if he found his way in, he'd never be spotted among the holofigures."

"They have tracking for human signals. I'll see that they use it."

"They're having a hard time with it. Something unintelligible about the increased wave range. Carolan says it causes dispersal."

"They—what?"

"Like I said. Nonlinearity and unpredictability of wave function changes. Actually, they weren't talking to me at the time. I was eavesdropping on some torrid technobabble between a designer and a Fed."

He knitted his brows. Made a fist and rested his chin in

it. These words joined with his earlier conversations about holes in the CNW, and suddenly fell into an ugly shape. "Shit," he muttered. "She didn't. She wouldn't."

Jaguar paused and let him get through his thoughts for a moment before she spoke. "Wouldn't what, Alex?"

"What? Oh. Never mind. Stupid shit. I'll take care of it."

*Are you sure?* her eyes asked. *Sure that it's nothing. Sure you'll take care of it.*

He saw her eyes asking, met her gaze, and held it. *Sure, Jaguar. Absolutely.*

She hunched forward and rested an elbow on her desk, full face in the viewscreen now. "Alex, did you ever find out who Philo used to be? If he has the capacity for Protean Change, we could be in trouble."

Alex chewed on this a minute. Protean Change was the psi capacity to take on different appearances. That was familiar. It went along, somehow, with the other detail he knew about him.

"He cuts off fingers," Alex said.

"Proteus," Jaguar cut in.

They stared at each other.

"Sweet Jesus," Alex said at last. "You're right."

Protean Change. Cutting off fingers. Scientific knowledge.

Proteus.

Jaguar leaned back in her chair and made thoughtful circles on her temple with two fingers. Proteus was one of the most elusive and most talked-about mercenary terrorists of the day. There were more anecdotes about him than about Jesus or Padre Pio or Jesse James or even Jaguar. He'd left his mark on bodies, removing fingers, but he'd never been arrested for murder, for arson, for bombs, for anything. People said he'd ignored the warning about a contract out on his mother—revenge for his bombing of a day-care center where a NICA employee had been planted to guard a diplomat's bastard son. They said he was a real son of a bitch, and good at it, too.

"He's been out of the loop for years, hasn't he? Nothing heard, nothing seen. Everyone thought he was dead."

"For three years, about. Fingerless women turned up, but so did copycats. He's been gone."

"Hiding out with Sardis."

"But what the hell is he doing with Revelation?" Alex asked.

"I think the better question is what has he done *for* them?" Jaguar said. "And I think that's something we need to find out pretty quick."

"That's my job," he said. "You get back on the site and deal with Sardis."

When she signed off, he spent a minute drumming his fingers on his desk. Then he picked up the telecom and punched the code for the training site. He requested tech director Stan Wokowski, and soon enough his long thin face appeared onscreen.

"Hey, Stan," he said. "Not much time. Listen, how good are you at interpreting logs for the VR site? No, the designers haven't quit. I just have a question I don't want to ask them. Yeah. Like that. I want to know if you can interpret cause of interference from looking at a log that indicates interference."

He listened while Stan explained in less esoteric and jargony terms what Dave and Andy had already told him. Certain transmission waves break holes in the CNW. But he knew that.

"Tell me what kind of monitors would do that. Then tell me what kind of monitors they're using in the Federal Agency Bureau these days. Then write it all down, with pictures, and wire it over to my computer. My home computer. Code Lakeshore Sunset 777@plan.com."

Stan complied, leaving Alex with even more ugly shapes to consider.

He flipped the telecom off and drummed his fingers more. Then he picked it up again and, with only a twinge of regret, called Carolan at her hotel to leave a message

canceling the dinner date they had for that evening. He had
a lot of work to do, and he didn't want to be distracted.

"Don't lose him," Madden said into her telecom, leaning
forward so that she could see the small muscles in his neck
and jaw working away. "We're very close to completion
of this project at one hundred percent success rates."

"I understand, sir." And she did. All that he wasn't saying, as well as what he did. Wasn't it just like a woman to
let a little jealousy get in the way of a big career move, to
hang on too tight, not understand that men needed room to
move. Carolan thought sometimes that if it wasn't for the
sex, she'd give men up for good.

"I won't lose him," she reassured her boss. "He can-
celed a dinner date, but I'll need him at the site later, so
I'll call him for that."

He leaned away from the screen and relaxed a micro-
hertz. "Okay," he said. "Good. Do you have anything else
to report?"

She shrugged. "The VR anomalies are worsening.
Mostly unprogrammed behavior. No new figures have appeared, but they do seem to be losing some programmed
ones."

"Losing them? How do you lose a holofigure?"

"They're dissolving. It is odd," she mused, "since the
readings on that are very different from the behavioral
anomalies."

"Different how?"

"Well, actually they're like the reading on the unscheduled holodemon. They appear on the scantron as bulges in
the CNW. It makes them look a lot like the readout for a
testing run on psi capacities."

"She's doing it, then," Madden said, breathing in deep
satisfaction. "Very good."

"I believe you're right," Carolan admitted.

"Keep monitoring. We might need the evidence. And
the prisoner?"

"Still talking about the End of Days. After what happened on the home planet, Supervisor Dzarny is very sure that the sect members mean to kill themselves.''

''And if they do, what've we lost, Shannon? The crazed children of a murderous God. We could do without it anyway.''

Carolan felt a wince of guilt at her own silent agreement with this point of view. They were all crazed to follow Sardis. Killing themselves. Killing children. Better to get them off the planet for good. Make everything a little bit cleaner. A lot of people would die, but in the long run they'd all be better off. And if they wanted to sacrifice themselves to their vicious, bloodhungry God, who was she to stand in their way.

''Continue the program, Shannon,'' Madden said. ''I'm heading your way tomorrow with a Senator McDanial for a VR review. He chairs the oversight committee. By then, perhaps, we'll have something interesting to show him.''

Proteus moved from a nondescript corridor, through a nondescript door, and stepped into a white room where a woman who chewed gum loudly scanned him for unauthorized weapons or materials and took his ID card.

''Who d'ya wanna be today?'' she asked. She snapped her gum three times, and then subsided.

''Um—what's my choices again?'' he asked.

She recited, as if from a list of beers, ''Shopping father bishop angel sales clerk 'r maintenance man.''

''Father,'' he said. ''It's a dress-down kind of day.''

He was issued a shirt and tie, jeans and sneakers, showed to a room where he could change, and handed a wad of bills.

''Don't pay for nothing,'' the lady told him. ''It's all free. Just hand these out now and then.''

Then she pushed him toward the door.

When he opened it, he was standing in the middle of a Moroccan bazaar.

As he wandered through it his sense of confusion grew deeper. There were angels here, walking by as if they belonged. He reached out to touch one, and felt the ethereal movement of wings against his hands. The angel smiled at his gesture, and he smiled in return.

They'd put her in heaven. Of course.

A virtual reality heaven. Beautiful.

He walked the streets of the bazaar until it took him outside whatever this central marketplace was and toward a stream that wandered prettily through grassy banks, at the bottom of a gently sloping hill. He sniffed the air and caught the scent of flowers blooming somewhere nearby.

He thought of his mother, and had a brief fantasy of meeting her here. He'd just walk right up to her and say, Hello, Mother. Sorry about those fingers. Here, though. I've got some spares for you, now.

He felt in his pocket for the finger he'd gotten from the girl in the park, then remembered he'd left it in his other pants. By the dead guard. Damn. That was sloppy. He'd have to be more careful than that if he wanted to finish his job and get out of here in one piece. He sat down hard, at the edge of a stream bank, to go through his next set of moves.

"Feeling poorly?" a voice said behind him.

He started, turned, and looked up. Then he jumped to his feet and started backing away, pulling his weapon from his pocket. It was a demon. A devil. Horns and all.

"No need to get touchy," he said. "You must be Philo, right?"

He lifted the weapon and fired directly into the demon's head. Nothing happened. The demon didn't even take notice.

"Pardon me for mentioning, but you could use a bath," he said, pinching his nose. "My name's Rider, by the way. Are you looking for someone?"

Proteus twisted his head this way and that. "How—how do you know?"

Rider took a step closer, and he backed away. "Okay, don't get in a sweat. Look, I'm just a poor little devil trying to work my way out of hell. I understand you're looking

for a woman named Sardis, and I thought maybe you'd like
to try elsewhere. She hardly ever comes here.''

''You're—a devil? In heaven?''

''Well, really more of a tormented spirit, locked into a
form not of my choosing. I'm told that I can earn my place
in heaven if I help you out. Sardis and all. This.'' He gestured around, then leaned in and spoke confidentially. ''Really, you can believe me when I tell you, it's absolute and
unadulterated hell. The worst tormentor is that Addams
woman. And she went that way.'' He pointed back past the
Moroccan bazaar, toward the car lot.

''That way?''

''That's right. Past the bazaar and take a left. She and
Sardis are selling used God at the new car lot. Or is it the
other way around? There,'' he said, ''that did it. I've earned
my wings.''

The demon assumed the shape of a dove, and flew away.

Proteus lowered his weapon and narrowed his eyes.
''What the hell was that?'' he asked the empty sky. A holofigure, for sure, since it didn't die. Not a real devil. There
weren't any such things as real devils. But who programmed a holofigure to know so much?

That wasn't good. Not at all. And Addams was with
Sardis, which meant he couldn't appear as Philo. Not at
first. He'd have to reconsider his plan.

He let his thoughts walk through options until he came
upon one that seemed possible. Tricky, but possible. A face
he remembered from his initial interview. A name he remembered hearing in connection with Addams. *Dr. Addams
works for Dzarny, if you know what I mean.* Said sala-
ciously by the worker who helped him at the computer.

It would be an easy aspect. He could assume it rapidly,
take care of his business, and get the hell out of here.

Time wasn't as abundant as it had been, he realized.
Time and luck both seemed to be running out.

When Jaguar got onto the VR site, she tried to call Rider
to her, and got no response. She wasn't sure what cued him

to appear. If there was something she felt or said or did, she hadn't noticed herself feeling or saying or doing it. At any rate, apparently she couldn't consciously will his presence to her. She just had to wait until he showed up.

Instead, she went in search of Sardis, letting the idea that had begun to formulate at her last meeting with Sardis develop. Her strolling and thinking ultimately led her to the car lot, where she saw Sardis perched like an ornament on the hood of a Z20 Benz. She was preaching beatifically to the salesman and a holofamily. The nuclear family. Jaguar wished heartily that they'd achieve critical mass and blow away.

And as she thought this the mother hefted her fist and whomped the father with a left hook to the jaw.

"Hecate," Jaguar muttered, "now what?" She broke into a sprint and got there just in time to see a nun in full habit steering a straight course for the salesman.

"A goddamn lemon," the nun roared, tying her hand round his throat and shaking hard. "You sold me a goddamn lemon, you prick."

"In the latter days the merchants shall cry woe for Babylon," Sardis noted, smiling on them.

The holofamily was on the ground, mother under father and children beating hard on the father's back. The nun and the salesperson were locked in a standing struggle.

Jaguar stood within the fray and turned this way. That way. Two angels had gone watery, their voices garbled in sour song. A group of women ripped off their dresses and cavorted around the angels, fondling them in inappropriate places. Was this part of the program?

"I don't think so," Rider's voice said in response to her thoughts. "I think you'll find there's been interference in the program on a number of counts."

She felt pressure on her shoulders, as of hands, and he twisted around full circle. "It's all falling apart," she whispered. "Did I do this?"

"Not all of it," Rider said. "Someone else started the thing unraveling. You just jumped into the fray. Dissolved a few angels. A few illusions. But how embarrassing. Love calls. Or maybe it's just lust.'' He pointed over her shoulder and she turned.

She saw a man walking toward them. A man in jeans and sneakers. White shirt and tie.

"Alex?" she asked, and took a step toward him. Rider's hand touched her shoulder.

"Careful," he said ominously. "Careful of the things that glitter."

"Rider, shut the fuck up." She shook his hand off and walked toward Alex.

When he reached her, he grabbed her arm. Human touch. Human, and distressed.

"Sardis—is she with you?" he asked, urgency in his voice.

"On the car," Jaguar answered, pointing.

"Good. Let's go."

"Wait. What's going on? What're we doing?"

"No time," Alex said, but she stopped dead in her tracks.

"No further until you tell me."

He took an impatient breath, then turned her to him. "We have to kill her. The End of Days. It's real and all the people are ready. If we don't kill her—Jaguar, they'll all die."

She kept her eyes focused on his, looked into the dark hollow of pupil, and let herself rest there. She felt the slowness of her thought, the reality of it. She saw it in these eyes, and she needed to see nothing more. The End of Days was real.

"Okay," she said. "Should I use my knife, or your weapon?"

"Your knife. I'll back you." He showed her the weapon he had palmed. "Let's go."

Fights curled around them in the static of heavy induction as they walked toward Sardis, still perched on the hood of her car, smiling at the crowd.

"Sardis," Jaguar called to her when they were close enough.

The cult leader turned to her and held out a welcoming hand, then drew back. "That man. He's with you."

Jaguar realized that Sardis remembered Alex's face as the man who kissed her in the mall. "Yes," Jaguar said. "I've captured him. See?" She slipped behind Alex, flicked out her knife, and held it to his throat. "Play along," she whispered in his ear.

"Right," he agreed.

In this position they moved toward Sardis, who inched away up the hood of the car toward the roof, looking afraid.

"Don't worry," Jaguar said. "He's not what he seems to be. You know him."

"I know him?"

"Sure," she said, tightening her grasp. "Philo, isn't it? Or do you prefer Proteus?"

She felt his surprise at her knowledge even before he moved, but then he moved quickly. He jerked hard under her hand and her arm came around fast to grab for his weapon, but he got his hand on top of hers and pressed between the small bones. Red hot pain seared her, and he twisted her arm, threw her to the ground, and raised his weapon toward her. His face was Philo again, just as she'd seen him in the interview room with Rachel.

Sardis let out a weak screech. "*No,* Philo. You mustn't. Not an angel." She dropped onto his back like a cat and hung on, her fingers in his eyes while he twisted to get at her.

He flipped Sardis over his back onto the ground at his feet. She lay on the pavement, wind knocked from her, sucking in air with a rattling sound like death. Jaguar scrambled to her feet and lunged for him, but not fast enough because Proteus was bending over Sardis and stroking her face with his weapon, crooning to her.

"There, there, Mother," he said. "There there. I'm with you. I'll take care of you. We have to kill that angel, though, because she's really a devil in disguise. You know that, don't you?''

"Father," she choked out. "I've—I've missed you so."

"Of course you have, Mother. And I've missed you."

Jaguar took a step toward them and he snapped his face up to her. "Don't," he said, his weapon resting at her temple.

She stood poised, waiting to see what move to make next, when she heard a voice speaking within her.

*I love these drama-rama moments, don't you?*

Rider. But she couldn't see him anywhere. She replied in kind.

*Shut the fuck up or help.*

*Help? Help save Sardis? Sardis, not Rachel? Are you sure?*

She had to choose? No. Not fair. And no time.

*Sardis for now. Help me, you shit.*

*Testy, aren't we? Step aside and let me through.*

Jaguar felt something push her forward, and Proteus gave her a warning glance. "No closer. We know what you are."

"What am I, Proteus?" she said, her voice low. "An angel gone bad? The Whore of Babylon? Which one am I? And which one is me, if you don't mind a little play with words."

She was pushed again, this time to the left, and light wavered, solidified into an image, and stepped out of her right side. Jaguar stood next to Jaguar, and smiled at herself. The other holofigures stopped their fighting, raised a unified cry, and flew away. Proteus's face went red. He raised his weapon and fired, hit one Jaguar directly.

"Horrible waste of ammunition, isn't it?" the other Jaguar said, and a third Jaguar appeared at her side. They began to shake hands all around.

Proteus scrambled to his feet and turned his weapon on one, then another, then another as a fourth one appeared.

"Confusing, isn't it? But you should know. You're the master of Protean Change, aren't you? Only, why'd you turn out to be such a bad boy?" One of the Jaguars walked toward him, dissolved, and re-formed in the shape of a middle-aged woman with soft eyes and a sweet smile.

Proteus mouthed the word *mother*.

"Why'd you do it, Johnny?" she asked, holding up fingerless hands. "Why'd you kill your own mother?"

His face went from deeply flushed to an ashen gray. Sardis sat up, clawed at his leg. He stared down at her without recognition, then he frowned.

"It's not real. None of it's real." His eye moved from his mother to the Jaguars. "You're not real, either. None of you."

One of the Jaguars took a step toward him. "Am I real?"

He jerked his weapon onto Sardis. "No. She's the only one who's real. And if you take another step, I'll kill her. What do you think'll happen then?"

Another Jaguar answered, "She'll die, Proteus. But you want that, don't you?"

He grinned. "So do you."

The Jaguars all stood still and listened.

"Yeah. You do. I can feel it in you." He stroked her head with his weapon and she rested in his lap as if this were normal, as if nothing were wrong on a perfectly heavenly day.

"I don't blame you," Proteus said. "You know what she did? I mean, at least I tried to save my mother. At least I sent her money to get out. But Sardis—ask her about her daughter, why don't you? Ask her what she has planned for the End of Days."

Proteus grinned at all of them. "Ten days, then three days of death and we meet at the Gates of the City. Into the cities." He nudged her with his foot at the small of her back, and she gasped in shock. "Everything's ready, isn't it, Mother?"

"Yes," she said, rolling on the pavement, clasping his ankle. "It's ready. They're ready. You've been such a help to me."

"That's right. And if I kill you, there's nobody in the world who can make it stop."

And he released the safety on his weapon.

"Are you sure about that?" a voice growled behind him.

Before he could turn to it, hands grabbed his hair hard and jerked his head back, exposing his throat. He twisted around and saw her face, green eyes filled with fire. Saw her knife glint red in the sun. Felt it slide cool and silken across his throat. Felt liquid wash warm and soft down his neck. He tried to pull away but couldn't control his motion and the knife slid into him again, easy as sex. He felt a tickle in his ear and he wanted to laugh because it didn't hurt, wasn't frightening or even interesting. He tried to laugh, but only a garbled sound emerged.

Blood poured out of his mouth, his face, distorted in its attempt at final laughter. Eyes wide. Seeing glory. Seeing horror. Seeing nothing as he dropped at Jaguar's feet.

Sardis bellowed wordlessly like a cow in heat or pain. She threw herself onto him, plunging her hands in his blood, hands smearing blood over her face, her throat, her breasts, moaning out quotes that Jaguar could barely understand.

Jaguar wiped her blade on his pants, retracted it up her sleeve, and took a step away. The others were gone. "Stop that," she hissed at Sardis. "Stop it, I said."

"All will be washed clean in the blood of the lamb," Sardis wailed, her voice a knife for Jaguar's ears.

Jaguar wrestled with words, found none she could pin down long enough to say. She grabbed Sardis and pulled her to her feet, pressed both hands around her head, and held on hard.

"What plan do you have?" She pressed in, looking, feeling into the tangled mass of Sardis's mind because one look in Proteus's eyes told her what she'd been trying to deny. The sect had a plan. And maybe it didn't matter to anyone else if all Sardis's crazy worshipers died and maybe it didn't even matter to her, but it was her job to stop them. Her job to stop them or die trying. She had given Alex her word.

*What, Sardis? Tell me the plan. When? And—why, Sardis? Why?*

There. The right question. At last. Why?

*Sardis Malocco—see who you are. Be what you see.*

The rush of wind told her she was being sucked into the barriers, the choking feel of them all around her as they circled her core, her center, who she chose to be.

There, again, this place. Sardis, a young mother, clasped her daughter to her and laughed.

*Such a pretty stone you brought me, Rachel.*

Over and over again. The same scene, starting and dissolving and starting again.

Then Sardis's face, smile freezing, twisting to horror. *No No No.*

Little-girl voice, screaming, *Mommy let me go I don't want to*

What? What?

Little-girl voice, screaming again, starting and dissolving in the infinite loop of Sardis's memory.

*Mommy let me go I don't want to I*

Bullets whistling, and Sardis didn't let her go. She didn't.

She didn't. Sardis held her daughter high in front of her, held her up to the gunman, hid behind her from the

Sweet mercy, was she doing that? Holding her daughter up, hiding behind her hiding behind her screaming in an ecstasy of blood and death as the

Whistling of bullets and flesh ripped, blood flying, child's arms flailing, eyes wide, small body convulsing, ripped apart. Jaguar, hands held out, crying *No No No.*

Laughter, wild and without remorse. Sardis's laughter.

*Worthy is the lamb who was slain. All, all will be washed clean in the blood of the lamb.*

Child body ripped by bullets, face showing more surprise than pain. Sardis, flinging the body down as she ran, ran for cover, for safety. Sardis, watching from where she crouched around the corner of a building as the dogs came, sniffing at her daughter, licking at the blood. Dogs, sniffing and licking at what was left. Dogs opening their mouths, teeth white and hungry.

*Rachel.*

Jaguar wanted out of this. Out of it, now. She didn't want to save this woman. Didn't want to help her or her people who fed the children to the dogs let them all die she didn't want this but inside her Rider laughed. Rider pushed her back, wouldn't let her out yet because there was more. More.

*More? More?*

More. More children.

Children held out their arms while adults draped jackets made of wires and boxes on them. A father patted a child on the cheek. A child pointed to a red flashing light on his chest and laughed.

They walked down city streets in groups of three and four while the adults waved good-bye. And behind every one was Sardis's daughter, bloodied, dark hair swallowing a face pale as a winter moon, eyes large as the night sky, and Jaguar could look into those eyes, feel the cold emptiness of forever and forever and forever. Put her hands through those eyes, that bloodied chest, and fall into forever, empty and cold and filled with nothing.

Only surprise. Never expecting this from her mother. Only surprise.

*No. No more. No more.*

Jaguar pulled away roughly, the contact broken with a twist and a snap.

No more. No more. She had to think. Sardis, squatting on the ground across from her, screwed up a grin.

Jaguar's voice trembled with rage. "You can't do this. You have to stop it."

Sardis tilted her bulk forward and scratched against the ground, moving toward Jaguar like a cat, bringing her face close as if she would rub it against Jaguar's cheek. "I can't," she crooned. "You killed me. With my death, it has begun."

Fury coursed through her like unreasonable fire. She made a fist, hauled off, and clocked Sardis in the jaw, feeling distinct satisfaction when she keeled over and hit the ground, silent at last.

"Shit," David Halpern said. "Now what?"

In the mall, the father of an Ethiopian nuclear family pulled out a knife and plunged it repeatedly into his wife. The children clapped their hands gleefully, jumping up and down and shouting, "Wheee!"

He turned to the computer panel and started punching in codes. As he punched he yelled over his shoulder, "Andy— hey, *shithead*—get in here."

The word *shithead* brought Andy running in. If Halpern was calling him that, he'd kill the four-eyed freak.

"Look," David said, nodding toward the computer panel. "It's going nuts on us. The holofigures. They're all going nuts. I can't hold it."

Andy eyed the numbers as they rolled over the panel readout. "Fuck me," he said reverently. "Massive program disruption. Turbulence." He resisted saying I told you so only because what was happening onscreen was so interesting. "But they aren't breaking apart. What the hell is it?"

"I can't even think of a fucking curse word strong enough," David snarled.

Andy leaned over toward the screen as if a closer view would change it. Then he shuddered. "Punch file control X7," he said.

David complied, and the viewer shifted to the car-lot scene.

"Fuck me twice," Andy said as he watched the events of that quadrant unfolding.

"Hard and dry," Dave agreed.

"Think we should warn that Teacher?"

"I think," Dave said, "we should kill that Teacher and warn the holofigures instead." He swiveled around to Andy. "Get the Feds here fast. We gotta pull her out of there now, before she destroys the whole fucking world."

# 13

CALM AND SMOOTH, LIKE HE'D JUST PUT HIS teacup down to talk about the weather, Rider's voice spoke in her ear.

"And do we feel better after our little display of temper?" he asked.

She said nothing.

"Well, never mind. It's a bit raw, I'll admit. You see the setup, though. Her God loves nothing better than a really fresh and juicy sacrifice. You can appreciate that, can't you? The blood of the lamb and all. Get it, Jaguar?"

She turned to look at Rider, staring grimly over her shoulder at Sardis, who lay still, splayed on her back, arms flaccid at her side.

"She killed her daughter," she said flatly. "Hid behind her, to save herself. She's hiding behind her still. All her rage and shame and guilt."

"That's right. And what's next?"

"I—saw something. What she did in Vermont, I think," she said, then shook her head.

"Come *on*, Jaguar," Rider cajoled. "Time is ticking ticking ticking."

"*Stop* it," she cut in. She needed quiet. As her intestines coiled into knots of queasy horror, she willed them into stillness "Okay," she said. "Sardis killed her daughter and she wants to justify what she's done. See it as a sacred act. But Rider, my God—''

"*Her* God, Jaguar," he corrected. "A God you'll never understand. And how will she manufacture a justification for her original sin?"

"She'll be the Messiah. I already said—"

"No," Rider said sharply. He walked a circle around her and Sardis, and stopped at her back, his impalpable hand on her shoulder as he spoke close to her ear. "Sardis won't be the Messiah. Worthy is the *lamb,* Jaguar. Her little lamb, and all that blood to wash everybody clean."

Yes. Her little lamb. Jaguar was lifted into the elation of sudden enlightenment. That was it. The core of Sardis's illusion. If Rachel died to save the world, then Sardis wouldn't ever have to face her guilt. Rachel would be the Messiah, and her mother made it possible.

"I get it, Rider," she said triumphantly. "I get it."

"At last," he said. "That's *why,* Jaguar. And knowing why should tell you how. How, Jaguar? *How* will little Rachel break the old glass ceiling on deity?"

"Through the End of Days," Jaguar said, her triumph vanishing into visions of children with boxes strapped to their chest. They would kill the children, repeating the offense to justify its rightness. More. No more.

She heard a brief clapping of hands. *"Brava,"* Rider said. "Which is to say assassin, female type. The Apocalypse promotes murder to sanctity. And why wait around, when it's so much easier to manufacture it yourself. And it is *cheap*? My dear, you wouldn't believe how little it costs. Just a few thousand children. But you already know that."

Jaguar continued to stare up at him, waiting for this to become real for her.

"I feel your thoughts moving into unpleasantries. But there's *more,* Jaguar. So much more than just a half a million crazy people choosing to leave this vale of tears with their unholy spawn. What did Proteus give your Rachel?"

"A nanosyringe," she said, and stopped, apprehension

crawling up her spine and into her brain. Of course. They had sophisticated weapons. Proteus, the ex-terrorist, was known for viral bombs. Chembombs. Ex-scientist making all their weapons for them. Boxes strapped onto the children who would go out into the cities.

*And her children I will kill with deadly plague.*

It was a real End of Days. Sardis meant it. Not just for the sect. For everybody. The End of the World, for real.

Jaguar pushed herself to standing. "Is it true, Rider?" she whispered.

"You know it is, Jaguar."

He lifted a hand and pressed the long fingernail of his little finger against her forehead. She felt the sweep of fire, heard the screaming panic, saw faces charred or melting in the agony of flesh-eating plagues. It was real. All of it about to happen. And they would meet at the Gates of the Cities to make it so.

Time. She needed time. "When?" she asked. "Do I know when?"

"The recently deceased told you. Ten days and three more."

She calculated from Sardis's arrival. No. From when she was arrested. That would be—one day? Two? She couldn't figure the time frame. Couldn't get her mind to work on it properly.

"Obsessing about details won't answer the big question. You know everything, don't you? Except how to stop her."

Jaguar pressed a hand against her lips, found they were numb.

"I have to take care of this," she said, indicating Sardis. "The Feds'll pull me from the VR. From Sardis. They won't believe me."

"What will you do, dear?"

She wasn't listening anymore. She had to get Sardis out of here. Could she revive her? Drag her? She had to leave. Had to talk to Alex. Nobody would believe her. Had to tell Alex.

"Jaguar, ticktock. Ticktock."

*"RIDER,"* she screamed at him, *"FUCK THE HELL OFF."*

He took a quick step back. "Oh my," he said in a small voice. "I guess you need a minute to get it together. Better make it fast, though."

He pointed over her shoulder, and she followed where his finger led.

"Xipe Totec," she said. "Kiss me because I'm about to get screwed."

Carolan approached hard, with two security guards trolling the wake of her well-heeled feet.

They'd take her in. Take Sardis away and time ticking on the home planet, on the bombs the children wore.

She turned to say something to Rider, but he was gone. She leaned over, hefted Proteus's body over her shoulder, and walked with her burden toward the oncoming troop. She came to a halt directly in front of Carolan, who stood and gaped, face frozen in speechless horror.

Jaguar slung the body off her shoulder and dumped it at Carolan's feet, splatters of blood and mucus spraying across the front of her soft pink suit in the process. Carolan stared at the blood on her breast, touched it with her finger, looked hard at her finger, and rubbed it off quickly onto her skirt, then stared at her skirt in disgust.

"Sardis is over there. I think she's all right, but you better see to her. Where's Alex?"

Carolan was so surprised, she answered. "He's at work— but he'll be here any minute."

"That's what you think," Jaguar said, kicking the body at their feet. Then she turned on her heel and left, ignoring the clamor of voices behind her.

Alex was walking down the corridor, ready to go home, when he heard Jaguar's voice, loud and clear and imperative.

*I'm at the breeding complex, standing at the jaguar cages, waiting for you. Get here fast.*

A message from Carolan on his belt sensor came next.

*Dr. Addams has gone off,* that message said, and requested his immediate presence in the computer rooms at the VR site. Nice to be wanted, he thought, and he took his wings to the sanctuary, running the path that led to Chaos, Hecate, and their namesake, Jaguar.

Jaguar stood facing the two big cats, talking to them in a language he didn't know, but when she heard his footsteps she turned to him, lifted her chin the necessary distance for their eyes to meet. Her face was smooth and there was no sign of tension in her body, but given the way her energy field was humming around her, that relaxation required a superbly disciplined restraint.

"Philo—I mean, Proteus—is dead," she said, voice measured and level. "He went after Sardis and I killed him. You have to make sure I don't get booted off the assignment."

Alex tilted his head back and stared at the sky. Let the information run through the mill.

"Why?" he asked at last.

"The End of Days. It's not a fantasy. And it's not just the sect."

"Tell me," he said, "All of it."

He saw relief wash through her. He wasn't questioning her judgment. He was accepting what she said. Apparently, she hadn't expected that.

Jaguar inhaled, pressed her palm against her forehead. "She killed her daughter, Alex. During the Serials. Threw her to a gunman. She's twisted by it. Dogs came and—now she'll take the others and Alex, she's going to feed the children to the dogs. All of them."

Alex stepped over to her, took her hands, waited until she lifted her eyes to his.

*Slow down. Hush. Just show me.*

He touched her lightly on the forehead, receiving the images as she had, direct and unmediated by explanation.

The sect children, strapping on their explosives and bio-bombs. The people gathering in cities all over the world.

So many people. Incomprehensible numbers. Death sweeping like a wind over the planet.

He released her, ran a hand through his hair.

"Do you know when?" he asked.

"Soon," she replied. "They followed a formula from Revelations. Ten days and three more, but I'm not sure if they count from her arrest, or when she came here."

With the difference between Planetoid time and home planet time, somewhere between twenty-four and forty-eight hours. Not much lead time, either way.

"Alex," she said, "the Feds won't believe me. The Board won't back me. You know that. They think I'm responsible for the VR breakdown, and for all I know, they're right."

"No," he said. "At least, not all the way. You're responsible for Rider, and for breaking up some holofigures, but not for the general breakdown. Credit for that goes to Carolan."

"What?" she asked, and he explained. His conversation with Stan had told him a few things. Specifically that yes, monitoring systems would punch holes in the CNW. The kinds the Feds used were small and unobtrusive, but very powerful. Too powerful to be used onsite without some kind of screening. Alex figured Carolan had used them. He'd go looking as soon as he left.

"But will the Board believe you?" Jaguar asked. "Will they do something?" She held a hand out, and let it drop. "You know what this is, Alex."

He did. Even half a dozen Immunoserum bombs would wreak havoc, and who knew what else they had. "You have to get Sardis to talk. She'll know where they are. We can't find them all in time unless she talks."

"She says she can't stop it because she's dead," Jaguar said, face twisting into frustration. "*We* killed her. We did it. Set it up so it was real for her. *Made* it real."

Alex felt his own skin crawl. Trapped by their own illusions. "Then you have to make it unreal," he said simply. "Can you do that?"

"I think so, but I have to get back on the site."

There was the problem. He'd have to get hold of Carolan's equipment. Get to Paul Dinardo, and have him clear her. He couldn't see a way to sneak her back on at this point. It'd be crawling with security. They had so little time, and it was so important not to panic.

"Okay. I'll take care of that. Stay with Marie. Just do nothing until you hear from me. It may take a while."

"Alex, we don't have a while," she said, her voice rising in pitch.

He raised his hand and stroked the air in front of her. *Bring it down a notch, Jaguar. Don't waste time on panic. Don't waste your energy. You may need it.*

He saw her breathe in and out deeply, calling herself away from fear, back to discipline. He took refuge in practical questions. Things he had to know before he went ahead.

"That's more like it," he said. "Keep it low to the ground. Tell me what you did with Proteus."

"I dumped him on Carolan," she replied.

Alex raised his eyebrows at her.

"Do you want the details?"

"I guess you better," Alex said, and she gave him a precise record of the events leading to Proteus's death, and her disposal of his body. Jaguar was right. The Feds and the Board would be all over her with warrants as soon as possible. He wondered what they'd be more upset about—the death on the site, her management of Sardis, or the trouble on the VR system.

That was easy. The VR system cost most. They'd be most upset about that.

"Jaguar, how did you know Proteus wasn't me?"

"He was carrying a weapon, and he wasn't wearing an earring. Didn't even have a hole in his ear. Besides." She reached to his side and lifted one of his hands. "He got your hands wrong. Wrong shape, wrong touch."

She let go of his hand. He felt it tingle, and marveled briefly at the human capacity for passion at the worst possible moments. People buried under volcanic ash were found clutched together in coitus. His hand tingled at the edge of the Apocalypse. He said nothing.

She took his silence for understanding, and turned away, but he put a hand on her arm. ''Wait,'' he said. ''Wait.''

She turned her face to his expectantly, open and ready, for once, to trust him. He held on to her with his hand, with his eyes.

''What?'' she asked. ''What is it?''

''Why did you leave?'' he found himself asking unexpectedly.

She blinked at him. ''The VR site? I told you—''

''No. Not the VR site.''

''I don't know what you mean.''

''Yes, you do,'' he insisted. And she did know.

Why did she leave his apartment without waking him up. When she found him sleeping with Carolan, why didn't she wake him up anyway?

She covered her uneasiness with a shrug, nonchalant. ''You were otherwise involved. I didn't want to disturb you.''

''Disturb me,'' he said. Yes. That was what he needed to tell her. Just that.

''What?''

''Disturb me,'' he repeated. ''Anytime, in any situation you might find me. That's your prerogative. To disturb me.''

''To—disturb you?'' she asked. He saw her trying to capture and subdue a smile.

''Yes,'' he confirmed. ''Always, under any and all circumstances. Understood?''

''More or less,'' she said, ''though I wonder how many times you'll regret having said it.''

''Many more than I care to think about. But I won't forget it, and neither should you. Go find Marie. Try and be patient.''

He released her, and she hunched down into herself, turned her face toward the path, and walked away.

• • •

Alex went directly to the VR site, where a state of moral indignation was the prevalent emotion. The Feds were there in force, standing politely and implacably at all entrances to the interior of the site, standing politely and obtrusively at doorways to the computer rooms, standing politely and officially in hallways.

Carolan had gone to her hotel room to change, a clean-cut young man told him. Alex was not to worry. They'd have a warrant for Dr. Addams's arrest in short order.

What, he asked, were the charges? The man she'd killed was a known killer himself—NICA had a ten-year-old dead-or-alive warrant on him. And she was acting in defense of her prisoner when she killed him.

It wasn't that, the young man told him. Sabotage and interference in governmental matters. The CNW was riddled with holes and bulges, and it was her fault.

Dave and Andy concurred with the Federal Agents. Clearly she was responsible, they said. When he asked how clearly, they blinked at him and said, well, who the hell else could it be?

He sighed. Of course.

While the room buzzed with talk and his presence was largely unnoticed, he spent some time walking through the computer banks, peering over the backs to see if he could spot something like what Stan Wokowski sent him a picture of. It would be small, probably gray and triangular. Plastic boxing with holes and three metal bands, one on each side. It would be easy to remove.

He found three before he stopped looking. He pocketed them, and requested use of a telecom to call Paul Dinardo, who knew about the situation. He told Alex that Karl Madden was en route and would be here in a few hours. Madden wanted Sardis turned over to his people. He wanted a meeting tomorrow first thing to discuss protocol.

"Let's pretend we're at that meeting now, Paul," Alex said. "Which side of the table are you sitting on—theirs, or mine?"

"Depends. What's your side got to say for itself?"

"Dr. Addams stays on the case until it's done."

Paul waited for more, but nothing came. "That's it?"

"That's the short version. An addendum is that the Revelation Sect is starting the Apocalypse, and we don't have much time to stop it. There's another addendum, but now's not the time or place to tell it."

Paul narrowed his eyes. "Gimme what you can."

Alex did.

Paul chewed on it for a while, and Alex could see the political wheels turning in his head. He might not believe Alex or Jaguar, but what if they were right, and he didn't listen? If they were wrong, he'd only offend the Feds, and maybe that wasn't such a bad thing right now. He didn't want Sardis taken from the Planetoids. It would look bad. And he was getting sick of the Feds. They had a way of politely and implacably implanting themselves and he politely resented that.

"Are you sure about the sect?" he asked.

"Yes. Proteus helped them set it up. Can you clear her to go back onsite?"

Paul pulled his hand down and his grim visage got closer to the screen. "Can she handle it?" he asked.

"Yes," Alex replied without hesitation. "If we let her."

"I'll have to smooth some feathers," he said. "You have no idea what trouble she's in, and with how many different people."

"Do what you have to, but do it fast. I'm going home. Call me there and I'll give you the rest of the addendum."

Alex signed off, not satisfied, but at least hopeful. Cautiously hopeful again. It was the theme of the case. Then, for courtesy, he called Carolan, who was sincere and sympathetic.

Obviously, she said, it was her mistake, putting Dr. Addams on the case, but she'd like the opportunity to rectify that if she could. She'd already spoken with her people, and they had arrangements ready to transfer Sardis to a Federal facility. Since he'd been on the assignment from the start, maybe he'd like to accompany her to the home planet and see it through? She understood that there was to be a meeting in the morning to discuss protocol.

I see, he said, and I'll think it over, and I see again.

He gave some time to wondering if they'd wanted this from the start, maybe wanted Jaguar's failure so they could get a piece of Sardis to chew on and spit out into their file banks, and some funding to set up their own VR site. Not that it mattered now. Not with what he had in his pocket. They wouldn't get any of it.

He went home and made coffee, took a shower, changed his clothes. Checked his telecom to make sure it was working. Checked it again.

"Dammit," Alex said to his machine. "What the hell is Paul playing at?"

He picked it up and punched in Paul's code.

"Working late?" he said. "And I do mean late, Paul, which you are."

Paul grimaced at him. "Alex, I know I said—" he began, and Alex knew they were in trouble. No. In more trouble.

Bureaucratic backpedaling at the brink of disaster, and Paul doing his administrative best to accommodate everybody's agenda. He said something about protocol. Something about the meeting Madden wanted.

Alex knew he shouldn't be surprised. The truth was so horrible, better to clutch the illusion of political control to your breast like a teddy bear to keep you safe in the night. And after all, you could look around and it all seemed pretty secure—your house, your vehicle, your life all there in front of you as if nothing could change ever and certainly this level of destruction just seemed too improbable. Too out of control. Too unreal. Better to stick to what you know. Call a meeting and talk endlessly around the horror in a nice suit at a big gleaming table.

"Do you know," Alex interrupted him, "how many children there are in the Revelation Sect? And how bad that many dead kids look when you're lobbying the Senate for increased funding? Not to mention the hell there'll be to pay in the cities. Why, taxes alone on cleaning up the bodies would run us for a year.''

"You haven't heard a word I said, have you? And what makes you so goddamn sure Addams is right?''

"You been talking to Carolan? About Jaguar?''

"I didn't tell her anything, Alex. I just solicited her opinion.''

"Great,'' Alex growled. "Tell you what, then. Why don't we just wait another day? If I'm right, we'll know soon enough. All those bodies ought to constitute proof, even with the Board. And with Proteus's background they'll have—hmm, probably VM3 splices, which spread like colds in spring, only they kill you. And, of course, Immunoserum bombs. We should be able to cross much of North America off the map in a few days. Then you can say I told you so to the only living people left—all of them right here. Won't that feel good?''

"Anyone ever tell you how manipulative you are?'' Paul asked acidly. "Okay. Madden wants a meeting and I convinced him to hold it when he arrives. Eleven o'clock tonight.''

"How about you just clear her for the VR site now, and explain it to them later?''

"Can't do it, Alex.''

"I have proof that the Feds' surreptitiously added their equipment to the VR, and that's what fouled up the works.''

"You can have proof of the existence of God and it wouldn't clear her.''

"Why not?''

"Speaking of funding, a Senator who's buddies with Madden just called me. Senator McDanial. He's on the oversight committee for the Planetoids. They've had kind of an eye on us since that nasty little incident with the Lear shuttle. Remember that? Him and Madden were on their way up here for a visit when the shit hit the fan, and now the Senator's real glad he came along. He reminded me how important it is to follow procedure. Used words like judicial restraints, impropriety, and so on.''

"Dammit, did you tell him? About the sect?"

"Yeah. That's when he started talking about probable cause and chains of evidence, and me with nothing to give him except the word of a woman who blows things up.'' Paul sighed. "Ever talk to a wall?"

"Paul, this is ridiculous.''

"Maybe it is, but we're doing it. I've got about twenty government officials to answer to—''

"You've got about ninety-six thousand children to answer to—and a lot of major urban population centers along with them.''

Paul's lips became a thin line. "Eleven o'clock,'' he said curtly. "You can bring your evidence with you, and I hope it's good, because you will not have a roomful of believers to show it to.''

"Paul—''

"Eleven. That's less than two hours from now. And what choice do you have?''

Alex felt his blood moving toward boiling. Wasting time to accommodate the administrative body. Shit. They just didn't get it, and he couldn't make them get it. He supposed he could only blame them as much as he blamed himself, because how long did it take him to get it? Even Jaguar had been tardy on this one, both of them distracted and confused.

He allowed himself the luxury of fuming pointlessly for a moment, then moved on to looking at his options.

He considered once again the possibility of sneaking Jaguar back onto the site. Or going there himself and taking Sardis off. But if he failed, they'd lose even more precious time, and he'd have even less leverage with the administrative body. Not that he had much now, with all the evidence regarding the sect's plans resting on Jaguar's word, and that from material she gleaned in empathic contact— which one didn't mention in polite circles outside the laboratory.

But he did have proof of what Carolan had done on the site. Evidence of her interference in a Planetoid program. And he had his manipulative nature.

He looked at his watch.

Less than two hours.

He'd try the meeting, and if that didn't work—he'd do what came next.

When Alex opened the door to conference room C he saw that Paul was seated with two other Board Governors on one side of the table, with Karl and Carolan plus a few polite and clean-cut young agents who were probably there to take notes and get coffee, on the other. Sitting at the far end were the VR designers. At the other end were two guards. Paul introduced him to Senator McDanial, and they shook hands.

Carolan gestured that the seat next to her was empty. He indicated a seat across from her, and went and sat next to Paul.

"Okay," Madden said, "let's start with a synopsis of events so far."

"No," Alex contradicted. All eyes turned toward him. "We'll start with upcoming events, since they're more pressing. The End of Days scenario isn't a fantasy. Sardis has plans to bring it about. We need to stop her. Or, more accurately, we need to let Dr. Addams stop her."

A great deal of sputtering ensued from both sides of the table, and Alex let it continue without responding to any of it or calling for a halt.

All a fantasy, spun out by a madwoman, Madden said.

Letting your teacher play into it, Carolan agreed.

How do you—this can't—where's your evidence—what could she possibly—nobody would ever—there isn't any—

Then Carolan, standing and banging her hand against the table for quiet. "Quiet, for God's sake *shut up,*" she shouted over the clamor of voices. The noise dimmed to a low rumble, and she looked directly at Alex, spoke directly to him.

"Look," she said reasonably, "I understand your loyalty to your workers, but you must know that Dr. Addams is still terribly angry over what's happened to her friend Rebecca."

"Rachel," he corrected.

"Rachel. Right. Sorry. It's been a tough day. Anyway, she's angry, and I can understand that, but she can't go on with the assignment. She's already killed Philo, she's been wreaking havoc on the holofigures, and we can safely assume that she'll go after Sardis since she already hit her—"

"You're more likely to go after Sardis than Jaguar is," Alex said, just as reasonably.

Her face went through its changes again as she held internal council. "Explain," she said at last.

"She'd do just about anything to save Sardis about now, because she knows Sardis is probably the only one who can call off the Apocalypse. Her life is worth a couple of million others," Alex said. "Your worldview doesn't even acknowledge the Apocalypse, so you don't value Sardis at all. Not her or her people, whom you'd just as soon—shall we say, lose?"

"There is no evidence that Sardis has any concrete plans for violence," Karl Madden chimed in. "Nor have you told us how you imagine she's to begin this Apocalypse."

"With the children," Alex said. "Like she did in Vermont, only this time they'll have biobombs strapped to their chests and they'll go public with them."

A sudden silence settled on them. That felt far too real. Far too likely. The truth had come to sit among them and they were made uncomfortable by its nakedness. He noticed that the Senator, an older man, had lowered his head and was staring at the table. He remembered the Serials, Alex thought. He understood.

"That," Madden declared, "is a puerile scare tactic. Sardis shouldn't have been brought here in the first place, and now when we finally prove that you can't handle her, you throw this at us, as if we'll fall for it."

"Is that what you came here for?" Alex asked quietly.

"Did you come here to prove we couldn't handle Sardis? Because you want her in your jurisdiction? Or was it about grabbing back a funding source you thought you lost?"

Karl shook his head. "Of course not, but—"

Alex interrupted him. "But in spite of that, you've been upping the induction waves at the site and putting in your own monitors, which you knew would unbalance the system."

"You have no proof of that," Madden hissed.

Alex reached into his pocket and retrieved the three monitors he'd pulled from the computer banks. He tossed them onto the table, and they skittered across the slippery surface like water bugs on a lake.

Andy made a dive for one and held it up close to his thick glasses. "Jesus," he said. "It's a v-line. Three of those'd punch holes in the system big enough to shit through."

Alex looked at the Senator, made sure the Senator was looking at him. "They carry Federal serial numbers, Senator, because they're Federal equipment. The Agency's equipment. They've been creating interference that's not only hurt the system, but also hurt Dr. Addams's capacity to deal with the prisoner. But I don't think Mr. Madden cared about the prisoner much, except as an issue of turf. In fact, that's what this job has been for them all along. Turf building."

He gave his gaze back to Carolan. "Along with recruiting, of course."

Carolan sat down hard. Her mouth dropped open, but she remembered to close it before anything too ugly fell out.

Paul cleared his throat. "Alex," he asked, "you have good reason to believe that this cult leader left her people with plans for large-scale violence."

"Global destruction is a more accurate term, Paul. I have what Proteus told Jaguar, and I have Jaguar's word," he said. "While she may be unconventional, she's not a liar, and she's not crazy. In fact, as you know, she has the highest success rate of any Teacher we have.''

The Senator raised his head to Alex, held his gaze, said the only three words he was to say throughout the meeting. "You trust her?"

"I'd stake my life on her word. I *am* staking my position on it, sir. Besides," he added, "if she's wrong, we can always fix the VR. If she's right—" He held his hand palm up, and let the sentence finish itself in their minds.

Paul tapped a finger against the table. "Is there anything we can do on the home planet to prevent it?"

Alex looked at Karl and Carolan. "We have a minimum of about eighteen hours, and a maximum of twenty-four. How long would it take you to round up all of Sardis's flock?"

"We made every effort to find out where they'd gone to," Karl said. "With that many people, you can't possibly fault us on it, and I resent the implication that our job here was simply a matter of establishing turf. I want that on the record."

"It's on," Paul said. He turned to the Senator, who closed his eyes, leaned back in his chair, and nodded.

Paul twisted his chair around toward Alex. "Get Addams back in. I'll call ahead to clear it."

Alex stood, and Karl protested. "You can't just—"

Paul jabbed a finger at him. "Watch me just," he said. "I'm Governor here, not you or your people. I *can* just, and I just have."

Alex exited on this line, knowing the argument would continue raging, as if it mattered at all. As if anything said at that table would change the straight course toward disaster they were all on tonight. Still, he was grateful for the rhetoric. At least it would keep them out of his way.

Rachel woke from a dream of falling to a room filled with light and the bustle of mid-morning hospital activity.

The world seemed unfamiliar, as if she hadn't been here in a long time and didn't expect to be here for an even longer time. But something in the dream asked her to wake up. She couldn't remember what, exactly. Just an insistence that she not go too far away just yet.

A nurse was checking her pulse, reading monitors on the machines they had hooked up to her last night. Just testing some things, they told her, though they never defined what things it was they were testing for. She felt the tubes go into her arm, but it didn't hurt. Pain had ceased sending signals to her brain, as if it didn't matter.

And it didn't. Not anymore.

Last night, she dreamed of falling into a space deeper than memory. Deeper than love. It was dark and cold, and Jaguar chased her through it. No. Jaguar threw her into it, then tried to bring her back. But she turned into a bird and flew away. Then she was a heavy stone falling.

No. None of this made any sense. But somehow she knew it was all true, and that was okay. Something important about it, and she had to wake up, leave that softer place where sleep filled her. Sleep, and no words to speak or hear or worry about at all. It was so peaceful there, she wanted to return. She heard her breath moving in and out of her as if it was a guest getting ready to depart, bringing bags in and out.

She wanted to go back there, where it was quiet. Why couldn't she? There was a reason, she thought. What was it?

Nothing was making any sense, but at least it didn't hurt.

The medic drew blood from her. She watched, then turned her face up to him, prepared herself to make sound, though it seemed unnatural to do so.

"Is she here yet?" she whispered.

He paused in his work. "She?" he asked.

"Jaguar. And Sardis. They. Are they here yet?"

The medic shook his head, smiled at her, patted her cheek. Delirium. People asked all kinds of odd things when they were this sick.

"Not yet. Get some rest. I'm sure they'll be along soon."

# 14

IT WAS PAST MIDNIGHT BY THE TIME ALEX cleared Jaguar's reentry onto the VR site, and asked if she needed anything else from him. Did she want him there? Did she need him.

No, she didn't. She knew what to do.

And what was that? he asked her.

Dispel the illusions, she replied. Of course.

And as the virtual stars sparked in the virtual sky, she walked the kingdom of God, barefoot and dressed in her ceremonial clothes.

She started at the stream, and made her way up the hill toward the formal garden. "Rider," she called out as she walked, "where are you? Ri-ider?"

She waited for a response, and got none. She went on her way. As she walked she went up to a tree, and placed her hands on it, pushing into it as hard as she could. It wavered and dissolved. She was capable of messing up the system. And the system was in her way.

A peacock strutted up to her, and she put her hands around its face. It fluttered, then fell.

Two virtual angels strolled ahead of her, speaking in low voices about celestial matters. She strode over to them and placed one hand on each face. She pushed hard and they fluttered their rapidly dissipating wings. Her head was beginning to go beyond the low chronic throb state, and into the nauseatingly painful state. She shook herself, and walked on.

Two small doves fluttered above her. She put her hands up, and they landed, so she let them have their first experience with empathic touch.

She went past trees and butterflies, flowers and small stones, touching them all, watching as they shimmered into nothingness, feeling her head jump with electric pain and ignoring it.

"Rider," she sang out, "Rider," she called, and saw that she was shouting in his face.

"How gauche," he said, peering down his nose at her. "Which is to say how clumsily done. How like performing with the left hand. How *sinistre*."

She took a step back, and saw that he was faded visually, though his voice still sounded clear and resonant.

"Am I getting it right, Rider?" she asked.

"Oh, when you catch on, you move. I'll say that for you. Dispel the illusions. It's the only way. Always was. But there's a few things you're forgetting."

"Like what?"

"Nothing," he said.

"I'm in a bit of a hurry, Rider. If you could grow less cryptic fast, I'd appreciate it."

He sighed. "It's a fast-food world, that's for sure. But I mean exactly what I said."

"What," she asked impatiently, "did you say?"

"You're forgetting nothing. The nature of nothing." He wiggled his hand at her as he dissolved. "See you round the shrink's office."

Jaguar shook off the feeling of discomfort that went with his words and continued on.

She worked her way through the entire Moroccan bazaar, dismissing holofigures and holoscenery as she went. It was time-consuming work, and her patience with it was limited. Her hands hurt. Her head throbbed, and small sparks of light appeared at the back of her eyes whenever she blinked. But she wanted to get rid of as much as possible before she found Sardis. It would be easier if she could work fast once she got to that point.

As she continued the dispersal, she could feel the gaps in energy left by Carolan's work, and how they were growing greater with her own. She put her thoughts into those spaces, expanding them and exploding them and watching them dissolve.

By the time she was at the used-car lot, she noticed that the figures were collapsing at the slightest touch. A good sign, she thought. The CNW was cracking. She moved through the mall, her hands numb now and her vision erratic under the pulsing lights inside them. Figures dissolved as she approached them, stores going liquid and washing away as she passed, so that by the time she found Sardis resting in the SleepTight store, there wasn't much left.

She sat down next to her on her queen-size bed, rested her head in her hand and her elbow on a pillow, reached over, and tickled her nose.

"Wake up, Sardis," she said. "It's a brand-new day, and you're going to stop the Rapture."

"Wh-what?" Sardis blinked, rubbed her eyes, then sat up fast and backed away from Jaguar. "What are *you* doing here?"

Jaguar grabbed her by the arms, pulled her up and off the bed. "I said, you're going to tell me how to stop the Rapture."

Sardis bared her gleaming white teeth. "Godless pagans," she said. " 'Thrust in thy sickle and reap, for my grapes are fully ripe.' "

"You're no goddess. Neither is your daughter."

" 'Blessed are the dead who die in the Lord,' " Sardis spit out at her.

Jaguar pressed a hand against the bed Sardis had been sleeping on, pushing herself, her knowledge into it, and watched it fizzle into nothing. Sardis gasped.

"Big surprise," Jaguar said. " You're not dead. You're just about to wish you were."

Keeping tight hold of her arm, she dragged her, protesting and stumbling over her long white nightgown, into the center of what was left of the mall. Only this corner, suspended in a sea of shimmering nothing, liquid at the edges, as if they stood on an island in the middle of empty space.

Jaguar caught hold of a potted plant and pushed it back into the ether it came from, feeling the spark and hiss in her hand as it dissolved from their vision. "Never did like plastic plants," she commented when it was gone.

"God help me," Sardis cried, trying to pull herself away. "What—what's happening?"

"I want you to help me count the crow I need to eat," Jaguar said, hanging on tight. "One for sorrow, two for joy. Three for a girl and four for a boy."

She pulled Sardis to her. "Five for silver, six for gold."

She held the burning eyes of the fanatic within the sea green of her own.

*And seven for a secret never told. Devil, I defy thee.*

Jaguar pulled Sardis in, deeper and deeper, as the system that enclosed them in this manufactured kingdom of God disintegrated around them. The sounds, the tactiles, the smells, all gone. The visuals fading and dissipating, flickering on and off around them. Jaguar focused, her head throbbing. She wrapped her consciousness around Sardis so that Sardis would see the nothing she perceived. She had a flash of Andy's face at the computer, blank and helpless.

Then, like a telecom suddenly gone dead, the connection was cut, and they were left, the two of them, standing in what looked like a cavernously empty airplane hangar, alone.

Sardis reeled back from Jaguar's hands.

"Where? Where am I?"

"You're on the Planetoids. You're my prisoner, and this is your prison. Heaven was all a lie. Right from the start, Sardis, all a lie."

She blinked at the emptiness around them, her hands clutching for what used to be there. "But—my plans. My daughter—"

"Dead, Sardis. You killed her. Not a celestial sacrifice. Not the new Messiah. Just a moment of irrevocable fear."

"But she's—the lamb. The blood of the lamb."

"No. She was a little girl and you killed her, Sardis. Her death is still your fear."

Sardis turned this way, then the other. She grabbed Jaguar's arm and shook it hard, then let it go and ran away from her to the center of the site, the sound of her feet echoing in the emptiness around them. Jaguar saw the terror in her eyes as the emptiness sucked her dream from her, her denial, her illusions all dissipating with the illusion of heaven.

She careened through the empty site, and her whirling fear brought her back to Jaguar, who was the only person left to blame for all this. "Whore of Babylon," she screeched, words torn from her throat roughly, "you did this. *You* did it. God promised—the Scriptures—they promised."

Jaguar whipped her hand up and grabbed the finger. Held on tight with her numb hand as Sardis struggled to release herself.

"Promised what? That killing your daughter was part of the divine plan? You've been lying to yourself for years, Sardis. It's all an illusion, except for those children you plan to kill—all those people who'll die with them. *They're* real, Sardis. And you can still save them."

"Save them?" Sardis asked. "Save them?" Her head swung back and forth in a wide arc. Jaguar saw that her whole body was trembling lightly, ripples moving through her. She was losing control. But too fast. Too fast.

Jaguar grabbed her finger, jerking her closer, making surface contact.

*Stay with me, Sardis. Breathe. Breathe.*

Sardis's trembling grew more pronounced, ripples growing to shock waves that coursed over her body. The illusions, so long held, were breaking apart, but Sardis was breaking apart with them.

Jaguar let go of her finger and lifted her hand toward

Sardis's face, slowly, meaning to soothe her. But the trembling increased and became more spasmodic, her face convulsed, and she exploded into motion, knocking Jaguar's arm back, swinging at her with one large arm and grabbing her around the throat with the other.

Strong as Medusa, Jaguar thought as Sardis lifted her up. She had a few seconds before she'd pass out or have her neck broken, and she took them, bringing her leg back and kicking hard into the softness of Sardis's belly, just below the ribs. Sardis let go and hugged her belly, and Jaguar moved in, squeezing hard at Sardis's temples, pushing into her in the way you weren't supposed to push in with empathic contact, shoving her way into the center of her own emptiness, where nothing else was left. Nothing.

Nothing. Just emptiness in the place where she'd killed her daughter and denied her death a home. The place where she hid murder under the tangled mass of the manufactured God she hoped her daughter would become. Nothing.

As suddenly and roughly as she'd entered the empathic space, Jaguar pulled out, and Sardis stood, teetered for a moment, swayed, and fell, her eyes rolling back into her head.

A wild wailing sound was ripped from her, screaming from her center as even the anger left her and emptiness moved in to stay in a place so hollow, not even the wind would bother to blow there.

"Shit," Jaguar said, breathing hard, rubbing at her throat. "Too much. I think—dammit." She bent to her and lifted her, smoothed her cheek. "Sardis, we have work to do. You have to—"

Sardis opened her eyes, looked at nothing. She moaned, and the moaning became low singing, a crooning, wordless song.

She rolled her head back and forth, crooning to herself, to her dead daughter, to the shadow of nothing. No illusions left, nothing to protect her from the truth, nothing to keep her emotionally intact. She rocked nothing in her arms, singing lullabies to soothe it to sleep.

"Sardis?" Jaguar asked.

No response.

Just more singing, a little laughter. A coldness washed through Jaguar. Sardis was gone. Gone too far. Over the line. And the sect getting ready to move.

*What did you think—she'd just snap out of it?*

She heard Rider's laughter inside her. She twisted to see him, but he didn't exist outside her now. Only the residue of his energy lingered in her psyche.

*I said you were forgetting nothing. She's a vacuum, and nature abhors a vacuum. She needs a fill-up quick, or she'll die.*

"If she dies, they'll all die." She closed her eyes and pressed a hand against them, feeling the onset of panic. They would all die, so many people.

What could she do? Show her God? Have God command her to call it off? Could she be God for her? Could she do that?

*Interesting thought, but I feel your resistance. Now, why is that? Wouldn't you like to play God?*

"I just don't know if it would work." Something else was necessary. Something she seemed to know, but couldn't find words for. Something.

*Aren't we evolving at an alarming rate. Of course it wouldn't work because it's not real. She needs something real to fill the void. Something real, Jaguar. Any ideas?*

Jaguar held a hand up to stop his flow of words. Voices moved inside her. Alex's voice. Her own voice.

*Let me take her out of here. Show her something real.*

*Like what?*

*Like Rachel.*

Someone real. Someone imperfect and real in her faith and her courage and her fear and her intent. A different daughter, a different Rachel whom Sardis had condemned to death. Rider's voice spoke with a gentleness that frightened her.

*Who can find a woman of valor, for her price is above rubies, and she is worth more than blood rubies. Keep going, Jaguar.*

Rachel. Empathic contact with Rachel. A moment of reconciliation with a spirit that was real. But Rachel was so sick. She couldn't possibly survive it.

"It would kill her, Rider," Jaguar said desperately.

And his reply came, cold and certain as knives.

*I know.*

To bring Sardis in to Rachel would kill her, and they'd be in a Death Walk. A Death Walk, inside Rachel, who lingered in that space where no lies could exist. Something real as Rachel, and something as real as death.

*Don't know if it'll work, but it's your only shot. Ticktock, Jaguar.*

"You were supposed to help me save her, Rider."

*You changed the deal. Traded her for Sardis. Your call.*

She stared down at Sardis, who keened for her daughter, and felt the stillness of truth, awful and complete. She said to Marie she couldn't imagine her spirits asking her to kill someone like Rachel. And now she was no better than Sardis, who lay in her arms, crooning sweetly to nothing, eyes staring ahead at the nothing around her. No better than Sardis. Only her arrogance had made her believe she was.

"There's no other way? You're sure?"

*Sure as shit, dear, which is what this is. Shitty choices. All yours. But cheer up. It'll probably kill you, too. Death Walk's risky business.*

She shook her head. She couldn't afford more risk. So much at stake, and no margin of error, and she'd already made so many errors. "I've never done this before. If I get it wrong—"

*Call a friend. Someone with experience.*

She frowned. Alex. She'd make contact on the way to the hospital, have him meet her there.

She pulled Sardis up to her feet and walked with her, catatonic and unresisting, toward the door.


Alex waited at his office for word from Jaguar, knowing he could do nothing but wait, felt his heart skip a beat when his telecom buzzed.

Then Carolan's face appeared. "Well," she said, "your teacher is gone. She blew the site system out, then left with the prisoner."

"Good," he said. That meant she knew what to do. That meant she was moving.

"What?" She gaped at him through the viewscreen.

"She has a plan, and she's moving on it. That means there's hope."

She pressed a hand against her cheek and held it there as if she was comforting herself. "Alex, do you really believe her? How can you put your trust in someone who sees holodemons and who would be so wantonly destructive?"

Alex gave a wistful acknowledgment to her smooth loveliness. Soft sweet skin and hair, all so clearly enjoyable. It was a pity, he thought. Then he let it go.

"Where should I put my trust, Carolan?" he said. "In someone who speaks courteously, never makes a fuss, and breaks her promise as soon as my back is turned?"

She brought her hand down and held it toward him. "You're angry about that. I don't blame you. But please understand the pressure I'm under. I had to do that. It wasn't anything to do with you. With you, it was different. We shared something good. The VR site—that was just a job, and I had my orders to follow."

"Then follow them," he replied, "back to the home planet. If there's anything left of it after the Apocalypse." He pushed the off button, watched her shocked face flutter away and disappear.

Harsh. That was harsh. But he didn't care. He had more important matters to attend to, and didn't want to be distracted by the glitter at the side of the road. He sat, still and open, seeking Jaguar. But she found him first.

*Alex, I need you.*

*Yes. Where?*

A slight pause, then her reply.

*At the hospital. In Rachel's room.*

Then she was gone, not leaving him any time at all to ask why.

# 15

## *day eleven (morning)*

WHEN JAGUAR ARRIVED AT RACHEL'S HOSPITAL room with Sardis in tow, the sky was beginning to lighten toward morning. An interstitial time, neither night, nor day.

The medical staff was changing shift, signing in and out, lingering at the desk to drink coffee or check on yesterday's incomplete disasters. With an almost catatonic Sardis in tow, she approached the medic at the desk.

"I'm here on Planetoid business," she said. "We'll be in Ms. Shofet's room, and we can't be disturbed."

The medic made some disapproving sounds, but Jaguar cut them off. "Call Governor Dinardo if you have questions."

She opened the door to Rachel's room and saw Alex already there, sitting by her bed.

"Sit there," Jaguar said to Sardis, and placed her in a chair next to Rachel's bed. She smiled briefly and tightly at Alex. "I need a minute," she said. "No—you can stay. Just don't ask anything yet."

She leaned down over Rachel, smoothing her face with her hand. Unconscious. Deeply so. Jaguar could feel the softness of it, fever in her hand. She touched her lightly on the forehead, calling her back to the living, and felt the rising of her thoughts from the bottom of this place.

She came back willingly. Waiting. She'd been waiting for Jaguar.

Her eyes opened wide, showing fear, then a profound calm. She spoke as if continuing a conversation they'd started long ago. "I knew you were playing big sister to me, but I wanted to be the little sister, too. It felt so much safer to stay there."

Jaguar continued smoothing her face. "There's nothing wrong with that, Rachel. Nothing at all."

"Only that I'm sorry if I was angry at you for being what I asked you to be." Rachel lifted a hand to Jaguar's and held it, stopping its motion. "I know why you're here. Sardis is with you."

Jaguar nodded. "I need to bring her in to you. Empathically."

"I know that, too. But I'm not an empath. I can't—"

"I can set it up. You just have to—" Have to what? Just have to die. Just have to let Sardis feel your death. Words halted, her throat blocked by something that felt like knives.

Jaguar saw a jumping motion in the heart monitor, but Rachel's eyes were serene, and there was no fear in her voice.

"It's okay, Jaguar." She tried a smile, but couldn't sustain it. "Just think of it as my Messiah complex. Another Jew out to save the world. This time a woman."

No, Jaguar thought. Not like this. Not fair. She felt all her gods laughing at her. At her arrogance, her supreme arrogance because she'd forgotten that thirteenth unaccountable thing. Laughing at all her scrambling to avoid falling into exactly the place she was now. All her spirits, laughing that she had to trade Rachel's life, which she valued above rubies, for Sardis.

"Rachel, I wanted to save you," she said, her voice dry and hard as her spirit.

"You already did," she said. "Now it's my turn."

No. Not right. She hated all of this. Hated it, start to finish. Not fair. Not right. Tearing and ripping at her and all her spirits laughing. She couldn't be Sardis, killing what she loved. It would twist her spirit, just as it twisted Sardis's, and she wouldn't live that way. Wouldn't consent to that no matter what her gods asked of her, she wouldn't give up her soul to save the world. She would rather die with Rachel than live twisted.

"Let it go, Jaguar," Rachel whispered like an ancient wind already traveling elsewhere.

But she couldn't.

And maybe that was the only difference between her and Sardis. In all the confusion, in the numbness of her hands and her heart, that felt like something real. Jaguar suddenly wanted to laugh at her gods. Inside this horror, she wanted to laugh because she knew what to do. What was right. She knew what Rider meant. At last.

"I can't," she whispered back, "I never learned how."

As Rachel retreated back into the depths of unconsciousness, Jaguar stood, and Alex stood with her.

*What're you doing, Jaguar?*

Jaguar gestured toward the door. "I need to see you for a minute."

When they stood in the hall and the door shut behind them, she pulled in a ragged breath and rubbed a hand against her forehead.

He grabbed her arm roughly and shook it. "Jaguar, what're you doing?" he asked again.

"Sardis—she's gone over the edge. I pushed her too hard or she's just empty. I have to bring her back. Give her something real. Rachel—"

She stopped. He filled in the blanks.

"What? Empathic contact between Rachel and Sardis? But in Rachel's condition, it'll kill her."

"*Don't* tell me what I already know." She jerked her arm away from his hold. "I need help. You said you did this before, right? Death Walk?"

She couldn't mean it. "Death Walk? With Rachel? Jaguar, you can't play God with Rachel's life."

"I'm not. I'm not playing God. That's exactly what I'm trying not to do and there's no *time,* dammit. Alex, I need your help."

But his brain stopped somewhere along the line. He couldn't comprehend that she would do this. No. It wasn't *what* she was doing. It was that *she* was doing it. That *she* could do it.

"Jaguar," Alex said, dropping the three words like stones into her belly, "she's your friend."

"You think I've forgotten that?" she said with ice in her voice. She turned feral eyes to him and let him look. He caught his breath.

"What you see here," she said, "that's the kind of woman I am. If you've been nurturing fantasies to the contrary, you'd better dispel them. Now."

Accept it. That's who she was. A cold bucket of water wouldn't have been as efficient as her words. That's why he gave her this assignment in the first place. She'd stop Sardis or die trying. Place this one sorrow, singular and profound, against massive destruction and hope the wall held. And she was right. There was no time. No time and so many lives at stake.

"Okay," he said. "Okay. You're right."

But Death Walk was dangerous. So easy to lose Sardis altogether. If they lost Sardis—no. No margin of error here. Jaguar had to learn quickly and well. He put his hands on her face and called her wild eyes to his. Saw her shudder with relief at his touch. Better. It would go faster this way.

*Hush. Listen. You remember the old stories. How it's done.*

*I remember. Innana. Demeter. Down into the darkness, naked. No protection. Entirely open.*

She knew. This much she knew, and she was willing to do it.

*That's right. Entirely open. Take nothing in. Try for no defense. The motion is a wave. Don't drive it. Just ride it. Ride it in and ride it out. It'll feel like falling a long way. Don't try to stop the fall. Trust me without reservation. Stay open so you can feel my life, listen to me. I'll know when to call you back. While you're there, swallow nothing. When you leave, don't look back. And for God's sake, Jaguar, don't try to hold on to Rachel. Is that clear? Do not attempt to bring her back.*

He felt her pause. Listened to the absence of her response. She wouldn't promise unless she meant it. When she finally spoke into him, her words did nothing to reassure.

*I understand the consequences. What else? Tell me.*

Understood the consequences. He knew what that meant, and how little point there was in arguing with her. He'd just have to keep an eye on her as she proceeded.

He let the wordless and necessary understanding pass between them. He would stay in the upper world, at the rim of her contact with Sardis and Rachel. His aliveness would remind her body to live. He showed her the feeling of pull, when to let go. The texture of the space she'd be walking in. The border between too far and not far enough. How to retrieve what she needed from Rachel and hand it to Sardis, keep Sardis in contact without dragging her beyond recall. The importance of a light hand.

Then he looked at her hard.

Was there nothing else he could give her? She was already exhausted, and the Death Walk took so much. There must be something else he could do. He touched her face, her lips, warm and alive. The old stories told how he could give something of his life energy to her, share that gift with her.

*Do it right, Alex. Kiss of Life.*

Kiss of Life. As an antidote to death, there was only this. An exchange of passion. The transfer of his energy to her, life flowing from his body to hers.

Would she misunderstand the gesture? Or was there anything to misunderstand?

No. Nothing. It would be clear to both of them. It would have to be.

"Jaguar," he said, reaching down to her face and pulling

it close to his. Then he pressed his lips against hers, kissing her with more thoroughness than he had ever kissed a woman in his life.

*Disturb me, Jaguar. Anytime. Under any circumstances.*

She accepted it, straining her mouth to his, drinking him, letting herself fall into him, tangling her hands in his hair, her body pressing hungrily against his like seeds deep in the earth, their bright leaves reaching up toward sun while their roots crawled deeper and deeper down toward water, toward the always burning center. She swam in deep earth, in clear water. She swam in him, in the waters of his eyes. They swam together, down and down, and he held her close as if they would never touch again. They spiraled through these waters that grew increasingly thick, increasingly secret and dim.

Then he let her go.

She went back into Rachel's room and sat down by the bed, placed one hand on Sardis and the other on Rachel. He followed her in, saying with her the ritual words that connected the three of them and allowed Sardis to feel Rachel's life and death through Jaguar. He drew the shades, leaving the room in the watery darkness of almost day. He locked the door, so they wouldn't be interrupted. He braced his back against a wall and lingered at the lip of their thoughts, watching and waiting.

Jaguar's right hand moved to Rachel's forehead. Her left hand rested on Sardis as Alex floated away, like new leaves, up and away toward light and air, while she remained deep under the earth, the sea, the dark dome of what it meant to attempt a Death Walk.

Alex could see both the nothing that seemed to be happening from the outside, and the motion within the three women. He couldn't go in to them, but he could view the sequence of events from this place, guide her with his thoughts, keep them connected to his life.

Rachel would have to feel Sardis's pain, know what she'd done. Sardis would have to feel the death that roamed

Rachel's body, and witness something of her soul. She would have to face what she did when she killed her daughter, when she killed the children in Vermont, when she sent Proteus out armed with death in his teeth. She would have to feel horror, and the possibility of light before she understood the need to stop the End of Days.

Jaguar had to make sure this happened, maintaining a constant balance between too far and not far enough. She couldn't let Sardis slip her grasp and fall into Rachel's death, but she couldn't hold her back too hard. As she moved between the two other women, there would be no room for him. It was a tightrope walk for three, with flaming swords.

Here, at the edge, he saw the dim shifting of colors, shades of feeling, ripples of energy pouring in and out. There was silence for what seemed a very long time. If Alex prayed for anything, it was that no medic should knock at the door.

None did.

The machinery in the room did not hum or buzz.

The noise of no traffic could be heard outside the window.

Colors shifted, and time did not move as Jaguar led Sardis into Rachel and both women felt the enormity of the abyss. Time could be measured in the unfolding of a leaf and the long release of one breath. He heard moaning, and felt the shock waves of sound as if it passed through his skin and went directly into his lungs and heart. Rachel's voice, soft and clear.

*I brought you a gift, Sardis. A pretty stone for you.*

Voices moved through him like whispering trees, talking stones, the groaning of an overburdened earth.

*Rachel? Is that you?*

Jaguar rode the waves of death between them, her face growing pale and beads of sweat forming on her forehead and upper lip. She hung on to Rachel, just at the edge.

*Rachel what have I done?*

Sardis's shame was a river that ran into an ocean, washing over Jaguar and Rachel. Rachel's breath labored under the watery weight of it.

*You did this, Sardis. This.*

Rachel's heart beat with increasing effort and less effect, her pain coursing through Jaguar and into Sardis, so she could feel it, taste it, and understand that Rachel did this for love. Love of the living. Love of Jaguar. Love of being alive. The power of death made moot by the absence of fear. No fear of it left. Only the washing fire of love.

The machinery of death moved through Rachel, slowly, like unglued time, like graceful giants in the night, passing from one world to the next. Jaguar dove into it, bringing it back like sparkling rubies to nestle in the dark corners of Sardis's heart, the gift that would heal her madness.

Sardis could feel the weakening of every cell in Rachel's body, the exhausted heart working too hard to maintain an already frail body under the weight of a woman who killed children without regret. Sardis tasted the lives she'd stolen, and the bitterness of the theft. Children strapped into bombs, their bodies tossed to the dogs.

*God God God what have I done? Can you ever how can you ever forgive me? Rachel. Forgive me.*

Sardis, her breath composed of grief that left her like a river pouring out. Jaguar, moaning, feeling Rachel's pain, the weight of grief. Death. The weight of it.

Rachel holding Sardis, her enfolding arms saying something no words would ever cover. Alex was stunned by the beauty of that gesture. He'd never seen such beauty as this washing fire. As Rachel, beautiful and simple and herself. A thing of beauty and sorrow, this death, this life, this choice, this grief and praise. That we grieve at all, so beautiful and astonishing. He needed to speak about it, tell someone. To be alone with it was madness.

*Jaguar, it's so beautiful.*

*Yes. Of course. Yes.*

She knew all along. Saw this clarity in Rachel and knew this is what Sardis needed to feel.

A breath of time and a shift that was no more than the unfolding of a leaf. Rachel released Sardis and began to drift away. Jaguar, her timing perfect in this, her hand gentle and smooth, guided Sardis toward Alex until his life called to her, drawing her back.

Jaguar should drop back now. Let go. Let herself drift back to the living.

*Your turn Jaguar. I'm here. To me.*

Rachel's breathing became increasingly shallow. The death rattle in her throat, unmistakable.

Jaguar should drop back. Now.

Colors floated away, and then the sound of cessation of breath, a silence louder than any other in the world.

*Let go, Jaguar, do you hear me?*

Monitors flatlining, breath ceasing.

*Let her go, Jaguar. Let her go you can't bring her back can't bring her back.*

Voices whispered, and she held on, dragged toward the edge of the abyss, his hands helpless to stop it, her hands reaching for Rachel. A sorrow, singular and profound, and the jaguar leaping to the abyss.

*Jaguar dammit do you hear me let go now. Now.*
*Now.*

But she didn't, and Sardis saw. Saw Jaguar hanging on to the impossible, to the couldn't-be-done, to this woman she loved when she knew it was impossible, would kill her, and it was so beautiful. So beautiful and terrible, this choice, this moment. She was so beautiful he felt as if the whole of the universe must stop and turn to witness this grief and praise.

But only Sardis watched, her rage and shame gone in the washing fire of love and Jaguar, not letting go not letting go.

*Jaguar don't do this don't don't do this*

A crack opened wide between here and there and it spit

Sardis back against the wall. She sucked in breath as if for the first time ever and covered her face with her hands, sobbing, sobbing.

A crack opened and Jaguar leaped into it, riding waves of light away from him, hands seeking Rachel as she fell down and down, away from him, away from Sardis, away from this room and this day and her life.

*No Jaguar. No don't not that sorrow not that*

His thoughts reached for her across that great yawning chasm, her breath getting ragged, going in gasps, eyes open like an injured animal seeing death but not running, her hands flailing air, finding nothing to hang on to as she stood and swayed, reaching for death as if it were her daughter.

He took three steps to her as her body began to jerk out of control as the convulsions tossed her back and forth.

*Now. Now.*

And his arms were there to catch her before she hit the ground.

"Jaguar, come back," he murmured. He had to stay with her. Rachel said he had to stay with her. She was in too deep and falling deeper. Barely breathing. Heart sluggish and recalcitrant. Thoughts swimming in waters too deep, too far away. He had to—

But someone in the room was sobbing. As he sat on the floor of the hospital room, lost in the watery light, he felt a hand on his shoulder, heard the sobbing voice behind him.

He blinked up over his shoulder.

Sardis. Looking stunned.

"I have to—to call," she said. "I need to stop this—I need help."

He stared down at the woman in his arms, knowing what she'd say.

*That's the kind of woman I am.*

He laid Jaguar gently down on the floor and went for a telecom.

•  •  •

There was falling, and darkness.

Better. No. No words. Falling, flung out by a great hand, and falling. No end to it. Here. Hands soft Jaguar hush. Here. There was falling, and there were hands no words this the hands place hands great hands.

Voices.

Lacy bones scattering. Hush. Leafy skeletons here. Hush. In the wind around her. Here. Hush. Hush.

Falling, and darkness. Rachel in the darkness falling. Jaguar's hands holding her, sweet skin dragged into the slow night.

Better. Here. In the no wind. In the no words. Falling.

Somewhere a hand, pulling her back.

Drifting. Floating. No words. No time anywhere. Her hands, touching nothing. Wind like breathing. Voice a song of water in her ears. Somewhere, a voice.

*Let go. Let go, Jaguar.*

Somewhere, hands, pushing and voices whispering the wind of desire of a claim on her life. Whispering desire. Whispering feet on the stone bones of the earth that crumbled and let go. Falling. Drifting. A song of water like arms lifting her.

A claim on her life. Whispering desire of many voices. Small. Far away. Laughing child.

Time a river. Her hands and that face. Her hands. A voice wailing wild screaming no you old man you old bastard you will not take her no I will not will not let her go.

Hands, and time a river. Hush. Better. Hush.

Whispering desire. Whispering desire into stone bones. Stone bones underfoot and a hand.

A hand. A hand sudden and white in the soft dark. In the hollow. A hand.

Somewhere whispering from a hand that pulled her.

*Hush. Here. Jaguar. Let go. Hush.*

Desire whispers a wind, and is singing. Hush.

Somewhere a sound. Somewhere her own voice. Here crying out. Flying. Falling. Laughter like glass breaking. Her own voice. Here crying out. Hush. Hush. Hush.

Somewhere, her own voice, crying out.

*Rachel.*

Her voice crying out, shattered at the center.

Somewhere a sound, like glass shattering.

# epilogue

*day fifteen*

ALEX STOOD AT THE FOOT OF THE BED, HOLDING
a glass of water and staring at Jaguar's recumbent form. It
was motionless and silent, as it had been since they arrived
yesterday. A thing of beauty and sorrow, grief and praise.

He turned away, raised the glass to his lips. A cry
shocked the silence, shocked him. The glass of water left
his hands and shattered on the wooden floor.

Jaguar lurched upright in the bed and opened her eyes.

Someone yelled. Was it her? She heard glass shattering.
A voice. Was it hers? She stared at the blur of world around
her, waited for it to focus itself.

Then she saw Alex, standing in the room with her, his
dark eyes wide and unsure. Bits of broken glass were scat-
tered at his feet, liquid spreading out from the center. He
looked down at it, and up at her. She blinked at the bright
sun pouring into the room.

"You caught me," she said to him with surprise.

The only possible response he could make to this am-
biguous statement was, "I always do."

He walked over to where she lay, and searched her face
with his eyes. Then he brushed the hair back from her forehead, a gesture of both affection and reassurance. She had
survived. She was here, tangible and alive. He sat down on
the edge of the bed, and smiled.

"Welcome back," he said, keeping it casual, not sure how much she'd remember of her journey. "How do you feel?"

She ran her tongue over her teeth. "Like my dentist would be happy if I flossed soon."

So. She was herself. Very much herself. "That was a helluva stunt, Dr. Addams," he said.

She pushed herself up on her elbows, her eyes cool and deep as an ocean. "Did it work?"

She was herself, and she remembered. Even better. "It worked. No Apocalypse this year."

She shuddered, then relaxed.

"You also blew the whole VR site to hell. It'll be months before they can put it back together."

"I'd call that a success, then. How close did we cut it?"

"Pretty damn close. Another hour and I don't know if we could've done it, even with Sardis. She reached all the houseleaders, but some of them thought she was the devil tempting them at the last minute and we had to send in the Sassies anyway. There were a few casualities, but nothing compared to what it would have been."

All those children, all wired, all ready to run through the streets of the major cities and die for the New Heaven and New Earth.

Paul went with Senator McDanial and surveyed the warehouse of weapons gathered from the sect. Bubonic splices, and neurotoxins and chembombs and worse. The Senator telecommed Alex afterward, and Alex could still see the beads of sweat on his forehead. He said he wanted to thank Jaguar personally. Tell her she was in line for a Medal of Honor. She deserved it, Alex thought, when he wasn't furious with her for almost killing herself trying to pull Rachel back.

The days following her Death Walk had been pure hell.

There had been a jumble of events as he'd arranged what Sardis needed, tried to explain to the hysterical medics what had happened to Rachel, get someone to keep Jaguar alive while he dealt with Sardis. When Sardis made her calls and

was taken away for aftershock treatment, he'd gone back
to Jaguar and spent a long two days struggling to pull her
back from the murky hollow where she wandered. There
were many moments when he thought she had slipped ir-
retrievably from his grasp into that abyss. Then, bringing
her here, the long shuttle ride and the longer night of waiting to see if she would revive undamaged, whole.

But she'd done it. She'd managed to pull it off. Sardis
was on Planetoid Two, where workers would continue a
more extensive program for her and see what level of rehabilitation she'd actually be capable of. Some prisoners
never made it all the way back home. Alex would lay no
bets on Sardis's chances. At least she hadn't done all she
was capable of doing. She wouldn't have to live with that.

"It would have been the End of Days, Jaguar. If it wasn't
for you and Rachel."

"Good," Jaguar said. "Then it was—worth it."

Alex let his hand rest on her face. "Jaguar, what I said
to you at the hospital—"

She closed her eyes, turned her face away. "I don't need
the speech, Alex. What I did, I have to live with it. And
Rachel—"

"Rachel," Alex said curtly, "made her own choice. Stop
seeing yourself as being in charge of her, would you? It's
so belittling to her courage."

Jaguar remained still, but he could see the muscle in her
jaw working, chewing on this.

"Look," he continued, "did you ever think that if Rachel hadn't gotten jabbed, we wouldn't have been able to
stop Sardis? If you hadn't slammed your hand against that
window, we might be on the home planet wiping up a few
million bodies right now. Both you and Rachel had the
workings of the universe at your back, and you both chose
right. Don't insult her by insisting on your culpability. It's
the height of arrogance."

He stood and walked away. Let her eat those words for
a while. He could stare out the window, which showed him
a landscape filled with heat and a sea of red anemones in

bloom, the great leaves of a fig tree, the sun dancing skittishly on their surface. Some minutes passed, and a bird sang a song he couldn't quite translate into human understanding. Perhaps it was the joy of creation. Perhaps just a call to dinner.

"Is there more?" she asked.

He stayed where he was and answered with his back to her.

"As a matter of fact, there is. Trying to hang on to Rachel after I told you not to—Jaguar, that was excessively dangerous."

"I'm dangerous, Alex," she said calmly. "Excessively dangerous. But so are you. Or didn't you know that?"

"I took no unnecessary risks," he protested.

"You assigned me to the case. You chose me. That was excessively dangerous."

He felt a muscle in his neck twitch. There she was, pinching his emotional neurons again. There would never be any safety with her, outside of the safety of truth. He'd staked a lot of lives on that knowledge of her. Her willingness to risk all for Rachel turned Sardis around, and almost killed her. It was the sort of risk she'd always take, until one day the risk took her.

*That's the kind of woman I am.*

She never lied to him, and now her words carried all the weight of a reality she wanted him to accept before he chose her again.

But would he choose her again? His hand moved to his mouth, where he could still call up the feel of her lips against his. She was right. That choice was excessively dangerous, though maybe it wasn't too late to see it as a passing insanity, the combined pressure of duty and drama calling him into places he wouldn't normally go.

That wasn't how the skin of his lips told the story, though. They'd choose her again. And again and again, in spite of any dangers. And if he listened to them, he'd be a fool. So he'd just have to find a way not to. He pressed them together, and asked them to remain quiet.

"Where are we?" she asked.

He gave her his profile, and pulled the curtain back from the window. "Rachavia. Israel."

She frowned. "For Rachel?" she asked.

"That's right. Her mother finally found her voice and insisted that she have her daughter back, no matter what her husband said. She won't be up and about for a while, but the medics thought it was safe to move her. She'll do her rehab here. It'll be a long recuperation."

Jaguar made a choking sound, and he whipped around to her. She'd gone pale and her eyes were wide and dark as the sea. "You okay?" he asked, going over to her.

"Her—rehab?" she asked, voice low and uncertain.

"Her rehab?" Alex repeated, not sure what she meant. "Rachel's rehab? Oh, she'll be fine. There's neural damage, but therapy should put it right. Jaguar, are you sure you're okay?"

"Alex," she asked carefully, "is Rachel alive?"

He sat down on the bed next to her. "Yes," he said. "Of course she is."

She leaned back against the pillow, and pressed her hand to her throat as if she couldn't breathe. She looked as stunned as he'd ever seen her, and for once incapable of hiding it.

"But I couldn't—I lost her," she said. "I slipped and was falling away from her. She's alive?"

"Jaguar, yes. I thought you knew. I thought you felt it."

"No. I only knew I couldn't hold on."

He put a finger under her chin and lifted it slightly, asking for her full attention.

"But she could," he said.

She groaned, and pushed her face into the pillow, not sure if she was going to laugh or cry. Alex helped her out by laughing for her.

"Listen," he said, "Rachel wasn't about to go over that edge if it meant dragging you with her. She refused to die. For you."

She turned her face away from the pillow and back to

him. "Alex," she asked again, needing to hear the words, taste them in her mouth, "Rachel's alive?"

"Very much. You'll be able to see her soon enough. You've been out for a few days, and I want you to rest. Stay here for a while. Take some time off."

She was ready to take any orders he had to give. She breathed in deeply, and let the breath leave her slowly. Alive. It was good to be alive. Maybe she could get in trouble at the Wall, with Rachel. Alive. So many people were alive, dancing under this sun. So many people, not sacrificed to Sardis's vision of God. Including Rachel.

"Will you stay with me?" she asked.

"No," he said quickly, and stood up, walked back to the window.

"Is something wrong?"

"Of course not," he said, keeping his tone casual. "I just have to get back. Someone has to deal with the bureaucrats."

"Is that why you're leaving, Alex?" she asked.

And for the first time since he'd known her, he looked right at her and told her a direct lie.

"Yes. Of course it is."

Jaguar's slow and quiet gaze rested on him. Deep oceans lived there. Clean deserts and high mesas and rolling night skies listened to his lie and heard the truth anyway.

He was leaving because too much had happened between them, and too much more could happen if he stayed. He needed time, time and space. She was right. They were dangerous. Fretful intelligences, swimming uneasily in profoundly swirling depths, complex and rich and potentially deadly. He needed time.

"When I get back," she said, "I'd like to write up a report with you on the appropriate role of Teachers in establishing VR programs."

"Good," Alex said, knowing she said it to reassure him that she would return. To reassure him that, no matter what, they were still working together. "Good idea. Maybe we can figure out a way to deal with the empath issue for VRs, too. When you get back.''

When she came back. There would be time then for whatever came next.

He stared out the window, past the anemones and toward the desert sand that danced in the sun. Somewhere out there, Sardis's daughter was dancing with it. Rachel's spirit, free of her mother's anguish, dancing. A dance of grace and courage for a laughing god.

And for now, that would have to be enough.